SEVENTEEN AGAINST THE DEALER

Books by Cynthia Voigt

THE BAD GIRLS SERIES

Bad Girls

Bad, Badder, Baddest

It's Not Easy Being Bad

Bad Girls in Love

Bad Girls, Bad Girls, Whatcha Gonna Do?

THE TILLERMAN SERIES

Homecoming

Dicey's Song

A Solitary Blue

The Runner

Come a Stranger

Sons from Afar

Seventeen Against the Dealer

THE KINGDOM SERIES

Jackaroo

On Fortune's Wheel

The Wings of a Falcon

Elske

OTHER BOOKS

Building Blocks

The Callender Papers

David and Jonathan

Izzy, Willy-Nilly

Orfe

Tell Me if the Lovers Are Losers

Tree by Leaf

The Vandemark Mummy

When She Hollers

SEVENTEEN AGAINST THE DEALER

CYNTHIA VOIGT

ATHENEUM BOOKS FOR YOUNG READERS
New York London Toronto Sydney New Delhi

ATHENEUM BOOKS FOR YOUNG READERS
An imprint of Simon & Schuster Children's Publishing Division
1230 Avenue of the Americas, New York, New York 10020

Also available in an Atheneum Books for Young Readers hardcover edition
Book design by Debra Sfetsios-Conover
The text for this book is set in Baskerville.
Manufactured in the United States of America
First Atheneum Books for Young Readers paperback edition July 2012
2 4 6 8 10 9 7 5 3
The Library of Congress has cataloged the hardcover edition as follows:
Voigt, Cynthia.
Seventeen against the dealer.
Summary: Dicey struggles to make a go of a boatbuilding business while facing family concerns, romantic problems, and the uncertainties of a drifter who offers to help her in her work.
ISBN 978-0-689-31497-1
[1. Family problems—Fiction.] Title.
PZ7.V874Se 1989
[Fic]—dc19 88-27488 CIP AC
ISBN 978-1-4424-5064-6 (hc)
ISBN 978-1-4424-2884-3 (pbk)

This one is for all of you
who have sat in a classroom
and let me teach you.

CHAPTER 1

Dicey?"

She heard him, but didn't hear him. His voice entered her consciousness the way the first sounds of morning enter a dream and become part of it, before you wake up into the real day. The smell of paint lingered, although she had cocked open the high windows and raised the wide metal door. The paint had a penetrating odor that hung on in the air. The curved sides of the dinghy shone with fresh color. She'd scraped and sanded the bottom before painting the sides. When this paint dried she'd put the boat up on the storage rack for the rest of the winter; and the job would be done because the bottom paint wouldn't go on until spring. Bottom paint was still wet when the boat went into the water. Green stains had splotched her jeans, her sneakers, her arms, hands, and face. Probably her hair, too, if she had a mirror to see it. She looked at her hands, the nails ringed with green, even after the scrubbing she'd given them in the shop's dank little bathroom. The hands she watched went right on with their work—as if she didn't exist—stroking the whetstone against the blade of the adze.

She was reviewing her plans. Dicey Tillerman always had things planned out so she could get to where she wanted. Where she wanted to get to was being a boatbuilder. Sailboats, she wanted to build sailboats. Not fancy yachts, but a boat a person could sail alone, or two people could sail.

Dicey knew you didn't get what you wanted just by wanting it. She'd worked the last two summers, over in Annapolis, to learn things she needed to know. She'd learned some carpentry, she'd cut and sewn sails, and this fall she'd hired herself out to a boatyard in Crisfield, never mind the rotten pay, to learn what you were contracting for when you offered winter storage and maintenance for boats.

The boats she wanted to build were wooden ones. She wanted to build a boat with a carved rudder to guide it by and the long, varnished tiller under your hand. Not plywood, either. Dicey Tillerman had an idea about a slender, soft-bellied boat built out of planks of wood fitted together so close it was as if they'd grown that way, sturdy enough for heavy winds but light enough so the slightest breeze would fill the sails and move it across the water.

"Dicey?"

For now, however, the shop came first, and the shop work—repair, maintenance, storage. She knew that nobody hired you to build a sailboat right away, first thing. She also had an idea for a dinghy, one that could be powered either by a motor or by oars. Her plan was to get herself a name for building dinghies, save up the profits, and then—when she was ready—start taking orders for sailboats.

So the next thing she needed, now that she had the shop and tools, and a bank account, was work. She didn't expect it to be easy. She knew that nobody had done what she planned to do, start her own boatyard, from nothing. At least, nobody she knew in Crisfield, or Annapolis, or the points between had done it. Boatyards were inherited, father to son, or bought out. Nobody just started one. But nobody had done a lot of what she'd done in her life, like getting her family down to Crisfield when they were all just kids, or even dropping out of college when she'd been offered a scholarship to continue. Just because nobody had done something didn't mean that Dicey couldn't.

Standing with her feet planted apart in front of the workbench, the light falling over her shoulder, wearing a sweatshirt no amount of laundering ever got clean, Dicey fingered the honed blade of the adze and then, satisfied, hung it in its place overhead, between the long saw and the squat broadax. All the blades above her gleamed like polished silver. She wrapped the oilstone in its cloth and set it aside in its metal box; the box she put on the storage shelf under the table's surface, beside the row of wooden-handled screwdrivers and hammers, and the pile of plastic containers that kept nails and screws sorted out by sizes, each container labeled with adhesive tape on which she'd made dark pencil marks—and gradually she heard him, standing still by the doorway just behind her. The sense of his being there rose up in her, as quiet and sure as a tide rising up along the shore. It was as if his silence awoke her.

The pane of glass shone dark behind his head, the darkness of early winter nights. His gray eyes watched her, had been watching her; she was glad to see him. "You're early," she said.

"Actually," Jeff told her, "I'm late. I thought you'd prefer that."

"Actually," she mimicked him, "you're right." She stretched her arms up high over her head, stretched the muscles along her back, then walked down the shop to turn off lights. It was like a cave, the shop. Square, about twenty feet by twenty feet, the cinder block walls rose up from a slab cement floor. The high windows snapped up shut, closing out the darkness; she'd pulled down the broad metal doorway that opened onto the water when the afternoon temperature started to fall; so the shop felt like a cave, too, it felt like a treasure cave. Some treasure, Dicey thought, and grinned. One dinghy, belly up on a rack at the center of the shop. Two more dinghies stacked on racks against the wall, waiting for the same caretaking. On the other hand, their monthly storage fees would pay what she wanted to give her grandmother every month, and because she was underpricing local boatyards, she could hope for more boats to winter next year—yeah, they were treasures.

Her tools were treasures, too, and they might in fact be worth something, at least to a collector. She'd picked them up over the last couple of years, in junk shops mostly, and at yard sales—hammers, screwdrivers, planes, and the cutting tools. She'd soaked and sanded those tools, honed and polished them, and even carved out a replacement handle for the broadax. She couldn't have afforded new tools, and, anyway, the new weren't made with the same care as the old. The old were made to last lifetimes.

And Jeff Greene, in a thick, dark sweater that rose up around his neck, standing waiting in front of the shop door, his thumbs hooked in his pockets, just watching her, probably knowing exactly what she was thinking . . . the thought made her smile.

"You look," he told her, "like the cat that swallowed the canary."

She reached up over the worktable to turn out the final light. "I feel like the cat that figured out how to get into a cream factory. That's how I feel. Cream is better than canaries. Canaries have feathers, and bones, and beaks, and claws, too. I'd think a cat that swallowed a canary would look pretty sick, Jeff."

He laughed, and turned to open the door. With all the shop lights out, the door's glass pane showed a whiter, mist-filled darkness outside. "You haven't hung your sign out yet," Jeff said, looking down at the carved wooden sign that leaned against the wall beside the door. "I thought you'd have it hung by noon on Christmas."

"If it's outside, I can't look at it." Her brother had made it for her, cutting the letters deep into a piece of mahogany, staining them dark so they would show up against the paler wood, and then varnishing it, coat after careful coat, so it would stand up against weather. TILLERMAN BOATS, the sign read. Dicey saw it clear in her memory, even though in the lightlessness she couldn't distinguish the letters. "It's a good thing Sammy took wood shop, or I don't know what I'd have gotten for Christmas."

"He's got clever hands," Jeff said.

"And he likes making things," she added. Sammy had even roped James into making a half-court, a backboard to play tennis alone on, one summer; at the garage where he'd been hired to pump gas, he now spent most of his time working on engines. It was Sammy who kept their old pickup going for them. It was even Sammy who'd found it, and talked them into it, telling them it could be got running, he could do it easily, and at the price, which was only $485, he said—ignoring Gram's raised eyebrows at the sum—they'd never find anything cheaper. "Who needs a wheeled vehicle?" Gram had demanded. "We do," Sammy had told her. "You do, and you need a license, too. Maybe we can't afford it, but that doesn't mean we don't need it. And we can afford it." Sammy had set his mind to it. Like anything else Sammy set his mind to, it got done. They insured it in Gram's name, because she was the cheapest; Sammy was the only one of them who didn't have a license at that point, and he'd turn sixteen in less than a year.

Jeff hurried Dicey along. "It's after six. They're waiting for us. Should I call and say we're leaving now?" Dicey shook her head and followed him outside. He waited while she locked the door and took a final look. The shop lay quiet, the boats thick black masses in the darkness inside.

She let Jeff pull her by the hand toward his car, telling her with mock comfort, "You'll be back tomorrow. It's only a few hours' separation."

"No, it isn't. Tomorrow's New Year's Day."

"Then the day after. It's only a few more hours. I don't know why you're in such a hurry."

"Why shouldn't I be? I know what I want to do, I've got enough money in the bank to pay six months' rent and utilities, I've got storage and maintenance fees coming in—and I've got probably the best set of tools in the county. Some of them," she added, "given to me by the man I love." She put her arm around his waist and felt his arm go around her shoulder. "What more do I need?"

"You could marry me," he suggested.

"I could but I can't."

"You mean you won't."

"I mean no, Jeff."

"No you don't," he corrected her, lifting her bike into the back of the station wagon. "You mean not now, not yet."

"I don't think I'd ever marry anyone else," she told him, fastening the seat belt. She had it planned—first the boats and then marrying Jeff.

"In that case," he said, half of his attention on backing the car around the parking lot, "why don't you marry me now and get it over with?"

Dicey turned her head sharply to look at him. "That wouldn't get anything over with, it would just start things up. Cripes, Jeff," she protested, and then laughed. "You make it sound so tempting." She could no more imagine him not in her life than she could imagine not having her brothers and sister there, or Gram. Jeff Greene, since the time she'd first met him—over eight years ago now—had got woven into her life so thoroughly that, she thought, picturing it—the warp threads and the woof threads, all the colors and the intricate design—if he weren't in it . . . everything would look entirely different, and feel different, too. Even the texture wouldn't be what it was without Jeff.

"Besides," Jeff said, "I'm still in school."

Dicey grunted her agreement.

"Although I'm graduating this year, so I'm almost through. But I'll probably go to grad school."

"I'd think so."

"So I don't have a job to support you with. Although we could easily live on my allowance. Think of the savings in phone bills."

"My phone bills aren't bad." They drove through town and turned onto a country road.

"I know. I know they aren't."

"I've been busy, you know that, Jeff. I've been working."

"If you married me, you wouldn't have to worry about being too busy to call me up," Jeff pointed out. "Or write me letters."

"Can we talk about something else? I don't like feeling guilty."

For a second, Dicey was afraid he would apologize. Instead, he told her, "You don't feel guilty."

He was right, she thought, grinning away, feeling good.

"And why should you feel guilty, anyway," Jeff asked, "for doing what you always said you wanted to do?" But he said this as if he was reminding himself, not telling her.

Then she did feel guilty. "You know I'll come home with you. Live with you while you're home. Whenever you say, I will— you know that," she reminded him. "Your father's away, we wouldn't be imposing on anyone." Whenever they had this conversation, she always hoped that this time Jeff would say yes.

"You know that won't work," he said, as usual. "I'm not good at half-measures, Dicey. Besides, it's too risky."

"I know how not to get pregnant."

"It's not about not getting pregnant."

She heard it in his voice, something angry, or sad, and turned in her seat to face him, to see his face. "What, sex?"

"I don't think of it as sex," he said. "I think of it as making love. And I think love deserves the best from me that I can give it. Which is a lot more than shacking up with you for Christmas vacation."

Dicey reached her hand across to touch the back of his neck. "I'm sorry—I said it badly—Jeff? I'm tired, I'm stupid with tiredness."

"It's okay," he said, and meant it. "You've been working too hard for too long."

"That part's coming to an end now, I think."

Dicey leaned back in her seat, while the dark night hurried past the windows and the dark road ran under the wheels. Work had laid the groundwork, and now the shop was started. She had always gotten things done; working hard, and harder, was what worked for her. She was bankrolling her own business because for the last six months she'd held down two jobs. Eight to four at Claude's boatyard, learning what had to be done and how to do it, meeting people who might hire her on her own, and then the night shift at the McDonald's up in Salisbury. Days spent sweating herself dry and nights togged out in a little orange-and-yellow outfit, inhaling the smell of grease and industrial-strength cleanser, taking orders and money from person after person, from an endless procession of people impatient to fill their bellies. Sometimes she thought if she never saw another hamburger in her whole life, it would be too soon. Sometimes, even, she thought if she never saw another human being, too.

Dicey was glad those six months were behind her, but she was even gladder for her bank account. She was on her way to where she planned to get to because of those months, which was what really mattered.

At the mailbox they turned right into the driveway, moving slowly. The two fields, one on either side, lay dark and empty.

The belt of pines that fenced the fields made a tall, dark wall. Then the driveway curved into the pines and Dicey could see the lighted windows of the house. Jeff drove around to the back and parked beside the pickup, in front of the barn. The car headlights shone briefly on the tarpaulin Sammy spread out to protect his tennis court, the beams of light reflecting off small black puddles formed by the mist, which gathered together if there was no soil to absorb it. Jeff turned off the engine and the lights, unbuckled himself, and then—as Dicey had hoped he would—he gathered her into his arms. The silky feel of his hair, and his strong young shoulders—the clean smell of him and the distant beating of his heart from deep inside his body— If she thought about it, Dicey didn't see how she was going to stand having Jeff go away again, back to school. She didn't think about it.

CHAPTER 2

When Dicey and Jeff got around to coming inside, they found Gram alone in the kitchen. She was pouring milk from a red pitcher into the six glasses set out on the table. The whole room was filled with the smell of some dinner Dicey had never smelled before.

A big covered casserole waited on the table along with a plate of butter and a basket filled with thick slices of bread. One pot bubbled on the stove—empty mason jars revealed what was in it, green beans mixed with tomatoes. Gram finished pouring the milk and put the pitcher into the sink before she turned around to greet them. "I heard you drive in."

Gram's hair was grayer now than it had been the first time Dicey had laid eyes on her, but except for that she looked the same, in a long, loose blouse over a long, loose skirt. Dicey checked Gram's feet to be sure she was wearing the mukluks Jeff had given her for Christmas. Gram would go barefoot all year round, whatever the weather, if you let her. They didn't let her.

"I'm wondering about you two," Gram said, her quick glance going from Dicey's face to Jeff's face. Over Gram's shoulder, on the sill of the window over the sink, a white cyclamen plant bloomed against the dark. This was Maybeth's Christmas present to her grandmother, and like everything else Maybeth cared for, it flourished. Half a dozen flowers, their silky petals blown backward by some invisible wind, shone white against the black windowpane. Windflowers, that was what their name meant, Dicey thought. The sturdy, delicate-seeming blooms with their fragile, sturdy-seeming stems and leaves—they marked the real difference, since the first time she'd seen her grandmother, the first time she'd stepped into this kitchen. Now the kitchen was crowded, or would soon be, with people and voices, with good food, with the tales and quarrels of the day—where before it had been silent and empty, like the windows of an abandoned house. That first day, Dicey remembered, she had been offered canned spaghetti—the memory made her smile.

"What're you smirking about?" Gram demanded, but before Dicey could begin to answer, she went on with her own thoughts. "I *do* wonder about you two. I don't think you spend half-enough time necking. Go fetch your family, girl—I'm almost starved and I bet Jeff is, too. Aren't you, Jeff?"

Maybeth had found a recipe called jambalaya, which she was trying out on them. With the jambalaya they had the green beans and tomatoes—simmered with some fresh oregano from the pots of herbs Maybeth grew at her bedroom window—and thick slices of Gram's bread, spread with butter. For a while, the only sounds in the room were eating noises, grunts and murmurs of appreciation, forks clinking on china, milk being swallowed. Jambalaya, Dicey discovered, was mostly rice, with occasional sweet surprises of turkey or ham, and little crisp bits of green pepper and celery. Inexpensive, filling, and flavorful, that's what jambalaya was. Dicey looked across the table at her sister. "Where'd you find this, Maybeth?"

"Mina told me," Maybeth explained. "It's something called creole, from Louisiana. It sounded good, so I looked in a cookbook."

"It is good," Gram said. "Was it complicated?"

"No. Easy."

"You think everything you cook is easy," James said.

"Cooking is easy," she agreed.

"Not if it's hard for you," James argued.

Maybeth thought about that. "But it's not hard for me."

James smiled, as if he'd known all along where this conversation would end up. And—being James—he probably had, Dicey thought. "That's a lucky thing for us," James told his sister.

Dicey was tired, good tired, from having ridden her bike across to the shop as soon as the light broke, from having worked a long day. She didn't have the energy to do more than nod her agreement and eat on. She didn't have to talk, anyway. They were all sitting at Gram's table, in Gram's home—their table in their home—and she was working her life out according to plan. She looked around at them all and the familiar gladness rose up inside her, like one of Maybeth's cakes rising up fat and rich in the oven, smelling so good you could almost lick the air.

Maybeth and Sammy sat across from Dicey. You'd know they were brother and sister, just looking at them. They both had Momma's golden hair and big eyes. Maybeth looked as if her face had been drawn with a finer pen than Sammy's, and she was growing her heavy hair long so the curliness had smoothed into waves, but one look would tell you those two were related. James, beside Dicey, was as dark-haired and narrow-faced as she was. And they all—all four of the kids and Gram, too—had Tillerman eyes, hazel eyes where the colors mixed up greens and browns and yellows. The Tillermans looked like they belonged together, and that was a book you could judge by its cover.

Jeff, whose profile she could see beyond James, was a book you couldn't judge by its cover—because he belonged, too, only not in the same blooded way. She watched his narrow wrist and the gray eyes you could look into and into and never touch bottom; she watched the way his hair, black as the water at night, fell down onto his forehead—cripes, Jeff was a treat to look at. Dicey couldn't ever see Sammy's chunky, sturdy body, even as big as he had grown, without wanting to hug him, and then pound small punches on his shoulder just to feel how strong he was, and then tickle him under the arms to watch his whole body collapse in laughing—but Jeff she could sit still and look at, for weeks, and never get tired of just seeing him, the way he moved and the way his skin had been laid out over his bones. Jeff was beautiful, inside and out; she'd always thought that, although she'd never let Jeff know she thought it. Jeff didn't think of her as having thoughts like that, and she didn't know how he'd react. Besides, he was right, most of her thoughts weren't like that at all.

Dicey's body relaxed as her stomach filled. Taking a forkful of vegetables, she thought about how the oregano in the green bean-tomato mix was sweet, and how its freshness made the vegetables taste fresher, too, and how Maybeth made up little packages of fresh herbs to sell at Millie Tydings's grocery store, downtown. The packages sold for a dollar and a quarter, of which Maybeth got seventy cents. It didn't sound like much, but it mounted up, over a growing season. The Tillermans knew how to bring money in, because they knew how to work. Dicey hesitated over her plate, wondering what to taste next, smiling to herself because she had so much to choose from, and picked up a slice of the crusty bread. She filled her stomach and listened.

Sammy would have gone on forever to Gram and Maybeth about some tennis camp he'd read about in the magazine Dicey had picked out for his Christmas stocking, somewhere in Arizona, where you did nothing all summer long but play tennis under coaches whose names Sammy seemed to know. But

Gram held up her hand to silence him when she heard Jeff ask James, "I thought premed meant you took science courses, like organic chemistry, molecular biology, that kind of stuff. And what are *you* taking? Philosophy, art history, Shakespeare, geology. That's not premed."

"You forgot math."

"And calculus," Jeff added. "What does a doctor need with those?"

"My scholarship isn't premed," James reminded him.

"Your ambitions are," Jeff answered. "I don't understand what you're up to. You tested out of all the distribution requirements with those AP exams."

"I'm not ambitious." James had his eyes fixed on his plate. It sounded almost like a quarrel he and Jeff were having; but what business did Jeff have quarreling with James?

Gram entered the conversation. "Yes, you are. Don't try to fool us, young man. We're your family."

"Not the way Jeff means. I know people like Jeff means, and— Anyway, what's the point of going someplace like Yale if you don't— I mean, it's this great liberal arts college, with a whole rack of good departments, not just a couple of strong ones— Why should I have to miss out on things just because I know what I ultimately want to specialize in?"

"Yeah." Sammy backed his brother up.

Jeff raised both hands in self-defense. "Hey, I wasn't saying you shouldn't. I was just wondering why you are. I assume you have good reasons because you always do. You should know I'm assuming that, James."

"I do," James said. "I guess you touched a sore spot, because I've been wondering myself how much effect not taking those science courses might have, when I go for a med school scholarship. But, Jeff, it can't be that doctors are allowed to know only about medicine. And they shouldn't just know that, should they? I mean, if a doctor has wider knowledge he'll be a better doctor for people—if he knows more about how people think, and are, about human beings, he'll see things in a broader perspective, too, so he can really see people and not just—not just whatever their diseases are."

Jeff studied James for a minute, then asked, "And you say you're not ambitious?"

Their laughter rippled over the table, over the scrubbed wood and the plates and bowls. But, Dicey thought, too lazy to say it, she knew what James meant. The Tillermans weren't ambitious. They wanted enough to take care of themselves, that was all. The Tillermans weren't greedy, to be rich or to own things, or to be famous, either. They just wanted to be able to take care of whoever they were supposed to, just to earn a living—because your living wasn't a present, it had to be earned. Even Momma had done that. She'd taken care of them until she couldn't anymore. But until she couldn't, she had done the best job she could, earning her living and theirs, too.

Dicey concealed the yawn that stretched her jaw muscles. She was feeling too good to want to be tired. She was too tired to eat any more, but she felt too good to want to leave the table, and the people. James talked on, getting excited.

"Did you ever take geology, Jeff? They measure things in billions of years, they round things out to the millionth—and they're measuring time. The odd three thousand years don't even matter, not in geological time."

"I know," Jeff said. "That's why I've never taken it. That point of view terrifies me—no, it does—because all the things I care about don't matter much, seen that way. It's all just a series of destructions and erasures, and there's so much lost . . . you know? So much just ended—and it's worth keeping, treasures of mind or art and—lost." He tried to shrug it off, with a movement of his shoulders. "And that scares me, I guess."

"Not me," Sammy announced. "I don't believe in it anyway because—it's always looking backward, all those billions of years backward. It's already finished with."

"I can't imagine billions. Of anything," Maybeth said.

"I can, millions," Sammy said. "I can grasp things in millions, like millions of dollars, or potatoes. And miles, if you imagine space. Can't you imagine millions of space miles?"

"Thousands," Gram said. "That's my outside limit. Dollars or potatoes or miles . . . and years, too. I can just about encompass a millennium. I can line up millennia in my imagination, but I'm still only counting in thousands. Which, as far as I can gather from James, is about what most people can imagine, which seems appropriate for a Johnny-come-lately species like man. But it all makes me about too tired to think."

"Yeah," Dicey agreed. Gram's eyes looked peaceful enough, and interested, but without any snap to them. "Yeah, I know. But I think I think in ones, anyway."

"That doesn't make sense," Sammy protested.

Dicey shrugged. It probably didn't, but it felt true.

"And the names," James went on, ignoring what people said, as he often did when he was worked up about an idea. "Precambrian, Jurassic, Cenozoic—they're such great names, heavy and thick, like layers of rocks resting on each other. You should have taken geology, Jeff. The dinosaurs, for example, they were around for one hundred and fifty million years. Man has been around for only, what? Maybe a million, give or take, and that's just if you define man as a tool-making hominid. What we know about, recorded history, isn't even ten thousand . . ." His voice trailed off as he thought about it. "And we think we're so important."

"Not important," Jeff corrected him. "Particular, maybe. Different from any other creature."

"What do you mean?" Sammy demanded. "That we're really just like ants?"

"Worse," James said. "Like caddis flies, that live only for a day, that have their whole lives in just one day."

"But if you look at it that way, what does one life matter?" Sammy asked.

"Looked at that way, it doesn't," James said.

"Then how am I supposed to take mine?" Sammy asked. He glared at his brother. "Anyway, it's not really true, or it's not the only thing that's true." He thought some more. "And anyway, if it really doesn't matter, then it doesn't make any difference. I mean, it doesn't matter that it doesn't matter."

That didn't make much sense to Dicey, but James was just staring at Sammy. "Cripes, Sammy," James asked, "how can you even think of wasting your life playing tennis?"

For a minute, Dicey thought Sammy might lose his temper. He'd grown tall, over six feet; exercise had given him thick muscles over his shoulders and chest; when he sat back, anger in his eyes, she thought it might be pretty lively if Sammy lost his temper. Then he shook his head, and grinned at James: "I'm not. And it's not wasting, anyway, to do something well. You don't think so, either, so don't try to kid me. Otherwise, why aren't you taking those straight premed courses?"

Dicey wished she had the energy to think about everything she was hearing and seeing. She was seeing, like dim, shadowy figures in a fog, the men her brothers were growing up into. They even looked a lot like men grown, at this point. She would have liked to get into the argument, because she had the feeling that she knew what her life was for. She had the feeling that what she knew and wanted was important. She was going to build boats, and she wasn't going to let anything stand in her way. Not even geology. Thinking that, her head resting against the back of her chair and her legs stretched out under the table, Dicey smiled to herself. As if geology was actually trying to get in her way, as if geology—all those millions and billions of years piled up on each other—as if it was going to pay any attention to Dicey Tillerman at all.

"Are you two through eating yet?" Gram demanded. "Because I'm about as uncomfortable as I care to get in this chair, and your sister is slithering away under the table—"

Dicey sat up.

"Isn't there dessert?" Sammy wondered.

"There's leftover pie," Maybeth told him. "But I thought we'd do the dishes first."

Sammy groaned, but it was only a token protest. James reached out to serve himself another large spoonful of jambalaya, and Sammy groaned again. "If you're not talking, you're eating. I thought we were ready to finish."

James ignored Sammy. "The courses I'm taking are fine, and I can pick up anything I need for premed later—except"—he put his fork into his mouth, chewed, swallowed—"I'm in trouble with the Shakespeare."

"But, James," Maybeth said, "you never have trouble in school. Are you worried?"

James nodded, and ate on. When he put his fork down, it was Maybeth he looked at. She was the easiest one of all of them to talk to, because she listened without interrupting—and that was because, Dicey thought, waiting to hear whatever it was James was going to say, Maybeth wasn't sure she could understand. The rest of them were pretty sure they understood things, and that made them bad listeners. Sometimes.

Gram, for example, interrupted James before he could start. "It can't be too serious," she decided. "Is there any reason we can't move into the living room? Where there are soft chairs and a fire burning. You didn't let that fire burn out, did you?"

In the living room Dicey took one of the big pillows Maybeth and Gram had made out of scraps of fabric and lay down on her stomach, facing the fire. The pillow was soft under her elbows and chest. The fire glowed warm on her face, a bed of gray ashes mixed with red-hot coals, with the black, burned skeletons of logs lying across it.

Sammy piled wood on the fire. Lying there, Dicey watched the little blue flames come cradling up around the new logs. Lying there, she could listen to her family's voices, and to the sounds they made shifting in their seats, and to the soft, plastic click of Gram's knitting needles behind everything.

From what he was saying, it sounded like James didn't know if he was going to pass the Shakespeare course, which would cost him his scholarship. Without that scholarship—which paid for everything, books, tuition, dormitory expenses—he couldn't go to Yale.

"I don't understand how you can be in trouble," Jeff said.

"Because of the professor."

"But, James," Sammy protested, "teachers always like you, because you're so smart."

"It's not that simple. It's not as simple as a personality conflict."

"And you like Shakespeare," Jeff said.

"Let me explain," James said. "See, Professor Browning—he's one of the old professors. This is his last year, and he's been teaching about ten years past retirement age because he really is good. He wanted to continue and they wanted him to. He's one of those professors who went to Yale as an undergraduate, and got a Rhodes scholarship—you have to be terrific to get a Rhodes."

"I know," Jeff said. "Why doesn't he like you?"

"But he does. That's the trouble. And I think he's good, too, and I like him."

"Then what's the problem?" Sammy asked. "You aren't making sense."

"The problem is . . . See, the course started out with the comedies. I did well because, well, the way Professor Browning looks at things, his worldview, is a lot like the comedies. The way the comedies say nothing is real or true, or trustworthy. Like, at the end of *Twelfth Night*, when the duke finally falls in love with Viola. You wanted that to happen, right? It was what would happen in a well-ordered universe, so you believe it. But if you think about it, there's no good reason, and the duke had said all during the play he'd always love Olivia . . . and Olivia had married Sebastien thinking he was Viola, whom she'd fallen in love with at first glance, thinking she was a boy and—all the couples, even Sir Toby and Maria, end up married, the way we feel they ought to, but—it's all chance. The whole play argues that love is irrational. You can't rely on it."

"I see how he's reading it," Jeff said. That was lucky, because Dicey knew the title but she'd never had time to read the play, even if she'd wanted to. Jeff could talk with James about this better than she'd ever be able to.

"Professor Browning cares about how I do, and what I think of the course. More than that, he really believes literature is important, not just because he teaches it, but because if people read and feel and think, they live better lives. Just because he isn't what he used to be, that isn't his fault. Just because he's old."

"Watch how you use that word," Gram warned him.

"You aren't old," James told her. "Professor Browning is kind of—crumbling at the edges of his mind? The trouble I'm in is—now we're talking about the tragedies, and will be for the rest of the year, and he has exactly the same way of thinking about them—as if they uncreate, destroy, make chaos. But there's more to them, you know? Always, at the end, the world of the play is made better, even though the individual is—lost. But if I think and write about the tragedies as having this re-creation aspect, I'll fail the course."

"He'll fail you because you don't agree with him?" Sammy said.

"I didn't say he was perfect. I said he's crumbling."

"I can sympathize with all that crumbling," Gram said.

"That's really dumb," Sammy told Gram, "and you know it. Let James talk, Gram, and stop trying to grab all the attention."

"I wasn't," Gram sputtered, "I don't—" Dicey turned her head and caught, as she thought she would, her grandmother's sudden smile. Sammy sat on the arm of Gram's chair, just grinning down at her, teasing. "That reminds me, Dicey," Gram said, "that man, Ken, from Annapolis called. He wants you to call him back."

"Okay, thanks." Ken Forbeck was a ship's carpenter who kept his eye out for wood; he knew Dicey was interested in becoming a boatbuilder. Tomorrow was a holiday, but she could call him the next day and find out what he wanted, find out if he had some wood for her to look at.

"Does this mean," Jeff asked James, "you're going to have to fail the course?"

She could take the truck up to Annapolis, so that if it was wood she could use, and she could afford it, she could bring it back with her. She had never tested exactly how much wood the truck could carry.

"If I did, it would cost me the scholarship. I have to maintain a B average."

"Then you *can't* fail it," Sammy said.

She hoped the weather would clear, because you didn't want to take good wood out on this kind of drizzly day, not for the two-and-a-half-hour drive, not open on the bed of the truck. But, she thought, James never failed courses.

"It would be stupid to fail," Sammy told his brother. "Losing everything because of one professor disagreeing with your ideas."

"And he'd really mind, too, if I did, because—he's decided I'm his swan-song student. The last best one. He really wants me to be brilliant for him. If I'm not—he'll feel as if he's failed, too."

"Can you do that well in it?" Jeff wondered.

"Sure. I can see how he's thinking. It's not even as if I'm sure he's wrong. I just don't look at it the same way."

"But to do that," Sammy said, "you'd have to lie about what you think is true. You can't do that, James."

"Why not? People do it all the time."

"Not you."

"But if I don't, I'll fail. I've never failed anything, in school."

"Yes, you have, in tenth grade, when you turned in that kid for cheating off of you, when you turned yourself in for helping him cheat. You failed that assignment with a zero."

"That was different. And besides, it was only one assignment, not the whole grade. I don't have anything lower than an A on my record, except for that one B. Ever."

"Those are just grades," Sammy said.

"Grades mean something. You know that."

"Maybe, but I don't care because—just because you get A's doesn't mean you're the best person. All it means is you're good at going to school. You can't use grades to mean anything, James."

"So you think I should fail it," James concluded. "Jeff, what do you think?"

"Can't you talk to your faculty adviser?"

"But I don't want to make any trouble for Professor Browning. It's not as if he doesn't work, or care, or isn't thinking about what he's doing; it's not as if he's a bad teacher."

"Well," Jeff summarized the situation, "it looks then as if you can pass, and belie yourself; or you can fail, and disappoint someone you would rather please, and lose your scholarship as well."

"That's it," James said. "I've never failed a course."

"Then pass it, get the A," Sammy advised.

"But I know how awful it feels to pretend to think what you don't," James protested. "It's like—like selling yourself into slavery, or—worse—selling your brothers and sisters, maybe, or your own children. I dunno, I don't have children—"

"I'm glad to hear that," Gram said.

"Because, if you can't be true to what you think . . ." James's voice faded away.

"Flunk," Sammy advised.

Dicey didn't have any opinion about what James should do. She rolled over onto her back. Behind the sofa, the top half of the Christmas tree rose, looped around with strings of popcorn mixed with cranberries. The strings looked like jewelry, like long necklaces around a shaggy throat, like rubies set in among some strange undiscovered gem that was part pearl, part sea foam.

"Gram?" James asked. "What do you think?"

"I'm sorry, James, I just don't seem to have any ideas."

"I wish I knew," James said. He leaned forward, resting his chin on his hands, his elbows on his knees. Dicey looked at the way his fingers laced together, and the bone of his jaw rested on the bones of his fingers. He really was worried about this. James looked at her and she shook her head—she didn't have any idea. He turned to ask Maybeth.

Maybeth sat curled up, her long legs under her, her hazel eyes dark with worry. "I'm sorry," she said.

James smiled. "It's not your fault."

"It's not anyone's fault," she said. "But I'm still sorry. Because—but—I wish I could think. If I could think—because—people who think keep thinking of things, when it doesn't seem as if there's anything but one way or the opposite. But I can't." Her hair fell forward, brushing her cheeks. "But I know James will be a good doctor. You will, James. I don't understand about counting up millions of years, and I can't remember the names you said, but—you can think, so you ought to be able to think of how to solve this. People who can think," she said earnestly, and nobody laughed at her, "can think of things." She reached up her hand to tuck the long, dark-gold hair back behind her ear.

"Maybeth's right," Jeff said. "We can't think of anything, but you should ask your adviser. Unless you don't trust him?"

"Her," James corrected. Dicey grinned. "No, I do trust her."

Gram was staring at Dicey. "I remember the first time I ever saw you, girl. You looked about this tired."

Dicey's smile stayed on her face. "You didn't," she told her grandmother.

"Well, I wasn't," Gram snapped. "I had all the time in the world, at that time, and it was too much time, that was how it felt. Geology notwithstanding, and all the ages, from Precambrian right up to the present, what is it, Helocene?"

"Yeah," James said, not sounding surprised that Gram knew the name.

Gram's hands were busy, knitting a blue sock. The three needles formed an exaggerated triangle, each line extended beyond its intersections with the others. The wool rose out of the workbag in a thin line and the tube of sock hung down.

"When I think about geology, it feels like time is so long—which makes my own time so short—I don't intend to waste a minute of it. The hard thing," Gram concluded, folding the needles together, wrapping the knitting around them, "is knowing what constitutes waste." She tucked her knitting into the workbag and stood up. "I'm going to bed. A happy New Year to you."

As she did each New Year's Eve, she leaned over to kiss each one of them on the forehead, Sammy first. Sammy reached up to hold her there, so he could return the kiss. They weren't frequent kissers, the Tillermans, but on New Year's Eve they always did, just as they always didn't stay up until midnight. This was their way of marking the end and the beginning, Dicey thought, standing up to wait her turn.

Maybeth, James, and Jeff, too—Gram kissed her family good night, and finally Dicey. At the door into the hallway she turned around, with a swish of her long skirt. Her eyes took them all in, and her head nodded briskly. "Those dishes are waiting. You three, give Dicey and Jeff a little privacy, you hear me?"

CHAPTER 3

New Year's Day was about a third gone when Dicey woke up. She didn't need any clock to tell her it was midmorning; she just looked out the window and saw the bright, cold sunlight sprinkling down on the garden. And she could feel the time in her body. She felt rested from sleeping so long and deep, she felt filled up with energy. She wished it weren't New Year's Day. She'd have liked to use this energy getting work accomplished.

Dicey thought about New Year's Day, as she went into the bathroom, about how unnatural it was. Spring would be a natural place to start a year, or maybe the first day of winter, the winter solstice. In the school year, September marked the new beginning. Last September was the first fall she hadn't been in school, so—she splashed cold water over her face, still celebrating not being in school, being done with it, finished for good—maybe she wasn't used to the change. But January first hadn't ever felt like anything new. Dicey had never paid it any mind. Although this year she'd have to, because she had a checkbook, and when she wrote checks she'd have to change the year.

She rinsed her teeth and ran her fingers through her hair. Catching a glimpse of herself in the mirror, she frowned. Even she had to admit that fingers hadn't done the job. She opened the cabinet door and took out a brush. She pulled the brush through her hair a couple of times, then replaced it. She didn't bother checking herself again in the mirror. If she'd brushed her hair, then it had to look okay. She didn't have time to waste double-checking, she had things she was supposed to get done this morning. She was hungry, too.

Dicey ran down the stairs, into what was left of the morning. Baking smells came up to greet her—sweet, warm smells, with nuts and vanilla mixed in—she followed her nose into the kitchen—apples, too, cinnamon, nutmeg. Gram and Maybeth were in there, both working away at the long table. Gram was beating something in the big bread bowl while Maybeth, an apron over her jeans, frowned at the grater she was rubbing an orange against.

Dicey poured herself a glass of milk and drank it down, watching the two of them. "You slept late," Gram observed, the big wooden spoon moving steadily even when she turned her attention away.

"I feel—terrific," Dicey said.

"Sammy's out back, chopping wood. People will be coming soon," Gram told her.

"I must have been tireder than I thought." Dicey kept moving around, stepping out of her sister's way, out of her grandmother's way, eating bread and jam.

"I thought so."

There was no use feeling impatient. Dicey had known that, like on Christmas, she would lose a day's work on New Year's. There wasn't anything she could do about it, anyway, because there were people coming over for the afternoon.

Over the years it had gotten to be a tradition, people coming to spend the first afternoon of the New Year at the Tillermans'. It wasn't official and it wasn't formal—nothing at the Tillermans' was ever official or formal—it was just something that happened once, and then again, and somehow got grown into a habit. You didn't dress up for it. Dicey wore jeans and a cranberry-red sweater Jeff gave her the first Christmas he ever gave her a present, a mix of cotton and silk that was so soft, every time she put it on she felt like a baby, wrapped around with care, or a royal princess nothing could ever happen to. She knew that was pretty stupid. The history courses she'd had to take had taught her that princesses were at more risk than ordinary people. Babies, she knew, were easy to neglect, or abandon, because they were helpless. But she wasn't a princess, so she didn't have to worry, and she wasn't a baby anymore, either. In fact, helpless was one thing she was sure she wasn't, she thought, running her hand down over the soft arm of the sweater.

At midafternoon, Dicey stood leaning against the door frame between the dining room and the living room. She was waiting for the hours to flow by, half of her mind in town at the shop—considering the list of tasks to be done, checking supplies—most of the other half wondering what it was Ken Forbeck had wanted, what he'd say when she called him. The trouble with holidays was you couldn't even make a phone call.

From behind her, she heard the voices of Gram and Dr. Landros, talking about something with Mina Smiths. She knew that if she turned around she'd see them, the three women sitting on three of the chairs that had been pulled away from the table, all leaning forward toward the others as they talked. Mina had come without Dexter, so Dicey guessed they were having one of the fights that had characterized the romance, now in its fourth year. She hadn't had a chance to ask, because seeing Mina unescorted, Sammy had dragged her out to the kitchen to talk about tennis camps.

The people in the living room had eaten and talked and were settling down to song. Jeff had his guitar ready. Maybeth sat on the floor in front of him, the fire behind her. James and his friend

Toby were playing chess at the desk; Celie Anderson stood behind Toby, watching. Those three had gone through high school together, old, good friends, the three of them, however oddly assorted. Dicey watched James shake his head, shrug his shoulders, laugh, and reach a hand up to Celie, asking her to make the next move. This meant that Toby had outplayed him and James saw his only hope in a move no practiced chess player would ever think of. Dicey never saw Celie's move because Louis Smiths, Mina's little brother—weighing in at about 170 now, not so little anymore, all muscles—moved and blocked her view.

Sammy sat in front of the big sofa, talking with Custer and Robin and the two girls they had brought with them. Both Custer and Robin had traveled with steadies since they'd taken up girls in the eighth grade. Dicey could never remember the girls' names, but that didn't matter, since the girls changed as regularly as the styles of dress they sported, which was pretty regularly. This year the style was layers, T-shirts that bore a curious resemblance to men's undershirts, hanging out under baggy sweaters, all hanging out over jeans, and hair in a mass of curls, so they looked like a pair of neglected poodles.

Jeff had brought his friend Phil Milson, who was getting a master's at an agricultural college in South Carolina. Dicey had wondered, opening the door to the two of them, why Phil was there. Not that she minded. She liked Phil. He had a lazy way of talking that was relaxing to be around, and he looked—with his thick blond hair, still bleached summer-white by outside work, and his lazy smile—healthy, like a good, healthy person who would be good to have around. Phil was sitting now in the stuffed chair across the fire from Jeff. When Dicey saw his eyes resting on Maybeth's face, she figured she knew why he was there. Well, Sammy wouldn't object to Phil asking Maybeth out, and neither would James, unless they thought he was too old. Dicey looked at her sister, cross-legged on the floor, her hands quietly folded on her lap, wearing an old blouse Gram had brought down from the attic, with its high lacy neck and long sleeves.

As she watched, Jeff lifted the guitar and started to play, one of the classical pieces he'd been studying since he went to college, quiet music, the notes clear, his hands moving along the frets and plucking gently at the strings. It didn't take long for all the chattering in the room to fade away. He changed the music then, to make the guitar a background for song. "'Should auld acquaintance be forgot,'" Jeff sang. Maybeth joined in about two beats after he started. Everybody sang, Dicey, too, "'And never brought to mind.'" Maybe it was morbid of her, Dicey thought, singing, but this kind of occasion, and this kind of song, always made her think of the people who weren't there. Old acquaintances, like Jeff's father, who was away teaching in Australia until spring. The Professor had sent them a case of kiwifruit for Christmas, and a card with a kangaroo that jumped out of it. Or an old acquaintance like Mr. Lingerle, who had moved away from Crisfield when the woman he met at a music teachers' convention said she couldn't live anywhere except Chicago, so if he wanted to marry her—which he did—he would have to move out there, and teach there—which he had.

And Momma, their mother, Gram's daughter. But it wasn't holidays that made Dicey remember her mother, it was singing. Dicey, as the oldest, had the most memories of their mother, and singing was the best of them. Momma when she sang—it sounded as if she stepped inside the song, the words and melody, and sang it out from its own self, like Maybeth when she sang, only Momma's voice was honey where Maybeth's was gold.

Maybeth was growing to look more like Momma, too, with her long legs and long hair; only Maybeth's eyes didn't have the lost, frightened look Dicey remembered in her mother's eyes. Maybeth used to have that look, all her life, until they found Gram and knew they were always going to live here. Dicey wondered if their mother had been shy, too; Maybeth still was, but it wasn't so much shyness now as quietude, because there wasn't any being frightened left in it.

Drawn by the singing, Mina came to stand facing Dicey. "'I'll take a cup of kindness now,'" she sang, raising her eyebrows at Dicey, "'for auld lang syne.'" She held the last note until her voice faded away. Because Mina sang with a chorus at college, she'd taken a semester of voice; the note she held, low and rich, like a bassoon, blended with the note Maybeth held high and clear, like a spun-gold thread. Mina had shown Maybeth what she had learned in her lessons, about breathing, about shaping the inside of your mouth around the letters of the words. In perfect communication, Mina and Maybeth cut the note off at the same time, allowing the guitar the last few bars.

Custer's girl asked Jeff if he knew "This Land Is Your Land." Jeff did, he always knew all the songs. Dicey asked Mina, "Why doesn't Sammy have a girlfriend?"

Mina shook her head; she didn't know. She had always dwarfed Dicey and, now that they'd reached their full growth, always would. Mina was wearing big, heavy, bright metal earrings, made in Africa, Dicey was willing to bet. When Mina shook her head, the earrings reflected little pieces of moving light onto her dark cheeks. "You going to start worrying about that now?" Mina teased. "I wouldn't. I wouldn't worry until it starts. Then I'd do some serious worrying."

"I've got more important things to think about."

"Are you sorry yet that you quit school?"

Dicey shook her head.

Mina studied her for a minute, while the Woody Guthrie song

played on. "You will be. Although, maybe you won't. That would be just like you."

"What would be?"

"Not ever to be sorry. To drop out and not miss it."

"You know I never liked school."

"No, I don't know that. I know you always would have rather worked on boats. That's entirely different—and entirely irrelevant, if you ask me."

Dicey didn't want to hear this again, even from Mina. "So where's Dexter?" she asked.

Mina hesitated, then answered, "In D.C. With some chick he met. He says, if he finds her so attractive he shouldn't be telling me he loves me. Can you believe the arrogance of him?"

"Yes." Half the time it was what Dicey liked best about Dexter. Of course, the other half, it made her want to walk out of whatever room he was standing stage center in. "Do you think he's getting even with you for going off with the chorus for another whole summer?" she asked.

"He's not that bad, Dicey. At least, I don't think he is. But you can't leave a guy on his own like that, not someone like Dex—he's a flirt, and he's so energetic, he's always got some idea cooking—my mother says if you leave a man alone too much he's bound to get himself into trouble."

"Do you think this girl is trouble?" Dicey asked.

Mina laughed. "For now, yeah—she's trouble enough. Do you ever think, when my mother was my age, she was already married and pregnant with Charles Stuart?"

"No, I never do think that," Dicey said, grinning.

"And Belle's been married for two years and she's having a baby in June. Whereas me— It'll be another year and a half before I graduate, then three years of law school. Sometimes I wonder if . . . it's not overwhelmingly womanly, if you know what I mean, getting degrees, practicing law, being ambitious, succeeding. Don't you ever think about that?"

"I don't have the time," Dicey said.

Mina laughed again. "Yeah, and besides, you tell me, what's so womanly about cleaning out the oven and hauling kids around, playground, play group, grocery store, doctors—right? So I'm not a failure, right?"

"You? No, you never could be. You aren't worried about that, are you, Mina?"

Mina thought the question over, then shook her head. "No. It's Dexter who is. Or, he says he is. When you put it that way, I guess he's just being an arrogant, manipulative . . ." She hesitated over the right word.

"Person," Dicey suggested.

"Person," Mina echoed. "You know what he said to me? That uppity man said to me that I was going to have to choose between him and law school. But the way I see it, he was really saying I'd have to choose between him and me. Which is no contest, right?"

"I wouldn't have any trouble with it."

"No, you wouldn't. And I shouldn't," Mina said, then, "so I won't. I think I'll aim to do the best I can for myself. How's that sound to you?" Jeff had finished the song. Before he could start another, and before Dicey could answer that question, Mina called across to him, "You know what I want to hear? A love song."

"What kind of love song?" Jeff asked. "True love? Love betrayed? Lost love, faithless love, or false love?"

"Let's go for true love," Mina laughed. "Never mind the odds."

Jeff looked at Maybeth, who nodded at him. He started to play a song Dicey had never heard before, but before she could wonder, Maybeth was singing. "'The first time ever I saw your face,'" Maybeth sang to a guitar accompaniment as single and clear as the golden voice Maybeth cast out around the room, where—like the animated drawing of a ribbon—it curled around and around everyone, then tied itself into a perfect bow. The song brought tears into Mina's eyes, Dicey saw, and had Phil Milson sitting so still, watching and listening so hard, that you could almost see the way the beating of his heart pushed the blood up into his cheeks, and turned them pink.

Maybeth sang, "'I thought the sun rose in your eyes.'" On the last word, her voice rose up a third and then down and around, a turning of melodic line as smooth as a curving ribbon. "'And the moon, and the stars,'" she sang on, "'were the gifts you gave to the dark and the endless skies. . . .'"

Dicey couldn't remember the first time ever she saw Jeff's face. Jeff's gray eyes, dazed with the song, were on Maybeth. Then he turned to look at Dicey, as if he'd known she was looking at him, and she knew that he did remember the first time he saw her. She thought she ought to be able to remember, but she couldn't, not the time. The season, that she could, but she ought to be able to do better than that. Then she stopped thinking and let the song wind itself around her, and pull her into the room to sit on the floor beside him.

All the long afternoon they sang, and talked, and ate, and Dicey didn't think about her boats, the ones she was working on or the ones she was dreaming about, except once, when they came to the line in Momma's old song that said "bring me a boat will carry two." She could see that boat then, as real as if she had already built it.

CHAPTER 4

Dicey took the turn onto Route 50, heading north, and moved the truck immediately into the right lane. The truck's top speed was fifty-one, the speed limit on the road was fifty-five, so even though she could see no other traffic, she kept in the slow lane.

The land spread out around her, flat under the broad sky. Fields lay empty, trees raised naked branches, the scrawny tops of loblollies looked even scrawnier than usual, and the few houses she could see from the road had a closed-in winter look to them. Dicey was warm enough, since Sammy had tinkered the truck's heating system into working order.

She didn't mind driving—the machinery did all the work. In a boat, you had wind and waves, tides, too, to work with or against; in a boat, you had things constantly changing, perpetual small changes that you needed to respond to, if you wanted to do it right and keep on getting where you wanted to go. In a boat, the sailor did half the work. It was a lot like living, sailing was, much more so than driving was. Driving, you got onto the track and steered along—accelerating or braking as the occasion demanded, but mostly you did what the signs told you to do. Driving was more dangerous, that was all, and it was dangerous because of the other cars and their drivers; maybe also, she thought, more dangerous because it was easier.

She kept an eye out, on the road ahead and the road behind, on crossroads, and let her mind work: It was a question of whether she should buy the wood Ken had called about. She'd brought her checkbook with her, so she could do that. Ken Forbeck knew wood, so if he said this was worth looking at, it would be.

"Close to nine hundred board feet," he'd told her, "and I'll let you have it for only what it cost me, five hundred and ninety dollars. That's a good price, Dicey."

"Why so cheap?" she'd asked. "Isn't it rift sawn?"

"Of course—the only reason I called is I haven't got any room to store it. I picked up a job lot. A shop in Carolina went out of business, and I bid on the inventory. He'd stocked Philippine mahogany, and some teak—this larch was in that. I won't need it. You'd be a fool to pass it up, Dicey."

If she spent $590, that would get her bank account down to just over $700, $706.87 to be exact, which brought her time limit down to three or four months, March or April. But if she built a boat over the winter and sold it in the spring . . . and in the spring there would be more repair work around, if she could get it . . . that was an awful lot of ifs to be banking on. Banking on ifs wasn't any too smart.

Not taking opportunities wasn't any too smart, either.

After Cambridge, and the long, low bridge over the Choptank River, the land opened out again. Dicey pulled the visor down to keep the sun out of her eyes. Cornfields, cropped to stubble, farmhouses with smoke rising out of their chimneys, and an occasional abandoned farm-produce stand—she passed by them without really seeing them, the speedometer needle steady at fifty. She couldn't believe what Claude Shorter had asked her that morning on the phone.

His call had interrupted her in the middle of hefting the dinghies around, which was no easy job. Moving boats was a two-man job. But the paint was still tacky and she wanted to get to work at least caulking on the next boat, so she'd been shifting them around to fit the two broadside on the rack, when the phone rang. At least, she'd thought, hearing Claude identify himself on the phone, he had been too lazy to come see her in person. She wasn't going to have to wait for him to talk himself out before he'd leave.

Claude Shorter was her landlord, but that didn't mean he thought she'd make a go of the business. He'd rented the shop to her because she offered to pay rent, and he hadn't decided whether he would be selling the property or not, now that he'd built himself a new shop, about four times as large as his old one. What he wanted from her that morning was to contract out some work to her. "I've got this order for thirty rowboats, finished, due the end of March," he said. Claude's business was mainly building rowboats for shipbuilders down in Norfolk, who didn't expect the little boats to hold up more than a year or two. "And the wife says I've got to take her down south. She's giving me hell."

Dicey had mumbled into the phone, not wanting to say anything. If she were his wife she'd give Claude hell, too. Everything he did was sloppy; his boatyard was a mess, his work—using the cheapest possible materials, skimping even on the marine plywood he made boat bottoms out of, and never getting anything better than household-grade plywood for the sides and seats. . . . Claude boasted about putting three coats of paint on his boats, but Dicey figured the only reason he did that was to glue them together so they wouldn't fall apart before he'd delivered them. She and Claude had entirely different ideas about the same job. Claude built boats to make money; he made money so he could buy things, like the trailer down in Florida he spent the winter in, or the diamond earrings he'd come around to show Dicey before he gave them to his wife for Christmas. The more money he made from each boat, the happier he was with his work. Dicey didn't want to make money. She wanted to earn her living building boats.

"I can't finish up the job," Claude said into her ear. "Not and take the missus south. We done the bottoms, and primer's on all of them. It's just the final sanding, then the painting."

"I can't," Dicey told him. The truth was, she didn't want to waste her time on his shoddy workmanship.

Along with which, Claude went on, not paying any attention to what she said, he'd supply all the materials needed, everything was already in his storeroom, sandpaper, paint, brushes, and even the turpentine to soak the brushes clean.

Dicey told him she wasn't interested. She was sorry but she wasn't interested.

"Besides, I'll leave the key to my shop with you—it'll be easy—and there's a trailer, so you can move them back and forth without any trouble. I know you don't have room to store thirty boats in that little place."

"Absolutely not," Dicey said.

His whiskery voice droned on. "Fifty dollars a boat, girlie. Think about that."

Dicey bit her lip—you couldn't take it personally, he called anyone female "girlie."

"Do the math," Claude counseled her.

"No," she said. "No, I can't."

"I'll give you a couple of days to think about it, before I offer the work to someone else. I'm doing you a favor," he explained to her. Looking at the two boats balanced askew on the rack, Dicey wished he'd do her a real favor and hang up. Driving along up to Annapolis, remembering the time-wasting conversation, she wished she'd had the bad manners to hang up on him. She wasn't about to take on work that Claude's sloppy planning left him behind on.

Up ahead, the little Kent Island drawbridge humped up high over the narrows. Across the bridge, the road ran between new shopping centers and new housing developments, to cross the island. Occasional inlets crept in close to the highway, the blue of the water so dark it looked black, and bottomless. The water looked as cold as the land.

Where the ramp rose up to the long Bay Bridge, and the bridge rose up, the sky took over. A setting sun lit up the long feathers of clouds that lay across the cold blue sky. The feathery clouds shone rosy orange, orangy gold. Two jet trails streaked across the open sky, long, golden lines cutting across the whole width of the sky. Then the bridge peaked and she began the downhill slope to the tollbooth.

She took the lower Severn River Bridge into the city. The Naval Academy edged the river like a medieval fortress, as if it had been built to protect the city behind it, or even to protect the whole country that stretched out behind the coastal city. It wouldn't be able to protect anything, however, so it looked like something it wasn't. She crossed the bridge over College Creek—just a hyphen between two roads—turned up the road in front of the college, rounded Church Circle, and then went down the long hill to the arched drawbridge over Spa Creek, where the Yacht Club watched over its long docks. The bridges marked her passage into, across, and out of the city.

She parked the truck beside Ken's van, but instead of going right into the office, she walked down to the creek. Looking west, she saw the creek flowing into the Severn, and the Severn opening out into the bay. At her feet, the water blew up against the pilings and bulkheading. Looking inland, Dicey saw masts, so many that they seemed grown as thick as marsh grass, all up the creek and along the labyrinthine docks built to serve apartment complexes. She began to get the choked and crowded Annapolis feeling. "A good place to live"—that was what Ken had said about it—"but a rotten place to visit." Ken liked to count up all the money those masts represented; but then, Ken liked money, liked talking about it and thinking about it.

She was only looking, Dicey reminded herself, she wasn't planning to buy, she was planning not to be interested in this wood. She didn't bother knocking on the office door, because off-season everybody went home at four-thirty, so there'd be nobody to hear her. She went right through the reception area, glancing at the photographs of work Ken had done—cabinets, tables, bunks, planking in varnished mahogany or oiled teak—and on into the shop. She couldn't afford to be interested in the wood, now she thought about it.

Half an hour later, she had the larch piled in the back of the truck, its projecting ends marked by a red cloth Ken had given her. She was using the hood of the truck as a tabletop, to write the check. "It's a good buy," Ken told her. He'd grown a red beard over the summer and fall, which made him look like a modern-day Viking.

She couldn't quarrel with him. It was a bargain price he was giving her. "Except, of course, you've got no use for it and you don't want to have to store it," she reminded him.

"So, you scratch my back and I scratch yours. Anything wrong with that?"

"Not by me," she agreed, passing him the check. She'd worked for Ken one summer, and they got along fine. As she was turning to climb back into the truck, two men came into the lot. One of them, in a sheepskin jacket and heavy mittens, she knew—Jake Mitchell, she'd stitched sails for him the summer before she worked for Ken. The other, in scuffed docksiders and jeans worn through at the knees, in a down vest over a flannel shirt, she'd never seen before. His clothing was pretty scrungy, but his face, even in the fading light, looked pinkly healthy, freshly shaved, and his hands had none of the thick calluses workingmen's hands had.

"I hoped we'd catch you before you went home, Ken," Jake said. "Hey, hi, Dicey. How's it going?" he asked, but didn't wait for her to answer before introducing her. "Tad Hobart, Dicey Tillerman."

"Call me Hobie," the man said, smiling at her. He was old enough to be her grandfather, and Dicey wouldn't dream of calling him Hobie. He didn't even want her to, anyway. If she hadn't already noticed his cheeks and hands, she'd have figured him out from the way Ken and Jake stepped back, to let him take the lead. A lot of wealthy people who had to do with boats dressed like workmen; but they always had something about them to make sure you knew what they really were. This man, pulling back his sleeve to see the time, had a heavy gold watch. "We were going to get a drink. I've been looking at the sails Jake's making for me, and a beer was starting to sound pretty good. How about it, Ken? And you, too—I'm sorry, I didn't catch your name."

Dicey shook her head. She wanted to get on back.

"Dicey's been slave labor for both of us," Ken said. "She came to pick up some wood."

"You're selling firewood now?" Mr. Hobart asked. "I know things are slow, but I didn't think they were that bad."

"Dicey," Ken said, in a mock confiding tone, "is going to become a boatbuilder."

He didn't need to say it that way, as if she were about three years old. Mr. Hobart looked at her from under thick white eyebrows, and smiled as if there were seven hundred things he knew, things that she'd never figure out. Dicey just stared right back at him.

"What kind of a boat are you going to build, Dicey?" Mr. Hobart asked.

"A pink one."

It took him a minute, and then his smile came back. "Something in rose? Or more lavender?" Reluctantly, Dicey smiled, and he asked again, "What kind of boat? Seriously."

"Just a fourteen-foot rowboat, one you could put a motor on if you wanted."

He kept his eyes on her, as if they were playing poker. "Round-bottomed?"

She shook her head. "Flat. I've never built one on my own before."

"Where did you learn how? Where'd you study?"

"Nowhere," she said. She knew what he was thinking.

"What kind of wood did Ken give you?"

"I bought it," she told him. She'd had about enough of this conversation, and she was tired of the way they kept looking at one another, like it was all a joke, and as if she couldn't see that. She turned around, to open the pickup door.

"Okay, okay," Mr. Hobart said. "What kind of wood did you buy?"

"Tamarack." Well, it was. Tamarack was just an obscure name for it.

"What's that?" he asked Ken. As if she didn't know.

"Larch," Ken told the man, his smile pretty much hidden by his new beard. Dicey put her foot on the running board.

"Hey, hold on, little lady," Mr. Hobart said. "What I'm thinking is, if you'll build it V-bottom, I'll buy it."

That stopped Dicey. She looked at Ken, but he was as surprised as she was. Behind Ken, Jake was smirking away, like the whole thing was some circus show that turned out even better than he'd hoped. She looked back at Mr. Hobart. He was waiting.

"That doesn't seem any too smart to me," she said, surprising him back. "Why would you want to do that?"

He shrugged, smiled, shook his head. "You've worked for Ken, so you must know something. You've worked for Jake, too. That's recommendation enough. I like your looks, I've got a boat they're building for me up in Norwalk, an ocean cruiser, and she'll need a dinghy. I believe in supporting local industry—"

"I'm from Crisfield," Dicey told him.

"What is it, you don't want an order?"

Dicey didn't know.

"Look, here's what I'll do." He reached into an inner pocket of his vest and took out a thick leather folder. Opening it, moving to rest it against the side of the pickup, he took out a pen he kept fitted in it. "I'll pay you fifteen hundred, five hundred down and the rest on delivery—say, the first week in April? How do you spell your name?"

Dicey told him. She didn't know why, but she didn't know why not to. He wrote the check, tore it out, and handed it to her. "Take this with you, and think it over. Let me know what you decide. You can rip the check up if you decide not to. My address is on it. Ask Ken and Jake, they'll vouch for me. I'll meet you two in a couple of minutes; I'll order for you," he said, and walked away.

Dicey had the check in her fingers. "He's not serious," she asked Ken.

"He's serious. He can afford to be. I'm not sure where his money comes from, I heard it was smart investments, but someone else told me he invented a gadget for sonar or maybe it was dishwashers."

"I heard he'd inherited it," Jake said. "Or his wife did."

"Whatever," Ken said, "he's got enough, plus more than enough, to do exactly what he wants."

"I'd take the money and be grateful," Jake advised.

Dicey shook her head. "It's crazy."

"Not to him. It's only crazy to people like us, who have to earn our living," Ken told her. He looked at Jake. "It would be nice, wouldn't it? If I'd had a chance like this, at your age, Dicey—who knows where I'd be now. Not still here, that's all I know. Not still scurrying around for orders. But if it makes you nervous, or you don't think you can do it—"

"Of course I think I can do it, I just don't *know* that I can. I don't like agreeing to do something if I don't know I can."

"How else are you going to find out?" Jake asked her.

Dicey folded Mr. Hobart's check into the pocket of her jacket. "I dunno," she said, biting her lip.

"Hey, Dicey," Ken said, "he's okay, he pays his bills and right on time. Building a dinghy for Tad Hobart—that could be the making of you."

Dicey nodded. She understood. She just didn't like it. She had thought—she thought she was planning to be the making of herself.

"Think about it," Ken advised her.

"I will."

"Keep in touch," he said. "Good luck."

She raised her hand in answer, climbing into the pickup.

It wasn't until she was off the Bay Bridge, driving through the light-spangled darkness across Kent Island, that it hit her: She was in business.

In business, she thought, the recognition floating around inside her head, like a laughter you've had to hold inside and finally you can let free, and laugh out loud. With this check in her pocket, she was in business to build a boat.

She settled down to think, moving along the road. She had some rough drawings she'd made; she'd better go over them. She didn't know how to draw up nautical plans, but it was only a dinghy, it didn't require the same kind of designing. But she'd never thought of a V-bottom, and she'd have to take a look at some, and then make a trip to the library up in Cambridge, to see what the books had to say. A couple of weeks, no more than a couple—she'd have the three boats in the shop done by then, but the supplies she'd need—white ash for the keel and frame, to begin with, and she had the tools but money was going to be a problem. It was expensive to build a boat.

She wondered, following the truck's headlights, as if the headlights were pulling the truck along the highway, if she *should* take on some of Claude's boats. But, come April, she'd have been paid for this boat, so money would be fine again. If she had Claude's boats, even only ten of them, she wouldn't have the kind of time she needed, to do this one right.

There were a dozen things to do, and she wanted to get to work on them right away, but first she had to go to the shop and unload this wood. She'd never felt less tired in her life. Besides, she was impatient to tell Jeff. She could call him from the shop. He'd be as glad as she was about it, and she couldn't even imagine what Gram would say; Sammy, she could. He'd think it was only natural that Dicey should do something like get an order so easily. "Good-o," that's what Sammy would say.

CHAPTER 5

Winter nights, Crisfield went to bed early. As Dicey drove into town, the houses she passed were black shapes with squares of yellow shining on the second stories, or, in the case of ranch-style houses, at the far ends. The pickup was the only moving thing that winter night in the dark and silent town. Cars were parked along the street, motionless as statues—if, Dicey thought, you wanted to make statues of cars, if you didn't have anything better than machines to make statues of.

Statues couldn't be like people, she thought, because people were always moving. If she met a person like a statue, she probably wouldn't like him. Or her. Striking a pose, or staying in one fixed position, those were things she didn't like in people.

Not only that, she thought, turning right, pulling into the parking lot behind the shop, turning off the headlights, enjoying the silence and her own thoughts, a boat was a kind of machine, too. You couldn't deny that. An older, simpler one, but still a machine. And a boat was beautiful. So she shouldn't go around criticizing anyone who wanted to make a statue of a car.

She shoved the truck door open with her shoulder. The night was cold, entirely still. The shop stood silent, deserted. No cars moved down the street, not at this hour of a winter night. No wind blew. If she stayed motionless and listened, she could hear the water moving gently, delicately, in continual motion like Gram's knitting needles.

Silent, solitary, content— Maybe that was why she didn't see it right away. When she saw it—the door to the shop, standing open—she didn't know why she hadn't noticed it as soon as she drove up. For a millisecond, she kicked herself for carelessness. But she *always* locked up, last thing; she couldn't remember doing it that afternoon, but she didn't remember not doing it, either, the way you remember you haven't done something you have the habit of doing—

Dicey ran. Something crunched under her feet. When she got the light turned on, she saw glass all over the cement floor by the door.

She didn't want to look around, so she turned her back on whatever might wait for her, or might not wait. Instead, she studied the door. Someone had punched a hole through the glass, or had hit it with a rock or brick, more likely, because you could cut your hand putting it through glass, even thin glass like the door into the shop. . . . Someone had made that huge hole in the pane and then reached in to twist the little knob that locked the door. Someone had reached in, to open the door. Why would someone do that?

Dicey turned around to answer the question. She felt as if she had only eyes, with no other parts to her body. She felt as if she were two big eyes and nothing else.

The one light cast long shadows. She saw that the two boats in the center of the room had been shoved aside, left askew. But not, she looked carefully, not damaged. The row of paint cans against the far wall, by the door into the bathroom, had been knocked around, spilling white and green blotches onto the plastic sheet she kept under them. The jars in which her paintbrushes soaked had also been knocked over.

Dicey felt like sitting down, in the middle of the floor, to feel bad for a while. Just a little while. She felt like getting angry and stomping around for a while. Why should somebody break in and mess up her shop, what was the point of it? It made her feel sick and it made her angry. But there was picking up to do, so she went to do it; there were paint cans, and the brushes—she'd just roll up as much of the mess as was entirely ruined in the plastic sheet. She'd have to replace it all, which would cost her close to a hundred dollars. When she thought about that, anger began to be the only feeling she had.

Dicey stood looking down at the mess on the plastic sheet, trying not to think, and thinking she was glad she'd put that sheet down because it sure made cleaning up easier. If the paint, for example, had soaked into the cement floor, how would she have gotten it out? Claude would probably be able to make her replace the whole floor, and she could about guess how much that would cost. So it wasn't nearly as bad as it could have been. It was bad, but it could have been worse. A lot worse.

She studied the shop, figuring out what needed doing first. Standing at the far wall, she could see what she hadn't noticed before, and the sick feeling in her stomach swelled up to push at her heart. It was as if what she saw didn't even hesitate at her eyes but went straight down to her stomach, as if her stomach had the eyes that saw this.

Her tools. They'd taken her tools. The rack above the worktable was empty, just a couple of long pieces of wood nailed into the wallboard. Adze, broadax, saws—they were all gone.

The shelf under the table was shadowed, so she couldn't see from where she stood if they'd noticed it or not. She didn't want to go down the length of the shop and find out, but she made herself.

And the shelf was empty, too. Hammers, screwdrivers, planes, straightedges—gone, all of them. The boxes of nails and screws had been left, but everything else—

All the tools she'd found, and stripped down to refinish, and taken apart and put back together, polished and honed, and the ones Jeff had given her, too—

Dicey leaned her hands against the worktable. Her head kept wanting to bend down and rest on the wood. Her body wanted to fold up. She didn't even have the energy to get angry.

Who would do this to her? And why would they? And what was she going to do?

Clean up, that was what. First things first. First she'd clean up and that would clear up her mind.

No, first she better call Gram. It was late and Gram would be wondering. She kept her back to the room while she made the call. If she wasn't looking at what wasn't there, it wouldn't creep into her mind. The phone rang only twice before Gram answered. "I'm back, at the shop," Dicey said.

"And you've eaten."

"Not yet. But I'll be a while yet here, so I wanted you to know that I'm back."

"Jeff wants you to call him," Gram's voice said into her ear.

"Yeah, okay, thanks. I'll see you in the morning, Gram."

When she'd hung up, Dicey got to work. First, she gathered up the brushes and jars, took them into the little bathroom, and lined them along the back of the toilet. She'd need to get turpentine in the morning, because if the brushes hardened up they'd all have to be replaced, too. Whoever it was hadn't gone into the bathroom, she guessed; a dozen clamps were still piled under the sink. They hadn't found the clamps. So at least they hadn't taken everything. They must have opened the bathroom door and decided it was so small and grungy, there couldn't be anything worth taking out of it.

Dicey rolled the plastic sheet up, from the outside edges, rolling up the empty cans inside it. She hefted it over her shoulder and took it out to the Dumpster. The quiet of her empty building, with all the other empty buildings around and the empty water beside, and the empty sky overhead, came creeping at her. She went back into the shop and closed the door, even though with the smashed window it couldn't keep anything out. It wasn't even keeping the cold air out.

She dialed Jeff's number and listened to the short buzzing rings. He'd be playing his guitar, probably, with a fire burning in the woodstove; or maybe reading, studying. The phone rang once, twice, and she almost hung up: She had to call Claude. After all, the shop belonged to Claude. But if she hung up and Jeff was halfway to the phone; and she didn't know how late it was, if Claude would be in bed already, and she didn't know what difference it made if Claude found out tonight or tomorrow, anyway.

Jeff picked up the phone on the fourth ring. "Hello?"

"What time is it?" she asked.

"Ten of nine. Why?"

"Can I call you back?"

She could hear his smile, as clear as if his face was in front of her eyes. She could see why he thought it was a funny conversation, but she wasn't finding anything particularly amusing.

"Sure. Or I'll call you."

"Okay, bye." She hung up. Claude's number was on the inside of a notebook she kept on the table, with numbers and prices and ideas for designs in it. His wife answered the phone. When Dicey asked to speak to him, Mrs. Shorter demanded, "Who is this?" But when Dicey told her, all she said was a bored "oh." Dicey told Claude that the shop had been broken into. "That's too bad," he said. She reported that her tools had been taken and the glass in the window smashed. "That's tough, girlie. I don't know why you're calling me, though. You should be calling your insurance agent. Although, I guess, the window'll come under my policy. Tell you what, why don't you take the cost of repairing it out of the next rent check? Did you change your mind about those boats?"

"No," Dicey said. She didn't have an insurance agent. She didn't have insurance.

"Well, don't take a break-in personal," Claude advised her. "It just happens sometimes."

She hadn't even thought about insurance. She didn't even know how you went about getting insured. The Tillermans didn't have anything worth insuring, except the truck. Dicey dialed Jeff's number again.

He answered on the first ring. "Dicey? What's wrong?"

"How do you know something's wrong?"

"You sounded—funny."

"Oh. I didn't think I— Someone broke into the shop," she told him.

He waited. "And?" he asked.

"They broke the window in the door. To get in."

"But that wouldn't bother you. Are the boats all right?"

"Yeah. And they took my tools," she admitted.

He didn't say anything. He felt the same way she did about her tools, she guessed. "I'll be right over," he said.

"No," she told him, "don't. I've got to clean up and then go home. I bought that wood, but I'll leave it in the truck overnight, I think. I'm not going to leave it here."

"That sounds smart. I'd like to come help out."

"I'd rather you didn't, Jeff."

"If you say so. But tomorrow—we'd better go out and replace them, or you won't be able to work. You're covered against theft, aren't you?"

"How would I be covered?" she demanded.

"Your insurance policy."

"I don't have one." He should know that. She didn't know why everyone thought she had an insurance policy when everyone who knew her should know she didn't. "I gotta go."

"Dicey? You know how sorry I am, don't you?"

She did, although what good sympathy did she didn't know. It just made her feel worse. She got off the phone and got to work.

It wasn't ten minutes later that she heard a car. She was trying to get broken glass up off the rough cement floor, practically scraping at it with a broom. She heard the engine, heard it approach, then idle, then stop. She'd *told* him not to. If she'd wanted sympathy she'd have asked him over, but it wasn't sympathy she wanted. Sympathy just made you feel worse and she didn't need to feel any worse. She stood up, ready to let him know how she felt about being ignored like that, being treated as if she didn't mean what she said. She stood there with her fingers clenched around the handle of the broom, ready to give Jeff an earful.

But it was Mina who walked through the doorway. At the sight of Mina, in a baggy sweatshirt, with flannel-pajama bottoms hanging out of the legs of her jeans, the crossness that had been puffing Dicey up evaporated. Mina stood just inside the door, looking around. "Yep," she said, "somebody broke in, for sure."

Dicey didn't see any need to comment on that.

Mina turned around slowly, to look at the empty worktable and at the empty rack above it. When she turned around again, her lips were stiff. "I gotta admit, I was hoping I'd heard Jeff wrong. Don't you ever wonder about people?" She put her hands on her hips, angry. "I do. Sometimes I could just—knock some heads together. We better finish this glass first." She pushed up the arms of her sweatshirt, as if getting ready for a fight. "What're you standing around dumbfaced for like that?"

Dicey shook her head. Mina stood right in front of her, big and dark and strong, with her sleeves pushed up, dressed out in her anger. "I'm glad to see you," Dicey said.

"Hunh," Mina answered. She pulled down the right sleeve of the sweatshirt, stretching it over her hand and then catching the overhang with her fingers, from inside. When she'd done that, she walked out to the open door and hit at it with her elbow. Pieces of glass fell out, then shards and sprinkles, as she ran her forearm around the window frame. Dicey stood, watching Mina punch at the broken window, elbow it and shoulder it and finally beat at it with her protected fist to beat all the glass out of it.

"Well, that makes me feel better," Mina said. "How about you?"

"I thought you wore nightgowns," Dicey said, which was the only thought in her mind.

Mina laughed. Her laughter was as rich as soup. Like Gram's beef-and-vegetable soup, her laughter warmed and filled Dicey's stomach. "You're right, I do. That is, when I haven't just dumped my long-time guy. All right. The only question is, what do we do next? You finish up the glass and I'll get some more lights on." She went down the room, reaching up to turn on the lights. "Where do you keep cleanser? There's wet paint on the floor here. What happened, did they dump cans of paint?"

"Yeah."

"Well." Mina surveyed the room. "I suppose it could have been worse. They could have trashed the place."

Dicey shrugged. They could have not broken in at all. But there wasn't any use thinking of could-haves.

She continued sweeping up glass while Mina scrubbed at the cement floor. Those two jobs done, they lifted the two boats back onto the rack. Dicey went carefully around each boat, checking for nicks or dents.

"We've got to figure out some way of covering that window," Mina said. "Probably a sheet of plywood nailed over it."

"They took all my tools," Dicey admitted. "Everything. I don't even have a hammer. So we can't nail anything."

Finally, Mina had another suggestion. "Dad keeps a toolbox in the car. We can use the flat of a wrench, and at least hang up a sheet of plastic."

Dicey just went along with whatever Mina suggested. She held up the plastic while Mina hammered little nails through it and into the wooden frame of the door. "Did you call the police?" Mina asked.

"What's the point?"

"To prove somebody stole something from you, for your insurance company."

Dicey shook her head.

"What does that mean?"

"I don't have an insurance company." Even Mina assumed Dicey had insurance. Dicey guessed she wasn't as smart as she thought she was, but she didn't much feel like talking about that. Not right now.

"How about your landlord?"

"He's not insured against theft of whatever's in the building," Dicey said. "Just the building."

They stood there, the two of them, in the damp, chilly air. Mina was worried, Dicey could see that. She didn't know what she was. Whatever it was she was, it was clogging her up inside, leaving no room for anything else. She was afraid Mina was going to make an angry, sympathetic speech, but Mina didn't. "You going to be okay?" was all Mina said.

"Yeah," Dicey said. She didn't see how she *was* going to be okay, because without her tools she couldn't build, and she didn't have time or money to go around finding another set, not to mention getting them into working shape—whoever had robbed her of the tools had robbed her of the hours she'd spent on them, too—as if they'd taken up a box filled with minutes and hours and days, and stolen it. She didn't even know what new tools cost, although her guess was she couldn't afford them. That made her realize she hadn't built up a big enough savings account before diving into this whole project. It had seemed like so much money, but it wasn't enough. She should have worked another six months, or at least three. She hadn't planned it realistically. Dicey didn't know what she was going to do now. But Mina, who had her own problems, putting herself through college, didn't need to hear about Dicey's troubles, especially since there wasn't anything Mina could do about them. "Yeah," Dicey said again, "I'm okay."

Then, as if repeating it made it true, she knew she would be. She'd faced worse, and gotten through it. She had money in the bank, and a check in her pocket. Besides, maybe no matter how much money you had it wouldn't be enough, because money itself wasn't enough. She had her plans and she knew how to work hard. She would be okay, she made herself that promise. "I'll figure out something," she told Mina.

"You always do." Mina stood there in the darkness, big and warm, sure of what she was saying.

And why shouldn't Mina be sure, since it was true. Dicey filled her lungs with energizing damp air. "Yeah."

Something made Mina laugh again.

"What's so funny now?" Dicey demanded.

"Sometimes, I look at the two of us and—I'm gonna leave old Dexter to his honey babe, and get on with my own life. You never liked him that much anyway, did you?"

"Half the time I like him a lot," Dicey said. "The other half—well, he's so arrogant and you do your supportive-female act and—I don't mind the arrogance, but I mind you—so I guess no, not that much. Although he's interesting—"

"Oh, yeah, that boy has brains enough," Mina agreed. "And ambition."

"For himself," Dicey pointed out.

"I know. Being Dexter's woman—I guess I just don't want to be any man's woman. I guess maybe that's what's really behind all the jive he says I've been giving him. I go back to school tomorrow morning. You know what I wonder? I wonder if all this school isn't a way of running away. You know? A failure to choose, and get down to the business of life. I don't think so, but I have the suspicion that a really free woman wouldn't ever wonder."

"I dunno," Dicey said. "Maybe that's true, but it seems like a lie, because how can you not wonder?"

"Well, I wish I knew how," Mina said, laughing. "I know what I want to do, and I think I know why I want to, but what if— Oh, well, if worse comes to worst, I'll work for you, okay? You can hire me. I know I don't know anything about boats, but I'm a quick learner."

Dicey wouldn't mind a bit working with Mina. "I can't afford to hire anybody," she pointed out.

"We can worry about that at the time. It's still a couple of years before I'll get a chance to fail to get into law school. By then, who knows? By then you may be the Sara Lee of boatbuilders."

"I wouldn't count on it," Dicey answered, smiling at the idea. She wasn't aiming for that, not even close. Earning a living, that was what she was aiming for.

After Mina left, Dicey turned off the lights and locked the door. She didn't know why she was bothering. First thing in the morning, she'd need to get a pane of glass and set it in. Except for the glass itself, she could find whatever else she needed—putty and a screwdriver to pry apart the wooden window frame, and a hammer to put it back together with—at home. She went on home.

Despite the hour, there was a light on in the kitchen. When Dicey had covered the larch with plastic sheets, she went inside. It was Gram who was awake, sitting at the table, drinking a cup of tea, wearing a faded plaid bathrobe. Gram had dark circles under her eyes. "You should be in bed," Dicey said. "You shouldn't have waited up."

"That's for me to decide, isn't it. You sounded on the phone as if something unpleasant had happened. Are you going to sit down?"

"No."

If Dicey sat down they would talk for a while, and Gram should be in bed asleep, she should have been asleep an hour ago. "I'll tell you in the morning," Dicey said. "I'm back, as you see, home safe—and I expect to see you get up from that chair and go to your room."

Sometimes you just had to boss Gram around, she was so stubborn.

As if she was pretending not to be doing what she'd been told, Gram got up, went to the sink, rinsed out the cup, and dropped the teabag into the garbage. Dicey just waited. She stood and watched and waited, not saying a word, until she saw the door to her grandmother's bedroom close. Then Dicey went upstairs to her own room, to take a look at her checkbook and try to figure out where she stood, to revise her plans.

CHAPTER 6

Dicey awoke the next morning with the sense that she was ready to solve problems, the way you often do, as if the time of sleep were a long journey to a distant country where alterations in geographical formations, in light, in ways of living, in language even, enable you to see your own world more clearly.

It was early. The sky outside her window shone dark, glassy blue. Night with its stars had traveled on, leaving the field of sky clear for approaching sunlight. But the sun had not yet arrived.

She crossed the dark hall to the bathroom. All around her, the house breathed gently in sleep. When she returned she sat at the desk. There, she pulled out paper and worked the figures: $75 a month for rent, including utilities, plus about $20 for the phone. That gave her, in the bank, more than three months, without taking anything out for supplies. Even with supplies her bank account could cover the next three months. Her income was $75 a month, from storage fees—and she'd sent out the bills for December, so that money should be coming in—plus an extra $150 when she'd completed maintenance work on the three boats. Although, she'd have to subtract from that the price of whatever supplies she'd used up getting the boats ready. Even after subtracting, however, she could look forward to the extra hundred-odd dollars.

That completed one column, one side of the paper. On the

other side, she had more question marks than anything else. She would have to get some insurance, she guessed, and some way of shuttering the door. Plywood would do it, a piece of plywood hung down over the inside of the glass. It was too possible that whoever had robbed her once might return, the same way a crabber returns to put his pots down in a spot that worked well once for him. She needed the extra security of some kind of window covering that could be put on and taken off. And she needed tools, but she didn't know how much to estimate for that. Maybe $250. She'd never bought new tools. She didn't have any records of how much she had spent on her old tools, over the years, her own tools that she'd—she stopped thinking along that line.

Dicey compared the numbers. If she took $250 out of the account, that would get her down to barely two months. The $75 she gave to Gram every month, for room and board, were seventy-five dollars she could ill afford. For a second, Dicey imagined that she might not give Gram the money, but she knew that she couldn't fail to pay her own way at home.

When she had the figures all written down in front of her, Dicey added in the $500 check that was in her pocket. That would pay for tools and supplies. She didn't like the idea of spending it, because it meant she was spending her profit before she'd made a single cut in the wood, before she'd even unloaded the wood into the shop. It meant she was spending what she hadn't earned.

Dicey leaned her head on her hands, and looked at the numbers. Looking at them, at how they didn't change, at their balancings between debits and credits, she made herself look again at Claude's offer. You had to balance time and money. She had to weigh the time she'd have to waste working on Claude's boats against the money that work would bring in.

Working full-time, which was about a nine-hour day, she could probably get the thirty boats done in two months. If she put eight or nine hours a day into Claude's boats, and if she were willing to work longer hours, then she could still spend two or three hours a day on the boat for Mr. Hobart.

Dicey could work, she knew that about herself. What she didn't want to do—and she didn't want to do it so much that it was the same as not being able to do it—was borrow money, even against future earnings, or fail to pay Gram the monthly room and board.

That looked like the decision, then. She couldn't call it a choice when there was nothing else she could really choose to do. All she was deciding was that she would be able to do what she knew she'd have to do.

Dicey took another sheet of paper and roughed out a work schedule: with eight weeks, she'd have to do three or four boats a week. It would be tight, because she had to allow time for the coats of paint to dry, but it could probably be done. She didn't want to do it, didn't want to spend her time on that kind of work—but doing it was the only way she could see to stay in business. At the end, she'd have three clear weeks to concentrate on Mr. Hobart's boat.

It wasn't a decision she liked, but it was a decision made, and she felt better for it. She lifted her head from the pages of numbers and looked out the window. The sun had come up, dragging low gray clouds behind it. Dicey got dressed, fast, and went downstairs.

Gram was ahead of her in the kitchen, with a batch of pancake batter in a bowl and the griddle hot, the table set, and the bottle of maple syrup warming in a pot of simmering water. That was one of their few extravagances. They bought real maple syrup, the cheapest kind, but still the real thing, and real butter, too. Everywhere else the Tillermans pinched their pennies, hard.

Sammy stumbled in while Dicey was still eating. He'd always woken up slowly and reluctantly. Dicey watched him clumsily pull out a chair, sit down on the edge of it and then slide cautiously over to the middle, look at the fork and knife as if he'd never seen utensils before; she lowered her face to hide her smile. The first ten minutes of Sammy in the morning were as much fun as puppies. After two plates of pancakes, his eyes brightened and he began speaking at normal speed. Dicey asked him then to help unload the wood at the shop, first thing. Maybeth, scrubbed and brushed, asked if she could help too. "There's a lot to do," Dicey said, saying it quickly, to get it over with, "because someone broke into the shop last evening. They took my tools," she told them, keeping her eyes on her plate, "but the boats are okay. I don't want to talk about it, if that's okay."

"Neither would I," Gram said. "Neither do I."

With the three of them working at it, the lumber quickly piled up beside the long side wall of the shop. Dicey looked at the crowded room and wondered how she was going to find enough space for Claude's boats, but she couldn't worry about that. She was going to do what she had to do, because she had to do it in order to do what she wanted to do. She'd always been able to live that way. That was the way of living that always worked for her.

She picked up the phone, intending to call Claude, but dialed Jeff's number instead. "If," Jeff said, "you come over here around noon, we can go up to Salisbury, to replace those tools."

Dicey didn't say anything, because her throat had closed up tight.

"Dicey? Are you there?"

"Yeah. Yeah, that sounds good," she said, forcing the words out.

"I'll put in a morning's work on this paper, and see you between twelve and one sometime."

It was just like Jeff to know what needed to be done. She hadn't known why she called Jeff first, but now she did—because she could count on him.

Claude, when she got ahold of him, was smug. "I knew you'd change your mind. You've got more sense than to turn away profitable work, girlie."

Dicey didn't bother to enlighten him.

"We're leaving Monday, so you better stop by before then to pick up the keys. I been thinking, I'll pay you by thirds. When the job's a third done, write me up a bill. It's a good thing you called back this morning. I was about to call a couple of other shops and give them the work."

Dicey almost wished he had. Why didn't you? she wanted to ask; or, Why don't you go ahead and do that? But she wasn't free to. "I'll be by later" was all she said. He didn't thank her and she didn't know why. She knew why she didn't thank him.

With Sammy and Maybeth's help, she went through the morning's chores. First, they got a piece of plywood and a couple of fittings, so that Sammy could make a cover for the inside of the door window. At the hardware store they also picked up a pane of glass and a box of glazier points. Dicey paid cash but kept the receipt in her wallet, to send along with next month's rent to Claude. Returning her brother and sister to the shop, to replace the window, she went back downtown, to deposit the $500 check and find an insurance agent. That took longer than she'd planned, because by now everybody she had business with had heard about the break-in, and wanted to say something to her about it. Most of them, especially the insurance agent, looked at her in that self-satisfied way people have when the bad luck is yours, as if they would have told you so if you'd asked them. Dicey didn't let any of them get through to her, not Gerry at the hardware store, who had graduated in Jeff's class from the high school, nor Mrs. Pommes at the bank, who dyed her graying hair a carroty red and wore long filigreed earrings, nor even Mr. Snyder, who filled out forms and told her where to sign, then took her hundred-dollar check for a year's insurance of whatever was in the shop, valued at $10,000. It was for a whole year's insurance, Dicey said to herself. She'd have to pay it only once a year. With the $500 for Mr. Hobart's boat she'd just put in, she had $1,107.87 in her account.

"Well, Dicey, you've got the barn door locked now," Mr. Snyder said to her, clipping her check on top of his pile of forms. Mr. Snyder had springy gray-white hair and a fleshy face; his little round eyes behind little round glasses looked as if they were laughing. Dicey didn't think there was much to laugh about. The whole thing was leaving a bitter taste at the back of her mouth and she felt as if she ought to apologize—

Apologize to whom, she demanded of herself. She was the one who'd been robbed. Since Mr. Snyder was making money out of the deal, she didn't see that she needed to tell him she was sorry and she'd never do it again. She'd made a mistake and she'd learned. She should have had insurance and now she did. She should have known, she guessed—if the dinghies had been damaged she'd have been in real trouble. She should have asked somebody what it was she ought to get done, in order to go into business. Anyone who knew would have included insurance on the list. But it was too late now, and now she had insurance so it wouldn't happen again.

Let that be an end on it, she thought, getting up from the wooden chair she'd pulled up to Mr. Snyder's desk, shaking his hand, not returning his smile. She ran down the wooden staircase, not because she felt like running but because it felt good to slam her sneakers down hard, and feel the whole structure rattle under her.

Some days, she wished she were a lumberjack. She would like that feeling, the swing of the ax, the bright cuts into the wood, the patient work and eventually the *crack*, the long breaking fall of the tree. Sometimes, that was the kind of work she wanted to do, up in some harsh northern country, moving through the silent forest, using her strength to bring down the marked trees.

CHAPTER 7

When she knocked on the door to the house Jeff and his father lived in, then turned the knob and entered the tiny kitchen without waiting for Jeff to let her in, it felt as if she was walking into Sunday afternoon. For a second, she felt dislocated in time, and cross with herself for forgetting that stores would be closed on Sundays.

Jeff was sitting where she knew she'd find him, at a long table that faced the big glass living-room doors. He turned around in his chair to welcome her. Books and papers were spread out over the tabletop. "Do you want to hear something wonderful?" he asked her.

Dicey shook her head. She let the peace of the room surround her, the big sofa and the enameled woodstove, some European model designed to keep Scandinavian houses warm through a Nordic winter. She let her eyes rest on the scene opening out before her, beyond the expanse of double-paned window, the brief colorless lawn, the tangled woods and motionless creek, the pale stretch of marshes, and the sullen gray sky overhead. From the stereo, orchestral music played quietly, rich, flowing music, Dicey didn't know the name of it. She went to stand behind Jeff, to put her hands on his shoulders. She looked down at the long yellow sheets of legal paper, but didn't read what he'd written on them. The opened books looked like poetry.

A double major, biology and chemistry, with a minor in philosophy, Jeff had taken five years for college, to study everything he wanted to. He also took one English course a semester—for the sake of the professor, he'd explained, because this particular professor really taught you how to read on your own, and meeting his mind was like meeting a good friend. Jeff had the time because he was doing the extra year, and besides, he had no social life to keep up with. "Good" was Dicey's response to that. She'd never taken a course she didn't have better things to do than, but she knew Jeff felt differently.

"No, listen," Jeff said. The music in the room washed around Dicey, like water at shoulder height, and the iron-gray creek lay looped over the flat, barren landscape like a line of melody. Jeff leaned forward, to read.

Our indiscretion sometime serves us well,
When our deep plots do pall, and that should learn us
There's a divinity that shapes our ends,
Rough-hew them how we will.

It didn't seem so great to Dicey. In the first place, it was bad grammar, saying learn instead of teach. In the second place, she didn't believe that fate decided what was going to happen to you. "I don't believe in fate," she told Jeff. "I didn't think you did, either."

"I'm not sure what I believe in," he said, "but rough-hewing, I know about that."

"Like wood?"

"Like wood. What I can't figure out about it is, if I'm supposed to take *ends* as conclusions, the end, death? Or as purposes, like the end justifies the means?"

Dicey had nothing to say about that.

"Or probably both. I mean, it's Shakespeare so probably both are probably right. Isn't it a great line, though?"

If it was Shakespeare, it was more than one line, it was three or four lines in Shakespearean verse. Dicey made a noise deep in her throat, and let him take it as he wanted.

He stood up, smiling. "Okay, okay, I'm ready. We'll leave right away. No more of this dillydallying in the realms of gold. I'm going to make myself a sandwich. You want one?"

Dicey shook her head. He knew she was coming to pick him up. He should have eaten before she got there. She didn't have time to stand around, watching him butter the bread and put slices of ham on it, spread mustard on one slice, then decide that, after all, he'd better make two sandwiches, adding a thin slice of Swiss cheese to the second. Dicey stood by the door, watching, chewing at her lip. She'd made a list of what she needed to get. She'd like to keep the cost at $250, tops, she'd decided that. But she knew she had no idea if that was a reasonable amount or not.

Eating at one sandwich, holding the other, Jeff turned around to face her. Now what? she wondered. "I'll get your jacket," she said.

"I've been thinking," he said. "Don't get angry, promise?"

"How can I promise that?"

"Promise. It's nothing serious or anything."

"No," she said. "I can't. I don't even know what you're going to say."

She wished he'd just spit it out, so they could get into the truck and moving.

"Tools are likely to be expensive." Jeff sounded apologetic, as if he was the one sticking the price tags on them. "I was hoping you'd let me buy them for you. Or, it could be a loan and you could just wait to pay me back until whenever you could pay it back."

He knew better than that. He knew Dicey wasn't about to borrow money. That was why she'd worked those two jobs and for so long, so she could pay her own way. If you weren't paying your own way, then you weren't earning your own living. "No," she said.

"But it doesn't make sense."

Dicey didn't care. The Tillermans didn't borrow money, it was as simple as that.

Later, she could almost have regretted that, writing the last of three checks at the last of three hardware stores. The figures lined up, inexorable as armies: 193.25, 210.22, 87.63. Total: 491.10. Dollars. And that didn't even include an adze. They couldn't find an adze anywhere—one store had once had a supplier in Kentucky, but that company had gone out of business; maybe she should try some of the antique shops? Nobody had seen an adze for years, but had she ever seen a drawl knife?

She bought the short-handled knife, not that it was a good substitute, but it would rough out the cut for her, she guessed, more slowly than an adze and without the smooth finish an adze—well swung—could give you. An adze you used standing up, with the length and strength of your arms and back, your feet straddling the wood. This knife you had to crouch over a board and pull at, little chopping strokes. Dicey didn't let herself think about the differences. She just wrote the checks.

She had spent almost $600 in one day and hadn't done a lick of work, either. All she'd done was get ready to work. If she didn't start working . . . she finished subtracting, down to $615.77 . . . and folded the checkbook back over itself, fast . . . in two or three months she'd have nothing but a big fat zero in that checkbook.

She declined Jeff's help, dropped him off at the end of his driveway, and unloaded her purchases into the shop herself. It wasn't as if what she'd bought was anything as good as what she'd lost. For all that money, you'd think she'd have something really good. The new wood was pale, unfinished, and even imperfectly sanded. She felt the roughness of sloppily sanded wood against her palms. Of everything she'd gotten the only thing she positively liked was the forty-eight-inch level—the several little glass tubes set horizontally and vertically into waxed pieces of wood, all the joints tight, the weight balancing in her hand—she would enjoy setting that level, reading it. But the rest were second-rate—and they'd cost her $491.10 of her hard-earned money.

She didn't have time for regret. As she'd said to Jeff when he asked her what she'd be doing that evening and the next day, all she had time to do was work. "If I don't get working," she'd said, but wasn't able to think of anything bad enough to explain what would happen.

Jeff understood. He never asked Dicey to be anything other than what she was; he never had. He was going back to school on Sunday, anyway. That was probably good, because the only thing for Dicey to do now was work hard, and harder, if she was going to have any chance at the business. At the thought of the jobs ahead, finishing the maintenance, figuring out how to build a rack to store the larch so there would be maximum working space left clear, starting in on Claude's boats, writing to Mr. Hobart to say she'd build his boat and then getting to work making some drawings: Thinking about what she was going to do, Dicey felt better. For the first time since she had opened the shop door and seen what had happened to her, she felt as if she knew what she was going to do about things.

It was always like that for her. She'd always had to decide what to do, then stick to doing it no matter what, no matter how difficult it would be. Things weren't easy, they never had been; in fact, things were often pretty hard. But Dicey was harder.

CHAPTER 8

First thing Saturday morning, Dicey wrote to Mr. Hobart. The address on the check was a post office box in Annapolis, as if he didn't want people to know which house was his. Before she could have second thoughts, she pushed the letter into a downtown mailbox. Then she drove on to the shop.

To hold the larch, she cobbled together a rack out of old pieces of wood she'd found in their barn. The best place to put the rack was in front of the big metal door that opened out to the water. In winter, she wouldn't be needing that exit. She could haul Claude's rowboats in sideways through the shop door if she lined the floor with plastic sheets so it wouldn't splinter the wood.

Dicey put off going to see Claude until just before lunch. If he had a meal waiting for him, he wouldn't spend so much time talking at her, giving her advice about things she already knew but not thinking of what she didn't know and could really use advice on. Like insuring the contents of your shop, for one example. All she planned to do at Claude's was pick up the key, take a look at the storeroom to find out which paint she should be using, and make sure his boat-trailer would hook up to the truck. Everything always took longer than you planned for, she had learned that, but then she'd learned how to plan for that. By midafternoon, she had the lumber stacked up high and neat, where it would keep safe and ready until she could start building Mr. Hobart's boat. Then she got to work finishing up the last dinghy.

It was long dark when she got home. Jeff had come for supper, and they'd kept a plate warm for her. Dicey was too tired for talk, but she sat up in the living room, listening, with a good day's work behind her and good company all around her. Jeff was going to drive James up to Baltimore with him the next day so James could catch a train back to New Haven. James and Sammy were looking over what Maybeth would have to study for her mid-year exams. Dicey listened, sitting close to Jeff on the sofa, until her head slipped down onto his shoulder and she heard Sammy say, as if from very far away, "They're both falling asleep."

Her eyes snapped open in time to see Gram's eyes snap open. "Go to bed, both of you," Sammy ordered them.

Dicey, who planned to be up by five-thirty the next morning and at work by six, didn't protest.

The cold, gray Sunday went by the same way, except that when Dicey got home Gram was with Maybeth and Sammy in the living room, taking down the Christmas tree, and she ate alone in the kitchen. Monday, school started and so did rain, a cold winter rain that slanted steadily down. But by Monday she was ready for the first of Claude's boats, right on schedule.

Gram drove Maybeth and Sammy to school Monday morning and then brought the truck over to the shop. Together Gram and Dicey went over to Claude's, hooked up the trailer, and brought over three of the rowboats, one after the other. They covered each boat with plastic sheeting for the short trip, then worked it sideways through the doorway to lay it on the floor of the shop. There, they would put more logs into the stove and warm their hands before setting out for the next boat. On the third trip back, they loaded the back of the truck with cans of paint. Gram set a stack of sandpaper beside her on the seat.

When the last can of paint had been set into its row beside the rack that held Mr. Hobart's wood, it was almost time for Gram to go fetch Sammy and Maybeth. Neither Gram nor Dicey had eaten lunch. Dicey didn't know about Gram, but she was hungry, and cold, and the only dry part of her was her waist. They stood by the tin stove, looking around at the cluttered shop. "I could happily kill whoever made off with your tools," Gram said. "And I think I'd better find you a kettle."

Too tired to figure out how her grandmother's mind was working, Dicey just asked, "Why?"

"Hot chocolate," Gram said impatiently. Then she sneezed. "I could use a cup of cocoa, or tea—even hot water—before I go back out into this weather." Gram hadn't even taken off her poncho. The bottom of her long skirt was dark with wetness. "We'd better get one of these boats set out so you can begin work on it. How desperate are things?" Gram asked.

"I'm okay," Dicey said.

"Don't sidle away from questions," Gram snapped.

"I wouldn't mind something hot myself," Dicey admitted. She should have thought of that, too. Water dripped down the side of Gram's face. "Moderately desperate," she said.

"Or you wouldn't be working on these"—Gram gestured at the rowboats they'd set along the shop floor, looking for the right phrase—"these boats no self-respecting rat would make a home in."

"Yeah."

"I like to think you know what you're doing, girl."

"Claude's paying good money, and I'll be building Mr. Hobart's at the end of it," Dicey reminded her grandmother. And reminded herself, too.

"There's only the one more boat to be hauled over tomorrow," Gram said. "That's a blessing." She sneezed again.

"Are you wearing socks?" Dicey demanded. Sometimes Gram stuck to her principles beyond common sense.

"What kind of a fool do you take me for?" Gram answered.

"No kind of fool at all. Just stubborn."

"Well, I am, two pair," Gram said. "For all the good that does in this weather. I'm going to send Maybeth with the truck to fetch you home, so don't think of riding that bike today. You hear me, girl? Can we unhook the trailer now?"

The rain held for two more days, but Dicey barely noticed. The sound of water drumming on the tin roof was soothing, joining in with the sound of the wood crackling in the stove and the sound of the sandpaper smoothing off the worst of the rough places on Claude's boats. She did the boats in pairs, inside first, then outside, sanding one down completely and painting it before starting the sanding of the second. The only human voice the shop heard that week was her own, yelling at Claude when a particularly bad join snagged the paintbrush.

The only difference the weekend made, besides occasional breaks in the rain, was that she could take the truck. She had time—because with the air so damp a coat of paint dried more slowly than she'd planned—to stop by the library and take out a couple of boat-building books. She had the first coat of paint on the second pair of rowboats, she had a kettle heating water on the stove for a cup of hot chocolate, and she had her notebook open in front of her, copying sketches to study proportions, on Sunday afternoon. At the end of the two hours, she raised her head from the papers she'd been concentrating on, and smiled.

It was as if all the long hours of work, all week long, had been to earn these two hours. And they were all worth it.

She rinsed out her mug in the bathroom sink and ran her fingertips along the side of a rowboat. She almost wished it wouldn't be quite dry enough, but it was. She pried the top off yet another gallon of paint, stirred it, dipped the brush into it, and got back to work.

What with the three storage boats racked up along the wall, the four rowboats, and the stacked pile of building wood, the little shop was almost impassably crowded. The days, too, felt crowded. Dicey worked through them. Her arms ached from the circular motion of sanding and the stroking motion of painting. Her shoulders ached from the hefting around of plywood boats. Her back and the backs of her legs, too, ached—from bending over, to sand and paint, long hour after long hour. She lost track of the days. She'd been this tired before—so tired you'd almost rather sleep than feed your hunger, tired with worry as much as from the mental exhaustion of cooking up ways to get what you needed and the physical exhaustion of following through on your own plans. That's what it had been like the summer she had brought her brothers and sister down to Crisfield, and this kind of tiredness was how tired she'd been, all that summer, all the long way from Connecticut to Crisfield. Like that previous time, Dicey had a place to get to. Knowing the place—what it was, this time, rather than where it was on a map—kept Dicey going.

She gave Mr. Hobart a week to answer her letter. When she noticed that a week and more had gone by, she figured that he'd been serious about the order. So the money in the bank was hers to spend. Gram caught a cold, probably from helping out those two rainy days. Dicey, eating breakfast alone in the six-o'clock kitchen, heard her grandmother, coughing away, behind the bedroom door. When Dicey opened the door, Gram was sitting up in bed, drinking a cup of hot tea. "I'm getting better," she announced.

"You don't sound it," Dicey countered. "You ought to spend a day or two in bed."

"You just worry about what *you've* undertaken, girl. I'll take care of myself."

Maybeth and Sammy were studying for exams, mostly for Maybeth's exams: science, math, American history, English—neither art nor chorus had an exam. History and English were the courses she absolutely had to pass, and Sammy, as a tenth grader, hadn't taken them. Dicey wasn't much help, either. She couldn't remember the things you had to know for American history. She could barely remember two days ago. She wasn't even sure whether it had been a week, or more, and if so how much more, that Gram's deep cough had lingered on, after the stuffed nose and runny eyes of the cold itself. Dicey kept forgetting exactly when it was that the exams would start. She kept forgetting in the evenings to return Jeff's phone calls, and not remembering that she'd forgotten until the next evening, when she was too tired to remember not to forget again.

She measured time in work accomplished. After she finished the first four rowboats, she spent a day hauling—hauling the painted boats back to Claude's shop, hauling back the next set of four. While she had the truck, she hauled a load of firewood from the farm, and stacked it wherever she could—in the bathroom, under the worktable, outside the door. The acrid, headache-inducing, lung-clogging, nose-offending smell of paint would fill the room if she didn't keep windows open. So she was burning a lot of wood, to keep warm. She couldn't afford to get sick.

Two of the monthly storage bills got paid. The third was a dentist in Salisbury who had said he wanted to be billed monthly. Dicey sent him a second bill. If she didn't have his money, she wouldn't be earning the seventy-five dollars for Gram.

When she had the time and energy, Dicey studied boat designs—or tried to. The trouble was, she couldn't read the designs, couldn't see from the flat lines on flat paper what the finished boat would look like. She studied the drawings and even copied one, line by line, onto another sheet of paper, but that didn't help. Besides, that wasn't what she wanted to do. She wanted to make her own ideas into this boat, to follow her own drawings. When she had time but no energy, Dicey simply worried; worrying gave her the strength to keep going.

Every morning, she forced herself out of bed. The alarm would go off and her body would want to go back to sleep. To keep that from happening, she lined up in her mind all the things she was in trouble over, and hadn't gotten done, or hadn't gotten done in time. This worked like hammering together a bed of six-inch nails and lying down on it, the way Indian fakirs were supposed to do. She would turn off the alarm and start remembering: the unpaid storage bill, the supply of sandpaper, the question of if she could have the truck, of how far behind schedule she was falling—driving the nails through the board she was lying on, like an Indian fakir reaching around to hammer up nails that would stick into his flesh. That got her out of bed pretty quickly.

The only time Dicey enjoyed was the time spent fussing over boat plans, thinking about the way a V-bottom was put together, or standing beside the larch she'd bought from Ken, with her hand resting on the pale boards, trying to feel the way they should be shaped. The golden lines of grain ran the length of the boards, almost as perfectly parallel as warp threads set out on a loom, ready for weaving. Looking down at her fingers resting on a board, feeling the wood, she was reminded of the Shakespeare Jeff had read to her, about shaping rough-hewn ends. When she had her fingertips tracing the lines of a board, Shakespeare's words felt real to her, because she was going to shape this wood to her own purpose, to her own design, into a boat she already had the buyer for.

Days passed. Dicey worried and worked.

CHAPTER 9

Half of the difficulties, she was thinking one day, as the wind blew bright and cold in the shop door and out the open windows, arose because Claude did such bad work. His bad work made her work harder. She had to sand more; sometimes she even had to replace badly driven nails or stuff paint thick into inadequately filled joints. She knew why she had to waste her time working on these boats—but even so there was in her a low, banked anger. She felt like some piece of skewered meat rotating over the heat of her own anger. Need for money skewered her, and lack of time skewered her, and she was being turned over her anger's fire as if every long brush stroke her arm made propelled her, rolling her around and around. It had been days since she'd been able to work on Mr. Hobart's boat plans, she thought. Although she wasn't exactly sure, it might have just been yesterday that she didn't.

The voice came from behind her, a laughing voice she didn't recognize: "'Why such impress of shipwrights, whose sore task does not divide the Sunday from the week?'"

Dicey straightened up and turned around, all in the same movement, holding the paintbrush up in front of her like a knife. A man was leaning against the door frame, the bright sunlight behind him shadowing his face. He had thick, dark hair with streaks of gray running through it. He looked, in his faded jeans and high-buttoned pea jacket, as if he'd been leaning lazily there for hours. His eyes watched her, laughing.

"What?" Dicey demanded. He'd broken the rhythm of her work. "What did you say? What do you want?"

"I was only wondering why you were working on a Sunday." He didn't move. The laughter was gone from every part of his face, except his eyes.

Dicey shook her head, impatient. "I know that. That was a Shakespeare quote, I know."

He took a step into the shop. *"Hamlet,"* he said.

Dicey shrugged: it didn't matter which play. "What do you want?" she asked again.

He moved into the shop and stood beside an upturned boat. Before he answered her question, he reached down and tested the paint with his fingers. Then he ran his hand along the long board that marked the keel of the flat-bottomed rowboat. "This one of yours?"

"No." Dicey disowned it quickly.

He straightened up. "Let me give you a hand turning it right-side up, miss. Or are you going to set it over there?" He indicated two rowboats waiting beside the stack of larch.

He had a noticing eye, a quick eye, Dicey thought. His light-brown eyes studied her, as if he had only one minute to learn everything about her. "I've got one more coat to put on it," she told him.

That seemed to surprise him, although she didn't know why it was any of his business to be surprised. "You've already got two coats on it, haven't you?"

She nodded. She didn't have time to waste, talking.

"Why three coats?" he wondered.

"The builder said so."

"It beats me," the man said. "Someone who slaps together a

boat like this—it's a P-poor piece of work—he probably wouldn't notice a missing coat of paint. Did you think of not doing the third coat? Did you think of the time it would save? Is he going to check up on you?"

For less than a minute, for just a few seamless seconds, Dicey thought of it: These two boats were numbers seven and eight, and she was two weeks into the job; she was on schedule—almost; well, she was falling behind almost imperceptibly; and there were twenty-two more of these waiting for her. . . . It wasn't the size of the job she minded. What she minded was spending her good working hours on such bad work. For a few seconds Dicey was tempted. Then she shook her head, as much to shake off temptation as to say no.

"Just because he told you to put on three? He won't notice if it's only two. Trust me, miss, he'd never know the difference."

Dicey, watching his face, thought she wouldn't trust him an inch. His face was made for mocking, a clever, mocking face. He looked lively, interesting, he looked like fun, but she wouldn't trust his advice.

"You always do what you're told?" he asked.

If he only knew, Dicey thought. "What *do* you want?" she asked.

"I want to see your boss."

"I'm the boss," she said.

That made him smile. She didn't like why he was smiling, but she liked his smile.

"I should have guessed. It's the bosses who work on Sundays, isn't it?"

"So, what do you want to see me about?"

"Work, I think. I could use a job, make a little money, and this place looks busy. Every other place around here is closed up tight."

"I can't afford to hire help," Dicey told him. "Sorry," she said. She turned back to the boat she was painting. It was an odd time of year for an itinerant worker to be looking for a job. Mostly they'd come around during spring and summer, and mostly they were kids. She dipped the brush into the paint and stroked down the side of the rowboat. She wished she *could* hire someone, and get this job over with.

She thought he'd leave, but he walked around to stand across from her. She looked up at him. "Really, I can't." It wouldn't do him any good to try to persuade her.

"Fair enough, miss. But it's a cold day out there, and you could offer me a hot drink. I see"—he forestalled her protest—"a kettle, and a box of cocoa mix, and I assume that's a sink in there. If you offered me a hot drink, I'd make it, and make you one, too. I'm pretty handy."

Maybe he was hungry, Dicey thought. His face didn't look hungry, but there was hunger mixed in with laughter in his eyes, so maybe he was too proud to ask. "Sure, okay," she said.

She painted while he ran water, then opened up the envelopes and poured mix into two mugs. The inside of this boat was already done, she was finishing up the final coat, and then she just had the one more coat to put onto the other, and this batch of work would be completed. Eight done, twenty-two to go. Dragging the paint can behind her, she worked up the curving side to the pointed bow. The man waited until she'd finished it and laid her brush across the top of the paint can before he poured steaming water into the mugs and stirred.

He passed her a mug, and she sat down on the dry boat to drink. The man leaned against the wall beside the stove, his jacket unbuttoned to show a thick white turtleneck sweater. "So this is *your* shop," he said. "I've never had a business of my own.

Never had the capital. Never had the chance. It must be nice, having your own business. You been at it long?"

"A couple of months." The instant cocoa wasn't anything as good as Gram's, but it was hot and thinly sweet.

"The great thing about a hot drink on a cold day," he said, "is the first swallow, the way you can feel it sliding all the way down your throat into your stomach. You know? It's about the only time I can really feel where my throat is, the length of it. So—you're Tillerman?"

She nodded.

"And you're not hiring."

She nodded again.

"I guess that's just my bad luck."

"Yeah."

"Tell you what, though, Miss Tillerman. I'll help you out. Gratis. A free afternoon's labor, what do you say to that?"

Dicey didn't know.

"You'd be doing me a favor. It's cold, there's nowhere else I can look for work until tomorrow—if I don't decide to move on—and I haven't talked much to anyone for a few days. I'm a man who likes talking," he told her, his eyes laughing, at himself that time.

"Yeah, but what if I don't? Like talking."

"Then you can listen. The truth is, I always prefer listeners to fellow talkers. You aren't going to turn down my offer, are you?"

Dicey thought about it. With another pair of hands she could do some actual work on Mr. Hobart's boat at the end of the day, before going home. She might even get home in time for dinner. "No," she decided.

"Good enough," he said. He took off his jacket and draped it over the stack of larch. He peeled his sweater over his head, and then pulled his undershirt down. He put his hand out for Dicey's mug, and she gave it to him. He washed both mugs in the bathroom, dried them, and set them back in place on the worktable. He moved around the shop with a catlike grace, never disturbing anything. Dicey got back to work.

He didn't need to be told anything. He opened a can of paint and stirred it patiently. He selected a brush from the glass jar where she kept them soft in turpentine, shook it out, then painted it dry on his jeans. He carried the brush and paint to the other boat and started painting the flat transom. Watching him out of the corner of her eye, Dicey decided he must just be lonely, which was why he was crouched there, painting with slow, careful strokes. He sure wasn't talking. He didn't look or move like a man who'd paint so slowly, so she thought he might be dragging out the time because he wanted company.

He broke the silence to ask, "Think it's going to snow?"

Dicey shrugged; she didn't know.

"Do you get much snow around here?"

"No, not much." She dipped her brush into the thick white paint and stroked along the side of the boat.

"Ever get blizzards around here?"

Dicey shook her head, her eyes on the moist line of fresh paint.

"I've seen blizzards, like you can't imagine. I was in one once, at sea—the North Atlantic and I'll tell you, Miss Tillerman, never more than once for me. For one thing, I was scared. Scared like nothing else ever. But—with the snow just pouring down and pouring down, and those waves, gray as thunderclouds, and the tops of them foaming, hissing, like it was blizzarding up, too—you ever see those little glass jars kids get for Christmas?" Dicey nodded. "And when you shake them, this fake snow swirls around?" She nodded again. "It felt like that, like I was inside one of those glass balls and someone was holding it in his hand, shaking it."

Dicey could almost see what he meant. For a minute, she could feel it as if she'd been there.

"And cold—cold so bad you couldn't breathe the air without freezing your lungs. No, it's true, we had to wrap scarves up around our chins and breathe through them, or our lungs would have frozen. Freezing from the inside out. Why do you think those ski masks—the kind robbers wear with just a slit for the mouth?—they cover up your mouth. It's the same anywhere the temperature goes down to—I dunno, somewhere below zero. Don't you believe me?"

"Sure," Dicey said. It didn't matter if she believed him or not. She had no way of finding out. Carefully, she ran the paintbrush up the sharp angle where the two sides of the rowboats joined at the pointed bow, then gently she painted horizontally again, so that all the brush strokes on the sides would go in the same direction. When she looked up, he was crouched there beside the other boat, watching her paint.

"That bit's unnecessary," he told her. "No one's going to notice it and I timed you, it used up about five minutes."

"That's *my* business," Dicey told him.

"Right you are," he said, not offended.

She carried her paint can to the bow of the boat he was working on, and began painting down toward him.

"Are you a Republican or a Democrat, Miss Tillerman?" he asked.

"What difference does that make?" She had, in fact, registered Independent, not that it was any of his business.

"Truer words were never spoken."

It took her a minute to figure out what he meant. He'd taken her words to mean something different from what they meant to her.

"The thing is," he said, "that there are three subjects everyone can talk about. The weather"—he counted them off—"politics, and education. I was trying politics, since you don't seem interested in the weather and you obviously aren't being educated."

"What do you mean by that?"

"Nothing personal. Just that if you were, you'd be in school now, not running a boat shop. You're what—maybe eighteen or nineteen?"

"Twenty-one," Dicey muttered. "And who says so, anyway, that those are the three topics?"

"Tolstoy." He answered so quickly she knew he'd wanted her to ask. "You ever heard of Tolstoy?"

"Yes. He's a Russian writer."

"Ever read him?" the man asked.

Dicey would have liked to say yes, but it would have been a lie. She almost said, But my friend Jeff did, and my brother, and she thought Gram probably had, too, remembering some conversations among the three of them. Dicey, however, hadn't. She shook her head.

"So what is there for us to talk about?" the man asked.

"I thought," Dicey reminded him, "that you were going to talk and I was going to listen."

"But I already know everything I think, and I'm bored with it. Whereas you, Miss Tillerman, are terra incognita."

Dicey glared at him. She didn't know what that meant and he knew she didn't, but she wasn't about to ask. She got back to work. Let him talk if he wanted to. She had work to do.

Another silence occupied them. They worked slowly toward each other at the center of the rowboat, where they would pass each other to move apart again.

"Miss Tillerman?" He sounded like he was barely not laughing.

Dicey didn't say a word, she just looked up.

"I wonder if I might make use of your bathroom," he asked.

"Sure," Dicey said. To his back, she demanded, "And why do you keep calling me Miss Tillerman, anyway?"

He didn't answer, closing the door behind him. He didn't answer, emerging, returning to the job, picking up his brush and laying thick lines of paint on with it. Finally he asked, "You don't like the name?"

"I didn't say that."

"I don't know your name," he pointed out. They were about opposite to each other by then.

"I don't know yours, either."

He didn't say anything, didn't look at her. She studied his thick graying hair and his broken nose; she studied the weathered tan on his skin, and saw that the ends of his wide mouth wanted to twitch up.

"Dicey," she said.

"How'd you get a name like that?" he asked, without looking up from his work.

Dicey shrugged. She wasn't about to say I got it from my father, or so I think, but I'm not sure because he took off years ago, so I never asked him. "What's yours?" she asked.

He hesitated. "Cisco," he said, looking her straight in the eyes.

He didn't look Spanish, Dicey thought. He didn't have a Spanish accent. But what did she know, anyway, about Spanish people; she'd never met any, or been to Spain. How did she know what he would look like if he were Spanish and had a Spanish name? But she knew he was lying, she thought; not that she cared what his name was.

"Kidd," he added. "Like the pirate?" Dicey had no idea. "Captain Kidd, but I never made captain so they called me Cisco, like the Cisco Kid on the television series. Or are you too young? Yeah, you're too young. Cisco rode around the Wild

West, righting wrongs, and he had a sidekick, Poncho, because Poncho was pretty fat around the gut. So they called me Cisco and it stuck."

He was talking as if all of that made sense, but it didn't make much sense to Dicey.

"You can call me Cisco," he concluded. "You know, it looks like those tools over there haven't been in use very long. In fact, it looks as if they've never been used."

"That's true enough," Dicey told him.

He waited, painting, then asked: "But you said you've been in business a couple of months. And you've got those three boats, over there, racked up like storage and looking like all the maintenance work has already been done, and there's that pile of lumber, as if you were going to build something, or patch it, but it looks pretty pricey for patching wood, and larch would be one of my first choices, if I were going to build a small boat. . . ."

He knew wood, and he had a quick eye, a quick tongue, and good hands, too. She didn't know where'd he'd come from, but she wasn't sorry he'd turned up for the afternoon. "I had some old tools, I'd bought them and refinished them, and—they were pretty fine, some of them were really old and fine. But I got robbed," she told him. "And don't ask me if I was insured, because I wasn't."

"Insurance is for people who like to play it safe, people who can't take risks," he answered.

Also for people who didn't want to take losses, Dicey thought to herself. She wasn't about to kid herself that she didn't wish she'd had insurance to cover that loss.

"Anyway, that's why I took this job. Originally I turned it down. There are thirty of these boats. It's for my landlord," she explained. "He needed to go to Florida, or his wife did—"

"Wives," Cisco said, sympathizing with Claude. "Women."

"Yeah, well, he's never too eager to work any harder than he has to, and I need the money."

"I didn't mean to be sexist," Cisco said, mocking.

"Yes, you did." Dicey couldn't think of any reason not to let him know she didn't believe him.

"Well, okay, maybe I did. Maybe I am. Do you think I am?"

Dicey just laughed. "How would I know? I don't know anything about you."

"Fair enough," he answered. "You don't know much about men in general, either, I bet."

Dicey didn't bother rising to that piece of bait.

"Because otherwise you would have thought of the most obvious thing."

Obvious thing? She had no idea what he meant.

"About being robbed. You mean it never crossed your mind? You never wondered if your landlord might have arranged the whole thing? So you'd have to work on his boats, and he'd be able to head on south and shut his wife up?"

"Are you saying that Claude's the one who stole my tools?"

"Probably not."

"Or hired somebody?"

"Does that sound like him?" Cisco asked.

None of it sounded like Claude, or anybody else she knew. She wondered about the kind of people this Cisco knew. "No," she said.

"My guess would be, it would be like Henry II having Becket killed. Your landlord would just sort of mention, maybe at a bar or something, that you had a set of tools that was practically antique, practically priceless, and if someone overheard him and decided to relieve you of them—well, that wouldn't be his fault, would it?"

"Is that what *you'd* do?" Dicey asked him.

"No. I'd take them myself, and get the money for myself."

For a second, she wondered if Cisco had actually done that. If he had heard Claude talking at a bar and heard about her tools, and stolen them. Then why would he come by the shop? Maybe he was playing out some elaborate game of his own. Then she realized how unlikely all of that was. It was the kind of complicated idea that might apply where there was a lot of money at stake, or some fantastic jewels, but not the tools in her shop. Cisco wasn't serious, he was just talking.

"What happened with Henry II?" she asked.

"Well, you know about Becket, don't you?"

He already knew she didn't, or he guessed so surely that it was the same as knowing. So she didn't bother answering. He wasn't surprised she didn't answer. He just went on and told her the long story. Dicey listened, and painted, letting his voice bring up alive in her imagination the man who changed his Lord Chamberlain's seal for a bishop's ring, understanding how that changed his way of looking at things. She could almost hear the footsteps of the knights come to murder him in his cathedral, the sound of the metal swords being drawn out of their scabbards. Cisco was, as he said, a good talker.

CHAPTER 10

The next morning, Dicey loaded the truck with firewood and stopped at Claude's to pick up the trailer, before going to the shop. In the dimmed brightness under an overcast sky, she emptied the truck bed, stacking the firewood under the worktable. Then she lay plastic sheets down over the floor and began working the first of the finished rowboats around to the shop door.

It wasn't cold enough to snow, but it was cold. She inched the boat carefully along, wondering if it would be possible to bring two of the unfinished rowboats at one time on the trailer. That would cut down at least on that end of the job. She thought about how with two people working, some things—like moving boats around, for example—took less than half the time, more like a quarter.

She wished she did have the money to hire someone. Not for all the time, just part of it. She didn't feel right always asking Sammy and Maybeth—and she hadn't even told Gram there were boats to be moved today. Gram's cold had cleared up, but she was still having trouble shaking the cough. Yesterday, after dinner, Gram had made a pot of tea, declaring her intention of floating the cough out to sea on a tide of tea. "You're no more tired of it than I am, girl," she'd told Dicey, which was probably the truth. "Have you returned Jeff's phone call yet?" Dicey hadn't, and didn't. There was too much to do, and by the time she got everything done, it was too late to call. Jeff's roommate went to bed early—well, early for a college student. She couldn't call Jeff after ten-fifteen. Besides, she thought, looking across at Gram over the list of biology vocabulary she was helping Maybeth memorize, she was too tired to have any kind of a conversation.

She couldn't ask Sammy and Maybeth to help her move boats, anyway, because they were on their last two regular class days before exams. She almost wished she'd had the money to hire that Cisco person.

She was lifting the first unfinished rowboat off the trailer when he returned. The boat's weight came into balance and she looked up; he was standing there, as if he'd always been there. "You sneak around like a cat," she said.

"You don't like cats?" he asked, the laughter barely below the surface of his voice, and unconcealed in his eyes. "It's pretty inefficient to do this by yourself."

"I told you yesterday," she warned him, "I can't afford to hire anyone."

"I heard you yesterday," he said. "So, where does this go?"

They carried it inside, then brought out the second of the finished boats, setting it down gently on the trailer's cradle. Cisco went around to the passenger side of the truck.

"I thought you were going to look for work," Dicey said.

"Nobody's hiring. I haven't got anything better to do."

She shrugged. She wasn't about to turn down help.

Wheezing at the weight of the load it was pulling, the truck hauled the trailer the half-mile to Claude's. Cisco, relaxed in his seat but refusing to do up the seat belt, commented on the sounds from the motor. "This truck's ready for the knacker's."

"The what?"

"You know, that's what they used to do with old horses. Send them to the knacker's to be turned into—oh, glue and dog food and probably cheap leather, too, now I think of it. Haven't you ever heard of the knacker's?"

Dicey didn't bother answering him. Obviously she hadn't.

"This truck must be about a hundred years old."

The low gray sky hung over them.

"It's probably a verifiable miracle that it's still running."

"My brother keeps it going." She shifted into third.

"You have a brother?"

"Two."

"Is that all of you?"

"No, I've got a sister, too."

"Are they all like you?" he asked. "Extroverted, talkative? Warm-heartedly convivial?"

Dicey looked across to meet his laughing eyes. "No," she said, keeping her own face straight.

"Oh. Well then, about cats. Did you know that the early Egyptians believed that cats were sacred?"

Dicey hadn't known that and now that she did, it didn't strike her as any too hot a piece of news.

"Certain cats, that is, not all cats. Like the Hindus with cows."

What about the Hindus with cows? she thought.

"You don't know about that, either?" He sounded pleased that she didn't. "What kind of an education did you have?"

"A normal one."

"Any college?"

"I quit, last May. After I finished my second year." Now he'd ask her why and she would have to decide whether to explain. She pulled the truck into Claude's parking lot and backed it around, until the trailer was in place, hoping he wouldn't ask her why.

"I don't blame you," he said. "I got out of school as soon as I could, myself. Listen, Miss Tillerman, I know you don't want to damage your paint job on the finished boats, but is there any reason we can't bring back two of the unfinished ones at one time?"

It was as if he could read her mind, or as if their minds worked the same way. "We can try," she said.

It didn't work, because the angle of the sides wasn't wide enough to allow an overlap that let the boats stack securely. So they spent a couple of hours moving rowboats around, leaning the finished ones on each other, like a row of circus elephants parading down the length of Claude's shop, bringing back the next group of four to Dicey's. Dicey didn't mind the time it took. She had figured to lose a day over this job. She figured now she was coming out ahead.

She split her lunch with him, giving him one of the two peanut-butter-and-jelly sandwiches and half of the wedge of pie. He declined any of the milk Gram had put into a thermos for her. He'd had enough dried milk to last him a lifetime, he said.

They ate sitting on the two boats she'd work on next, facing each other, both pairs of knees in worn jeans, the two pairs of feet in sneakers, only his were the thick-soled kind. He ate the way he did everything else, quickly and neatly.

"Why don't you go home for lunch?" he asked her.

"It takes longer. Besides, my grandmother needs time to herself."

"You live with your grandmother?"

"Yes."

He waited, but she had nothing more to say.

"It's funny, you've got instant milk, which is about as skimpy as milk can get and still have the name, but this bread is homemade and the pie—" He put the final bite into his mouth and chewed contentedly.

"Instant milk is cheaper and just as nourishing. Homemade bread is cheaper, too. Gram buys flour in hundred-pound sacks."

"Is it okay if I make myself a cup of hot chocolate?" he asked.

"Sure." She listened to him as he filled the kettle with water and set it on top of the wood-burning stove. She heard the clink as he set a mug down, and the tiny ripping sound when he opened a packet of mix. His voice came from behind her.

"If you live with your grandmother, what about your mother?"

Dicey's eyes were on the rough joints where Claude had nailed household to marine plywood, the cheap materials hastily assembled. She was reminding herself—eight done, the next four beginning, when she finished these there would be twelve done, which was almost half of the job— "She's dead," Dicey said.

"I am sorry." He sounded like he meant it. Well, Dicey was sorry, too, but there was nothing she could do about it. "So you live—there are four of you, right?—with your grandmother. Did you ever think," he changed the subject, "of how many lives Louis Pasteur saved?"

Dicey shook her head. She never had.

"If there's a heaven, and if good deeds get you there, he's probably in heaven."

That was too many ifs for Dicey to have anything to say about.

"You do know who Pasteur is, don't you?"

She turned her head to look at him. He wasn't looking at her. He was standing, watching the kettle, so all she saw was his tall, lean body, and the broad shoulders under the white turtleneck sweater, and the thick, gray-streaked hair growing long down over his weathered neck. "I'm not stupid." She let him know that.

He turned his head, to grin at her. "I never thought you were stupid, Miss Tillerman. Only uneducated."

Dicey stood up, crushing the two folds of wax paper that had wrapped the sandwiches, balling up the foil from the pie. She tossed them like baseballs into the wastebasket, and then folded up the paper bag, to take it home with her at the end of the day. She had work to do, a long afternoon's work.

"What do you do next?" he asked her.

"Sanding."

"I could stay and help out."

"I keep telling you, I can't afford hired help."

Steam came out of the kettle's spout. He poured water into the mug, then stirred it with a spoon. "So, I could work a few hours, and then when you get paid you could pay me."

Dicey shook her head. "I don't plan to owe anybody any money."

He studied her, his eyes peering over the top of the mug. Dicey made herself go over to pick up a couple of squares of sandpaper. She didn't kid herself; she didn't want to bend to this particular job. She especially didn't want to do the sanding, partly because of the tedium of the task, but also because it was only the first step, and the first step on the first boat. Until she'd begun, she wasn't doing the job. But she had to, and she knew it, so she leaned over the boat and got to work. Getting to work, that was the only way to get the job done.

Cisco drank hot chocolate and watched her work. He didn't say anything. She ignored him. It took all of her concentration to keep on with the sanding, forcing her hand to hold the stiff square of sandpaper, forcing her arm to reach out and gently circle the floor of the boat. And this was only boat number nine. Dicey had never played any sport herself, but she'd heard that there was a point where if you pushed yourself past it, all the exhaustion disappeared. Maybe she was at that point. She hoped so, because at that point she couldn't even dangle the picture of Mr. Hobart's boat in front of herself, like a carrot dangled in front of a mule, to keep the animal moving.

It made her angry, too—she could take about two more minutes of having someone stand around while she worked, stand around watching somebody else work, as if he was . . . an old-time plantation owner, strolling through fields where cotton was being picked. Dicey was surprised, now that she thought of it, that overseers and owners hadn't been beaten to death by the slaves. There had been enough slaves. They had outnumbered the white men. If she were a slave, and someone watched her slave away, she'd have murder in her heart.

He went into the bathroom and rinsed out the mug. At least, she thought, working mechanically, he was tidy. At least, she thought, he'd be leaving now and she wouldn't have someone standing around; she could at least be alone while she worked. At least, she recognized, she was now working mechanically, without having to make herself do it.

He wasn't leaving, however. He was getting a piece of sandpaper and getting to work on the second boat. In a minute, she thought crossly, he'd start talking.

And he did. "Why are you in such a big hurry with these?" he asked. He had a light voice, and you could let it float right on past you if you wanted to ignore it. She didn't want to, but it was the kind of voice that let you decide. Gram's voice was like a grappling hook; it went right into your head and caught your mind. Maybeth's voice, like their momma's as Dicey remembered it, went its own direction, like an arrow from a bow. You had to reach out for Maybeth's voice, with your mind, to try to ride along on what it was saying. Jeff's voice, she thought, smiling to herself, spread out from the middle of your mind, of her mind at least. She ought to call Jeff. He'd left enough messages. She made a mental note to call him before supper, before he left to spend his evening at the library.

"You going to tell me?" Cisco's voice asked. "Or is it some deep, dark secret?"

"Tell you what?"

"I'd asked you a question, but you were way off somewhere else. What were you daydreaming about? Some boyfriend?"

"Voices," she snapped. What she was thinking was none of his business, and she didn't know why he didn't go away, anyway.

He laughed—amused at Dicey didn't care what. "You're in a real charming mood today, Miss Tillerman."

Dicey just gave him a look.

"If looks could kill" was his only response. "What is it with you, anyway—you on the rag or something?"

Dicey straightened up. It was almost a relief to have something clear to be angry at. "If you mean am I menstruating, the answer is it's none of your business. I assume," she went on, almost enjoying herself, "that you meant to be pretty vulgar. Rude, too."

He had straightened up to face her, and he wiped his face clear of laughter, although he couldn't control his eyes. "Sorry, Miss Tillerman," he said quickly. "I'm sorry, and I apologize. Accepted?"

She didn't want to accept. She wanted to be angry. She didn't move a muscle.

"It would be childish to sulk," his light voice pointed out to her.

She wasn't sure she cared about that.

"I'll not repeat the error—not in any form. I know when I'm outgunned."

Dicey bent back to work.

"So," he asked, "what were you thinking about voices? We

can't hear our own, because they echo inside our heads, did you ever think about that? That's why deaf people have so much trouble learning how to speak. And that's why it was such a remarkable thing that Helen Keller, who was blind and deaf, and therefore effectively dumb, could be taught to speak. Do you know about Helen Keller?"

Dicey shook her head, so he told her the long story. Having done that, he asked her again why she was in such a hurry with these rowboats. She told him about the order Mr. Hobart had placed with her, about the boat she was going to build. Because he was curious about it, she explained how the money for the business worked out, between Mr. Hobart's advance and what she'd earn from Claude and the maintenance-storage income. She even told him about the dentist's overdue account.

"Want me to call and demand payment?" he offered.

"I've already written, twice. He's never even answered."

"Yeah, but—now, don't get your dander up about this, because it's only a fact of life—sometimes if it's a man, they'll take it more seriously. Listen, are you willing to give up the money? I'm serious, because if it were me, my boat here, I'd figure to just pay you when I picked it up in the spring. I'd let you wait and keep the money in my own pocket. I wouldn't pay you until I absolutely had to. Not because I couldn't afford it but because it would make me feel more powerful, in control, getting away with something. If I could get away with it, I would. So if I knew you were going to just dump my boat somewhere—into the water?—then I'd be more likely to pay my bill, because I'd feel as if I had something to lose."

"I've already put hours of maintenance into it," Dicey protested.

"It's a gamble," he advised her, not looking up from the sanding he was doing. "You gamble the risk of losing what you're owed against the pleasure of not being taken advantage of."

Dicey thought about it. "Yeah," she said, "I'm willing. It makes me mad."

"Do you have a contract I could look at, to figure out penalty prices?"

"Contract? No, we just agreed." Dicey considered that. "What do I need a contract for?"

When he didn't answer, she felt pretty stupid. "Nobody has contracts," she said.

He didn't say anything. Cisco's saying nothing said a lot.

All she wanted to do was build boats, and it seemed like every time she turned around something got in her way. She didn't know what she was doing that was so wrong. She felt like she was always, over and over again, cutting a path through to where she wanted to go, and as soon as she cleared out what she thought was the final part of the path, she'd see something else, sprung up to get in her way.

CHAPTER 11

Dicey got back to work, and so did Cisco. Before long, he was talking again, about space, and the stars, whether there was time in black holes and whether space was endless, about the chance of intelligent life elsewhere in the universe. "If you consider man intelligent life," he said.

Dicey grinned. It was only the first coat, so they worked fast, and carelessly, covering the insides of the two rowboats. "My little brother is talking about maybe being an astronaut," she said.

"Then he's got more courage than I do."

Their brushes made soft stroking sounds, laying paint onto the wood.

"Either that or he's a real dreamer," Cisco said.

"Maybe both," Dicey said.

"Maybe, but it's an unlikely combination, you have to admit it. What about the other one?"

"The other what?"

"Brother. You said you had two, didn't you?" Cisco was crouched low inside his boat, his eyes moving quickly between her and his brush, keeping an eye on her, keeping an eye on the job.

"He's in college." Suddenly, Dicey had the feeling she was telling him more than she was telling him. She didn't know how that worked, but she wasn't sure what was going on, and she wasn't sure how she felt about not being sure.

"Yeah? What year is he?"

"Freshman." The questions seemed innocent enough.

"Yeah? Where's he go?"

"Yale."

"Yale? Yale in New Haven?" She nodded, without looking up. "You're lying," Cisco decided, which didn't seem to bother him.

Dicey didn't say anything. He could believe what he wanted.

"Okay, you're not lying. So he must have a scholarship, so he must be incredibly smart."

Dicey didn't say anything.

"Tell you what, Miss Tillerman. I'm impressed—here I am working for a blood relative of a member of the social and intellectual elite."

She didn't know why he took it that way and then, looking at him, she saw that he wasn't taking it that way. "No you're not," she said.

"Okay, you're right. But I am impressed with this brother of yours. He must be quite a kid. Unless your grandmother is rolling in money."

"What is it you're trying to find out, Cisco?" Dicey asked carefully.

"Nothing," he told her. "Nothing. I'm just talking. Talking's a good way to help the hours pass when you're working at a rote job. Or singing. Do you sing?"

"Not without accompaniment."

"I used to play the guitar," Cisco said.

"What happened?"

"I hocked it— I needed the money; it may have been Melbourne."

"What were you doing in Melbourne?"

"Looking for work, like always. The job I got there—I usually do come up with a job—usually paid work," he pointed out, but it was a joke, not a complaint. "In Melbourne I was a short-order chef. Okay, I was just a cook. I've done about everything, I've been about everywhere. I've been about everything."

Dicey decided, looking at his face, at the laugh lines and the age lines and the set of his mouth, that she believed him.

"But do you know that some scientists are working on the theory that there's a second sun in our system?"

"That's ridiculous," Dicey said.

"Because we can't see it? But that doesn't mean anything, you should know that. The evidence of our senses is unreliable, philosophers have proved that, and psychologists. These scientists hypothesize a second sun from the way meteor fields act. They've even named it, which is pretty funny if you think about it, naming something you think *might* be there. Nemesis, after the Greek goddess."

"I don't remember any Greek goddess named Nemesis," Dicey protested. "I've heard the word—it's the force that brings you down, isn't it? Like doom?"

"Nemesis was an honest-to-God goddess," he told her. "Interesting that she's female, isn't it?" And he was off again, telling her something, talking about the Greeks and their sense of fate, and the Norse gods, with their Götterdämmerung. When he wound down, Dicey said to him, "How did you learn so much?"

"I read a lot," he answered.

Then why, she wondered, did he just wander around picking up odd jobs? Why didn't he do something seriously? She knew if she asked him that he wouldn't tell her, even though she also knew he knew what she was thinking.

They worked, and talked, all afternoon. Cisco suggested, when the first coat of paint was drying, that they go ahead and sand the next two rowboats. They could just set them out on the floor, he said. That way, they wouldn't have to sit around twiddling their thumbs, waiting for paint to dry. They could use the time. Unless Dicey needed to take a break?

Dicey didn't. It was full dark by the time they ran out of unpainted surfaces, and the two boats on the racks had second coats of paint drying, while the two on the floor had first coats applied. They rinsed out their brushes and set them into a jar of turpentine. "Now," Cisco said, "let's make a phone call." He seemed to be enjoying himself.

Dicey gave him the number, and the dentist's name, and stood there listening. Working at this rate, two boats a day might get done. She was tempted to hire Cisco, she really was.

"I'm calling from Tillerman's Boatyard, where you have an overdue account," Cisco said. He listened. "That's as may be," he said, "but it is still an overdue account. So that, if the check isn't in our hands in two days, we'll be putting your boat back into the water." Cisco's light voice was cool, unconcerned, and oddly threatening. He looked around at Dicey, the phone to his ear, and raised his eyebrows twice at her, and then he winked. She muffled a laugh, as his cool voice, entirely belied by his mocking face, spoke into the phone. This was like a game Cisco was playing. "Yes, we can extend that to four days. We will, of course, send you notification of where your boat is—when we have the time—should your check not arrive."

Cisco hung up, grinning. "How much money do you have on you, Miss Tillerman? I've got"—he reached into his back pocket for his wallet—"ten dollars here. I feel like a pizza. Don't," he warned her, "try that old joke, about not looking like a pizza. I expect better of you. How much do you have?"

"Nothing. I almost never carry cash. Just checks."

"Okay," Cisco said, "I'll swing for the whole thing, as long as you don't drink scotch. Will you join me?"

Dicey shook her head. "I've got to get home." She put on her jacket and wrapped a scarf around her neck. She hung the wooden shutter over the glass of the door. Cisco watched. She turned out the lights and opened the door, motioning him through. It was going to be a cold walk to wherever home was, she thought, climbing into the truck. "Can I give you a lift?"

He reached over to catch the end of the long scarf Gram had knitted for her. "D'you know how Isadora Duncan died?" he asked.

Dicey had no idea.

"A scarf. A long scarf like yours. It caught in the wheels of the car she was riding in. Which was a Lamborghini."

"Ah," Dicey said. She didn't even know who Isadora Duncan was, but she wasn't about to get Cisco talking again. "Listen, thanks for all the help. Really."

That seemed to be what he was waiting for. He gave a gentle tug on the scarf and then stepped away from the truck. She pulled the door closed. He didn't say a word. He didn't do more than grin at her, his teeth white in his shadowed face.

He was a strange one. He drifted through the world, showing off all the things he knew. But he was a good man to work with, and she was sorry she couldn't hire him on, at least to finish Claude's boats. With Cisco working, too, she could get eight or maybe even ten boats done in a week, and then the money would be in and the time would be free and Dicey could get to work.

She almost stopped the truck and turned it around, to go back and ask him. She had no idea where he was staying in Crisfield, so if she was thinking seriously of hiring him—but she couldn't, she reminded herself. To do that would be to spend money she hadn't earned yet, the money from Claude; she'd already done that once, buying the tools with Mr. Hobart's check, and that wasn't any way to do business.

Cisco would say—she could almost hear him—that was just

the way to do business, and probably cite seventeen examples to prove it. Well, she was glad she'd run into him, and she wished him well along his way.

But he was there at the shop the next morning, when she rode up on her bike, his breath floating like frost on the cold air, where he waited for her, leaning against the door. Behind him, over the shop, the sky glowed yellowy orange in front of the rising sun.

"Hello," Dicey said. "But—"

"Come on," Cisco cut her off. He was looking pretty pleased with himself. "I want some cocoa, and I feel like burning off some energy on manual labor. You didn't think I'd split before that guy sends you the check, did you? He'll send it, I'll put money on that."

Dicey just stood there. She knew she worked well with him, she didn't mind his constant talk—in fact, it was interesting and she could probably recite back to him almost everything he'd said, from Henry II on; so why was she reluctant to open the door for him?

Impatient with herself, she dug the key out of her pocket and unlocked the door. "I didn't think about it at all," she told him.

"You know, Miss Tillerman, in all respect, I'd say you don't think much as a general rule."

Dicey, taking off her jacket, hat, and scarf, shook her head. "You'd be wrong. I'm always thinking about what's next. I've got today all thought out."

He shook his head, and loaded wood into the stove. "That's not thinking—that's planning, or scheming. I mean, think about things."

Dicey looked around the shop, feeling good about all the work they'd gotten done yesterday, and were going to get done again, since he was back. At this rate . . .

"What is there to think about?" she asked.

"You're kidding." He turned around, without straightening up, so he looked like some dwarf-character out of a fairy tale, twisting his face to look up at her as he bent over to put logs into the stove. "Just the little things. Life. Time. Love. Death. God. The nature of man. The nature of political structures. Power. Just the odds and ends of the world you live in."

"Who was Isadora Duncan, anyway?" Dicey demanded.

Cisco threw back his head and laughed, a sound like pebbles being tossed against rocks by the waves. Dicey couldn't help it, she could hear how she sounded to him, and she joined in his laughter.

Dicey didn't mention her odd itinerant worker at home. There hadn't been much occasion to talk to anyone, for one reason. Generally, by the time she got home for dinner everyone else had settled into the evening's work. They saw one another, enough to be sure everyone was all right; but work was what Dicey thought about. That was another reason for keeping silence about Cisco. It was almost as if she was holding her breath, to see every day if Cisco would turn up again. If she talked about him, named him, it would be as if she was laying claim to him. Dicey figured, someone like Cisco, laying claim was a pretty sure way to scare him off, and she wanted to keep him around, if she could, for a while. The difference that second pair of hands made, in getting work done—it was almost as if she held her breath, afraid that like some magicked creature out of a story he would disappear if she counted on his being there.

It wasn't smart to talk about good luck. If you talked about it, it turned its back on you. So Dicey put aside the plans for Mr. Hobart's boat and concentrated on getting Claude's job done. With Cisco's help.

With Cisco's help, it would be only two or three more weeks, she thought, riding her bike through town on the first light of Wednesday morning, if he continued showing up. But for once he wasn't there waiting. He hadn't arrived by the time she stoked the fire and settled down to painting. Then, once again, he stepped out of a gray morning, as if he'd been there all along, had been working with her for years. She guessed he just liked to pick his own time. She guessed he liked to do just exactly what he felt like. She wasn't paying him, so she couldn't make any demands, and she guessed that was the way he liked it. She could see why he'd never settled down to anything, except maybe the particular day's work, to which he settled down energetically.

And talking. The man's talk was like constant rain, the words falling and falling. It was lucky, Dicey thought to herself, that he was so interesting, that he knew so much, otherwise he'd drive her crazy with his talk.

As he said, he'd been everywhere and done everything, and he liked showing off to her. She didn't mind. She heard about paintings in a museum in Florence, Italy—"Firenze, that's its real name. Like the way Peking is really pronounced Beijing, only the Brits when they had their empire established Peking as the transliteration. Oh, but the colors, Miss Tillerman—that's what those Renaissance Italians knew. The books talk about perspective and neoclassicism, but for my money, it's the colors. Of course, I don't have any money," he pointed out.

Dicey looked up in the middle of one of these monologues, in the middle of the afternoon, as they were putting the final coat of paint on boats eleven and twelve, to ask him, "Is there anything you don't know?"

He took the question seriously. He stopped talking to think about it. "Molecular biology," he finally said, "but I'm going to get some books the next time I'm in Baltimore. Or London."

Dicey lowered her head, to hide the expression on her face. She didn't mind the touches of vanity in the man. But he'd mind knowing that she saw them.

"And languages," he said. "You'd think I'd be good at languages, but I never can get the hang of them."

He was there Wednesday, and Thursday, too, and Dicey waited for him to show up on Friday. There was a set of finished rowboats to be taken back, exchanged for a set of unfinished boats. When they'd done that, she promised herself, she would write out a bill for Claude, for the first third of the job. That meant five hundred dollars. If she mailed the bill out that afternoon, then Claude would have it next week, and the week after that she'd have the money. While she waited for Cisco to show up, she attached the trailer to the back of the pickup, then backed it around to the shop door. By the time Claude had paid the first bill, she'd be about ready to send him the second. She already had two boats finished from the second ten, so that in a couple of weeks after that, by the middle of February—her mind raced on over the month, until it arrived at four clear weeks to work on Mr. Hobart's boat.

She decided not to waste any more time waiting for Cisco, and started moving the boat herself. When Claude's check came, she might just pay Cisco something, no matter what she'd said. A hundred dollars, she decided. She thought maybe she'd tell him she was going to do that, but then she thought she'd wait, and just hand it to him.

If, she thought, working the boat through the doorway, he ever showed up again. The sun shone pale white behind a thin curtain of clouds, a little pale circle of light that seemed no stronger than the moon. The temperature wasn't bad, only down to the high thirties, so she didn't need gloves. Maybe he wouldn't show up again, Dicey thought to herself, just as he came into view, walking carefully around the puddles accumulated at the roadside.

She stood up to greet him, glad of his help. But that morning he hadn't come to work. She saw that right away. It wasn't that he'd changed his clothes, because he hadn't. His face looked different, that was what she could see, as if he had swallowed some secret. She couldn't tell if it was a good secret or a bad one; she suspected that his face would have looked that excited, his eyes that eager, whatever kind of secret he had learned.

"I came to say so long," he said.

Dicey nodded. He waited, but she didn't have anything to ask him. It wasn't as if he was being paid for his work, and she had no business thinking he ought to stay.

"I'm going up to Atlantic City," he said.

"Oh," Dicey said.

"Now, don't you go all moralizing on me, Miss Tillerman," he said, as if Dicey had even thought about that. She hadn't. His life was his business. "Here, I'll give you a hand loading this."

"Thanks."

He shrugged. "Do you want to stake me for some?" he asked her. "That way, you'd get a percentage."

"A percentage of what?"

"What I win. If I win."

Dicey couldn't help it. He made her laugh. "No," she said, laughing.

"You ever gamble?" Cisco asked.

"I can't afford to lose."

"But that's the time when you should," Cisco told her.

CHAPTER 12

It took Dicey most of the day to move the rowboats around. Before she got down to sanding, she wrote out the bill for Claude, put in the receipts for the cost of replacing the broken glass and a reminder to deduct the next month's rent from his check, addressed it, and walked into town to mail it. If it took four days to get down to Florida, and four days to get back, then she'd have the money by the end of next week.

Dicey had expected to feel the difference when she was hauling boats alone, but she hadn't expected to hear the silence in the shop so loudly. It was pretty funny, she thought, with the only sound the rasp of sandpaper on painted plywood, the way she had had to get used to the constant talk and now she was having to get used to the constant quiet. She hadn't realized how quickly she'd adjusted to having someone else around, occupying her attention, while she got tedious work done. She wondered if Cisco would be back, and she thought he might. But she figured, probably he wouldn't, and especially not if he won. She was beginning to know Cisco.

When hunger cut too sharp, she made herself a mug of cocoa. With the edge of hunger blunted, she could ask herself to do another hour's work, or more. Dicey leaned against the stack of lumber, drinking, looking around her shop, noticing that her supply of firewood was getting low again. Sunday or Monday she'd have to replenish it.

Night lay black outside the high windows. Night at the windows looked as flat and black as if the glass had been painted to keep all light out. There might be stars and moon out there, bright in the dark winter-clear air, but she couldn't have seen them because of the way the interior light reflected off the glass. She thought about Jeff. She hadn't talked to him, or written to him, or heard from him either, for a while. How long, she wasn't sure of. She hadn't realized how long it had been, however long it had been. Too long. She'd never totaled up how many phone calls she hadn't returned, but if she did she'd probably feel bad.

She went to the phone and dialed his number. She hadn't meant to let so much time go by. The phone rang and rang. Finally, it was answered; but it wasn't Jeff's voice asking hello. "Roger?" Dicey asked. "It's Dicey. Is Jeff around?"

"No." Roger sounded surprised. "He's gone."

"When'll he be back?"

Another hesitation. "He's gone for the weekend."

"Home?" she hoped. She wouldn't mind seeing Jeff.

"No, skiing. He's in Pennsylvania—it's a bunch of people, the midwinter weekend break."

"Oh." Dicey hadn't known it was already time for the long weekend.

"He'll be back Tuesday night."

"Oh. Okay."

"Any message?" Roger asked.

"No," Dicey said. "Just—tell him I called. Thanks, Roger."

She didn't know why it should surprise her that Jeff had gone skiing. She knew he liked to ski. She knew she didn't expect him to hang around his room all the time, on the off chance that she might return his telephone calls. Thinking about it, she didn't much like the way she'd been ignoring Jeff. Especially since she knew perfectly well how she felt about him, she didn't like the way she hadn't taken any trouble over him. With Jeff, you had to be careful not to take advantage; he didn't ask for much, he didn't make demands, he made it easy to neglect him.

Dicey's stomach felt overfull, with bad instant cocoa and bad feelings. Before she went to bed, she would write Jeff a long letter, telling him everything about the past weeks—about Cisco mostly, because Jeff liked odd characters, and about the work she'd been doing. When you could make someone unhappy, that was the person you should be most careful of.

She got back to work, making herself do it. Anyway, she told the swollen, disappointed feeling of her stomach, she knew how to make herself do things she didn't like, do the work. Sometimes, she didn't like herself any too well, but she always liked the way she could count on herself to get down to work. She heard the sound of a car engine outside. Before she could hope it was Jeff, she knew that it was their pickup.

Maybeth and Sammy came in, each carrying an armload of firewood. "Where do you want this?" Sammy asked her. "We thought you probably needed wood, so we loaded up. Beside the stove?"

Dicey looked at them, then back to the work. "Under the worktable. Thanks, Sammy. Thanks, Maybeth. You were right, I do."

"We finished dinner, and the kitchen, and neither of us had anything going on tonight," Sammy said.

The two of them worked quietly, going in and out. There was the sound of sandpaper, and the sound of footsteps, and the sound of chunks of wood being dropped down onto the floor, then stacked neatly. There was no sound of anyone talking, until Dicey stopped her work and turned around to look at the two of them, parading in and out, arms loaded, arms empty. The two of them, in heavy sweaters, weren't looking at much of anything, as if they were looking inward, not outward. The two of them were coming in and going out of the shop as if they weren't where they were. Usually, when the two of them—especially Sammy, but Maybeth, too, in a different way—were in a room, you felt the air in the room change. The air in the shop wasn't changing.

Dicey straightened up, Maybeth, arms piled high with firewood, followed Sammy into the shop. She waited until his logs were stacked before dumping hers onto the floor and crouching down, to add them to the growing pile.

"Hey," Dicey said. "What's wrong?"

"We came to tell you," Maybeth said.

"Let us finish this first, it's only a couple of more loads," Sammy interrupted. "Then I'll make us some cocoa or something. You go ahead, Dicey, you don't have to stop work."

"Okay," Dicey said, worried a little. "Gram knows you're here, doesn't she?"

"Sure," Sammy said. "We told her we were bringing over some wood."

"So she wouldn't worry about if we were bothering you," Maybeth explained.

"Are these those boats of Claude's?" Sammy asked. Dicey had the rowboats spread around the floor of the shop. She had done the insides, the hardest part of the job, first, then flipped them over, to sand the outsides. She nodded.

Sammy inspected the boat at his feet. "Piece of shit," he said.

"Yeah," Dicey agreed. Maybeth got busy making the hot chocolate. Dicey didn't much want another serving of the mix, but she thought she'd better let them play the scene the way they'd written it.

Sammy wandered around the shop, picking up tools, running his hands over the sides of the dinghies, studying the stacked larch. "Are you going to be able to build this one?" he asked.

Dicey nodded her head.

"How many of Claude's do you have left to do?"

"When I get through with these? Fourteen."

"How many in all?"

"Thirty."

"So you'll be more than halfway done? How long will it take?"

"That depends," Dicey said.

Sammy didn't ask any more questions. Dicey sanded away, and listened to Maybeth rinsing out the mug Dicey had used earlier. "This is nice wood," Sammy said. "Good grain, rift sawn."

"Yeah." Dicey straightened up. That was it, all the rowboats were sanded, that job was done. All she had to do was wipe them down with a damp cloth, to pick up sawdust, and tomorrow she could start painting. She went over to stand by Sammy, and put her fingertips on the pale wood.

"It must have cost you a lot," he said.

"Ken gave me a good price. How about helping me damp-wipe the boats?"

"Sure thing." Sammy looked down at her, but he was looking at himself more than at her. Dicey, looking up at her little brother, the fatigue spreading across her back, decided that while they sat down to drink she'd better find out what was troubling him. For now, however, she just said, "Thanks."

They sat on the boats. Maybeth and Dicey shared a mug, because there were only two. Sammy sat across from them. He pulled a letter out of his back pocket, and passed it to Dicey. It was from Yale.

She looked at the front. "It's not addressed to me."

"Gram thought you might be interested. It's James's grades."

"Are they good?" she asked. She already knew what the answer would be. Looking at James's report cards got pretty boring. She was proud of her brother, and she thought he was going to be able to do just about anything he tried for, but she didn't see any sense in looking at yet another terrific report card. Especially since James wasn't there. You had to be more careful of people if they were right there, watching your reactions.

"The usual," Sammy said. "Take a look."

"Later. I can't even make sense out of the address at this point." She passed the envelope back to Sammy. "I'm so tired, I'm not even thinking straight."

"We know," Maybeth said. Looking at her sister, Dicey thought she probably did know. How or why Maybeth should be able to know, Dicey didn't have any idea. It was as if Maybeth could see from inside other people, the way she sang from inside a song.

"Let's close up here and go home," Dicey said. "Will you give me a ride?"

"That's why we're here," Sammy said. "It's cold, and dark and—"

"We wanted to give you a ride home," Maybeth said.

They sat three abreast in the cab of the truck. Dicey leaned her head against the window and closed her eyes. Her mind drifted, planning out the work of the weeks to come, one way if Cisco were there and the other without him. "Hey, Sammy, thanks for helping." Beside him, she felt his shrug. "You, too, Maybeth."

The figures in Dicey's checkbook appeared before her mind's eye, the present balance—$615.77 wasn't an awful lot, but it was enough to be going on with. She could always go back to work at McDonald's if she had to. If she had to, she could make herself do that.

Things used to be so much simpler. Clearer, things were clearer when she was younger and didn't know as much as she did now, about the way things happened. Easier, too; she remembered life being easier. Right now she was as tired as if she had walked all day—like that summer seven years ago—or was it eight? She didn't have the energy to fit the right number to the memory—when she *had* walked all day, with the little kids to take care of, too. Remembering it, comparing, she thought it was easier then. Or at least it was clearer, simpler. Maybe troubles you remembered, or bad times you'd gotten through, always looked easier than the trouble you were living in right then. She wouldn't be surprised, although she didn't see what good figuring that out would do, even if it was true.

Dicey sat up, opened her eyes, turned her head to look at her brother and, beyond him, Maybeth's profile. "Have you two gotten your exams back? How did they go?"

"Everything was fine," Sammy said. "No surprises."

"My lowest grade was a forty-nine," Maybeth reported. "Last year it was a thirty-seven on the midyear exams. *And*, I passed the biology exam—"

"Good," Dicey started to say, but Maybeth kept on talking.

"—and the English exam, too. I've never passed two exams before."

"Good for you, Maybeth," Dicey said, and meant it. She didn't know how Maybeth kept it up. This was her third year in high school; Maybeth was a junior. Twice a year, January and June, Maybeth studied for exams that, twice a year, she mostly failed. She never gave up on studying. She never flunked a whole course, because she worked as hard for every day as she did for exams. But twice a year, June and January, Maybeth got told she wasn't as good as everybody else, and no matter how hard she worked, she wouldn't be.

If Dicey year after year got stuck onto the flypaper of money, and never did get to build boats because every year she had to work as hard as she could just to pay her share of the living expenses, to pay the rent on the shop, to buy supplies and tools, to pay the phone bill: That's what it would be like. She could imagine how that would make her feel. Dicey wondered what kept Maybeth going.

"There are only three more sets of exams you have to take," Dicey said.

"I know." Maybeth's voice had a smile in it. "I can do it three more times. Maybe I'll graduate from high school."

"Is that something you want?" Dicey asked.

"Yes," Maybeth answered. "I might not be able to, because everything keeps getting harder, but if I could I'd like that."

"Why?" Dicey wondered.

"It would make a good ending," Maybeth explained.

"Ending to what?" Sammy asked.

"Ending to me being in school, because—when you do something, it's better if there's a good ending." She explained what she meant: "Just because you work hard doesn't mean you'll get your good ending."

"If it's possible," Sammy said, in a voice that made Dicey wonder what was going on in his mind, in his life.

"I'd like to graduate, and have everybody come to see me graduate."

"I'll be there," Sammy promised. "You, too, won't you, Dicey? We'll be there with bells on and banners flying and—you know, Maybeth, I used to think you shouldn't have to go to school—"

"But I want to. How else would I learn something? Just because you're not good at something doesn't mean you don't get to do it, does it?"

"What gets me," Sammy said, "is when you *are* good at something, and still don't get to do it."

Dicey could sympathize with that. She didn't know how good

she was at building boats, and she kept trying to find out, but things kept getting in her way, things like time and money. Not people—the people she knew knew better than to get in her way.

It wasn't until she lay in bed that night, falling into sleep, that a question drifted across her mind. She was too tired to catch it. It was like when you see something out of the corner of your eye, some movement in the shadows at the far boundary of vision—that's what the question was like. By the time she had noticed it, and said to herself that there was something there she might want to see clearly, and found the right muscles to turn her mental eyes to catch it, and seen what it was—she was asleep.

CHAPTER 13

The alarm cut through the darkness like a spotlight suddenly turned on. Dicey was up and dressed, washed and fed, and out the door, with the day's work outlined in her head, before anyone else stirred in the silent house. She rode her bike through filmy gray predawn light. Air sounds were all she could hear—the whirring of air through the tires of the bike, the rush of air by her ears.

She had figured out a way to work on all four of the rowboats at the same time. Maybe. If she moved the low wooden rack at the center of the floor over to the worktable—and she wasn't using the worktable, so it didn't matter whether the space around it was clear—if she spread out plastic sheeting to protect the cement—she should have room for all four of the rowboats on the floor of the shop. If she had all four spread out, she would waste less time waiting for a coat of paint to dry. If she painted the ones nearest the stove first, then the heat would make them dry faster. A good morning's work, that was what she needed.

A good morning's work was what she put in, band after band of paint streaking off her brush. When she finally straightened up—it was early afternoon, to judge by the messages her stomach was sending her—the insides of all four boats had been painted with their first coats. The two by the stove were still slightly tacky to her fingertips, and she decided she'd go home, have lunch, and then maybe bring the truck over after a couple of hours, so she could drive home when she was finished for the day. Maybe she'd bring Maybeth, too, to help her flip the boats; that would make more sense, having Maybeth to help turn them over and shift them around.

In the meantime she could write Jeff, a long letter, the kind of long letter that felt as if she was talking to him. Since she couldn't actually talk to him she'd write—which cost a lot less, anyway. She hadn't talked to Jeff since—it was only two weeks, she figured it out, but it felt much longer.

Gram was in the kitchen when Dicey got home, Gram sitting down for once, with a teapot, a mug, a jar of honey and a lemon, and a thick book. Dicey was too hungry even to toast the bread for her peanut butter sandwich. "What're you reading?"

"Dickens. What are you doing home?"

"A coat of paint is drying. It'll take another couple of hours. Is Maybeth here?"

"She went shopping, up to Salisbury, a gaggle of them—somebody's having a sale and somebody else has some money. You know how girls are."

Gram knew perfectly well Dicey didn't know how girls were, and, furthermore, Gram knew Dicey knew she knew that. "How about you?" Dicey asked. "How are you feeling?"

"Not worse," Gram said, "and that's something these days. I think I've broken the back of this cough." Gram's cheeks were too pink, and her eyes were too bright; her voice sounded rough-edged, too deep; her voice sounded chesty. Gram said she was getting better, but Dicey wasn't sure about that. She didn't feel like quarreling with Gram, however, so she asked instead, "What time does Sammy get off work?"

"I expect him momently," Gram told her, and then smiled. Gram's smiles moved so fast across her face, if you weren't watching you'd miss them entirely. "Do you know how long I've wanted to be able to use that word—momently—in a normal conversation?"

Dicey smiled back. "No."

"That's a relief. I sometimes think—sometimes I'm afraid you can read my mind. And there are a lot of things going on up there that are none of your business, girl, or that I'd just as soon not trouble you with. So I'm glad to know you can't read my mind. Although," Gram continued, "sometimes I think I can read yours."

Dicey thought about the same, and it didn't trouble her.

"D'you mind?" Gram asked her. "I would."

"No. Because you can't read it, not really," Dicey said.

"Probably a good thing, too," Gram said. "There's mail for you. And don't bother yelling at me about going outside—Maybeth brought it in. I haven't stirred out of my own doors for—a week now, almost. It feels like a year."

The mail wasn't a letter from Jeff, but it *was* a check from the dentist in Salisbury, for twenty-five dollars. If Cisco came back again, Dicey thought, she could tell him he'd succeeded. She signed the check over to Gram. Gram didn't refuse to take it, although from the look she gave Dicey, Dicey wondered if Gram didn't have a pretty good idea of how tight money was in the business. "I'm due over three hundred dollars, from Claude," she told her grandmother. "I finished the first ten of those boats, and I sent him the bill." Sammy entered the kitchen at that news and pronounced it satisfactory. Saturday was payday for him, and he took ten dollars out of the envelope before handing it to Gram.

"Looks like we can make it through another month now," Gram said. "If your sister will let me out of the house to go to the bank and make a deposit. That was a joke," she said, looking from one to the other of them. "Don't bother telling me how bad a joke it was. Go away and let me read."

"I wanted to ask Dicey something, anyway." Sammy's face was red from the long bike ride home. He blew on his hands. "I should've worn mittens. The January thaw is sure over."

"But it's just the beginning of January. How can the thaw be already over?" Dicey asked.

"Cripes, Dicey, where is your mind? It's almost February. No, I'm serious, it is. In fact, it's almost"—he grinned at his grandmother—"Valentine's Day."

Gram humphed. Dicey spoke quickly, before Gram could get going on what she called the proliferation of holidays, appearing like rabbits all over the calendar. Somebody, Gram maintained, was making a fortune out of all of these brand-spanking-new holidays, with the paint not dry on them. But Gram was too busy trying not to cough to get started on her speech.

"I was going to ask if you could help me out for a while this afternoon," Dicey asked Sammy. "Moving boats around. I'll give you my full attention about whatever. It won't take long to move them. But we'd have to ride our bikes."

"I have to be back for dinner," he said.

"Nobody has to be here for dinner," Gram snapped, and then she started coughing, a deep, chesty cough. She waved her hands at them to say she was all right, and coughed. She tried to drink some tea, and coughed. Dicey looked at Sammy, and felt him asking the same unspoken question she was, which neither of them could answer. In a couple of minutes the coughing subsided. Gram sat bent over for a minute, as if she was catching her breath after some race, some running race. Then she drank off her mug of tea. "And don't you two look at me like that. I tell you it's getting better."

If this was better, Dicey thought, worse must have been pretty bad.

"I *want* to be home for dinner," Sammy got back to the argument.

"Nobody ever said you didn't," Gram answered, pouring herself another mug of tea, squeezing lemon into it, spooning honey. "I don't even like honey and lemon in my tea," she complained.

"Then let's get going," Sammy said to Dicey.

At the shop they shifted the rowboats around and turned them over. "This is like turning the mattresses in the spring," Sammy said. "Want me to put masking tape along the waterline for you? You do one side and I'll do the other, and I could tell you."

"Great," Dicey said. "Thanks." She got to work, peeling off tape, setting it evenly along the top of the painted bottom, ripping an arm's length of tape off the roller. "So, tell," she asked. "Tell me whatever it is you want to tell me."

"They turned me down."

"They what? What they?"

"That tennis camp."

"The one you were talking about?"

Sammy nodded.

"The one in Arizona?"

He nodded.

"Did you actually send in an application?"

"Yeah. That part was okay. It's when I asked for a scholarship that they turned me down. It was a nice letter, they sounded sorry, but they said no. The list of tournaments I've played in, and how I placed, didn't give them enough to go on, for all that money. Because the scholarship is for a lot of money. Because, if I were in Arizona they'd know what the competition was like. Or California. But because I'm not—and they've never seen me play."

"That's hard on you," Dicey said.

"Maybe they're right. I mean, maybe I'm a big fish in a little pond here, in my pond, but I wouldn't be such a big fish in their pond. I just wish—"

Dicey knew what he wished. He wished he could go to that tennis camp.

"The letter really was nice. They said they hoped I could find a way of being able to enroll, even without the scholarship."

"Can you?" Dicey wondered.

"Dicey." He looked at her across the flat-bottomed rowboat, half-amused; half-annoyed. "Do you have any idea what it costs? It costs sixty-five hundred dollars."

Dicey just stared at him.

Sammy just stared back at her.

"Oh, Sammy," she said. There was no way any of them, even putting everything together, could afford that. For a summer camp. Nor even for a tennis camp, not even for Sammy could they come up with that kind of money. "That's terrible."

"Plus the airfare there and back," he added. "I just wanted to tell you," Sammy said.

"I know."

"Because what really gets me is, I could work, if I dropped out of school, and if I worked a couple of jobs I could save up the money—not for this summer but for next—and then I could afford the camp, but if I did that then I wouldn't be playing tennis in the meantime, not competitive tennis, so . . ."

Dicey knew what he meant, but didn't see any purpose in repeating that. She didn't have any ideas, either. She could probably, if she had to, work nights in the spring and earn his airfare, and she wouldn't mind doing that, for tennis camp, for Sammy. But coming up with sixty-five hundred dollars—

"All I can do is work," Sammy said, working steadily while he talked, "and even then, even if I do that, it won't get me what I want."

They taped in silence for a while.

"I should stop wanting it," Sammy said.

Dicey didn't know about that.

"But just because you aren't good enough, or rich enough, to be able to get something, that doesn't mean you have to give up wanting it, does it?" he asked her.

Dicey didn't know.

"And I *am* good enough," he said.

Dicey nodded.

"Anyway, I just wanted to tell you." He was waiting for her to answer him, but she didn't have any answer for him.

"All I can say is—I know what you mean," Dicey said.

He lifted his head and grinned across at her. "Yeah, I know. I guess that's what I wanted to hear."

Sammy, Dicey thought, took his knocks standing up. While she was thinking about how to say that to him, to tell him how proud she was of him, he changed the subject. "What about Phil? I think it's okay for Maybeth to go out with him, and so does James. Do you?"

"Has he asked her?"

"Once, before he went back to school, but Maybeth says he will again, she hopes, maybe."

"You're worried because he's so much older? I always liked him."

"Except he seems like the kind of guy she might fall in love with."

"Would you mind that?"

"Not a bit. Except, I figure Momma must have fallen in love, too."

Dicey thought she understood what he was asking her. "But Maybeth isn't going to have to run away from home if she wants to love someone, not like Momma did. It's not the same at all."

"You're really sure about that, aren't you?"

Dicey was.

"So am I," Sammy said. "But then, I was pretty sure the tennis camp would give me a scholarship, and they won't, so I wanted to hear what you thought."

Dicey said just what she was feeling. "If you went away for the whole summer, I'd miss you."

"Cripes, Dicey, that's what it's all about, isn't it? Going away? You did it."

"I came back," Dicey protested.

"It's not the same. Even if you come back it's not the same. You don't come back the same. I mean, how many times have you been home for dinner this month? You're away from home right now. You live here in the shop. All you don't do is sleep here."

"Who'd want to sleep here?"

"Not me. I've gotten used to a bed, and sheets, and good food on a regular basis. But I wouldn't put it past *you*."

Dicey looked around the shop. You could fit a cot in, or a sleeping bag, with the stove for warmth and cooking, and with a bathroom, you could live here. She'd lived under worse circumstances, and Sammy had lived in them with her. She remembered Sammy then, Sammy little, as she looked at Sammy, now fifteen. Remembering, as she watched his strong hands smooth masking tape along the waterline of a boat, just helping her out because she needed it, she told him, "You ought to be able to go to that camp."

"Sixty-five hundred dollars," he reminded her. "Thinking about trying to get that much money, it's like—wanting to fly to the moon."

"But that *is* what you want," she reminded him. "That's what astronauts do. Fly to the moon."

He looked at her, and his eyes had laughter in them. "The stars, actually. Farther than the moon, more than the moon, that's where I want to go. All the way, the farthest."

Dicey didn't know *what* she should say to him about that.

CHAPTER 14

Sometimes work was all you could do, just put your shoulder to the wheel and push, and keep on pushing. You could barely see the wheel moving, but after a while you could see that you'd gotten somewhere. So Dicey worked, patient brushstroke after patient brushstroke, keeping the stove burning hot enough to dry whatever boats were near it, shifting the boats by herself, not wasting any of her working time.

When she had to wait for paint to dry, when she had that time, she prepared the bills to send out: fifty dollars for maintenance work, twenty-five for storage. She couldn't mail the three bills out until Friday, which was the last day of the month, but she had them all ready to go, stamped and sealed, by Tuesday morning. On Tuesday, she hauled back the four rowboats she'd finished painting and picked up the next four; that job ate up most of a day. Working the boats out of the shop, then up onto the trailer, working them off and onto the racks in Claude's shop . . . the day wasted away on her. That was the time she really wished Cisco was around. She'd half-expected him Sunday afternoon, and was nearly surprised when he didn't show up on Monday morning. She'd given him up by Tuesday, figuring he must have won his bets in Atlantic City, because she was figuring he wouldn't return to Crisfield unless he lost. He hadn't said anything about coming back—and why should he? But he hadn't said anything about not coming back, either.

Dicey knew that it was her own convenience his presence suited, not his. She would lift her head sometimes and look down the length of weeks ahead, and think of how long it would take her to build Mr. Hobart's boat. When she did that, she could feel the end of March rushing at her, too fast. She could feel how short the week was, and how—thinking of the eight or nine weeks that were left to her—and those boats of Claude's she had to do so slowly, doing them alone—she didn't let herself think of it.

It would have been easier with Cisco's help, that was all. But Dicey figured he wasn't anyone you could rely on and he certainly hadn't made her any promises. He didn't owe her anything. If anyone had asked her, that would have been what she said, all along. It wasn't as if she'd hired him, or was paying him, and the job would have been in worse shape, she knew, without the days of labor he'd given her.

If all went well in the mail, then Claude's check might arrive before the end of the week. She'd asked him to take the rent for February out of the money he owed her, so that was taken care of, and only the nineteen-dollar phone bill was left to be paid. That was okay, everything was okay. As long as Dicey could keep on working she'd be okay.

Dicey concentrated on getting done what had to get done, each day. No wishes, no regrets, just the job at hand. That was why, when she returned from Claude's shop late Wednesday, the back of the pickup loaded with cans of paint, she was surprised to see Cisco there, leaning against the door to the shop, a duffle bag at his feet.

Dicey, smiling despite herself, feeling as if it had been years, not days, since he'd left, climbed down to say hello. "I guess you didn't win."

Cisco laughed. "I guess I didn't. Well, to tell the exact truth, I did, but not enough, and not for all that long. How's it going?"

Dicey shrugged. "The usual."

Cisco reached in to help her take paint out of the back of the truck. He waited for Dicey to unlock the door. When they had the gallon cans lined up along the wall, he offered to make her a cup of hot chocolate. Dicey, feeding logs into the stove, thought that sounded good. Before he did that, however, Cisco went back outside to get his duffle. He carried it slung over his back, the way Jeff sometimes carried his guitar.

"Brought you something," Cisco announced. "A souvenir from Sodom, a gift from Gomorrah—a little memento from the cities of the plain."

Cisco looked so pleased with himself as he listened to what he was saying; he looked so smug and self-satisfied and sure of himself that Dicey said, "But I thought you were going to New Jersey."

He wasn't sure if she was saying something stupid that showed she didn't understand what he'd said, or saying something smart that showed she thought what he'd said was stupid. She helped him decide: "And Atlantic City is right on the coast."

Cisco dropped his duffle behind him, and started to laugh. Dicey tried to keep her face blank, to keep him guessing, but she couldn't. When he laughed, the lines and wrinkles of his face gathered together, around his eyes and mouth. "I almost missed you, Miss Tillerman, while I was away. If you were a man—" He went to fill the kettle with water.

"If I were a man, what?" Dicey asked him.

He looked at her for a bit, wondering if he wanted to say it. "I'd say, Come on along with me for a while, a few days, or months—years? Time has a way of disappearing underfoot when you're journeying. I could show you the whole world, spread out—and you'd like that, wouldn't you?"

"Who wouldn't?" Dicey asked him. Right then, the thought of the whole world, spread out and waiting—right then, it sounded like what she'd always wanted.

"Most people wouldn't. Most people don't. I thought I was right about you. But," he said, bending over to unzip the duffle, "since you aren't, I can't, and you'll have to make do with this." He held out a long, narrow candy bar, in an odd triangular shape. "Best chocolate in the world," he promised her. "I'd be happy if you shared it with me."

Without passing it to her, he peeled back the thin cardboard box and then the thin foil covering. He broke off a big chunk, and handed it to Dicey. "I love this stuff," he told her, breaking off a chunk for himself, placing it tenderly into his mouth. He set the kettle on the stove, took down the mugs, and emptied cocoa mix into them; then he stood watching the kettle, waiting for the water to heat. Dicey studied his back for a minute, swallowed the candy—which was okay but not all that great—then took off her jacket and hunkered down beside the row of paint cans. She pried the lid up with a screwdriver, then took the electric paint mixer she'd borrowed from Claude, turned it on, and watched it get to work stirring up the separated paint.

Crouching down to hold the mixer steady, looking up at Cisco, at his long back and the faded jeans that rode low on his narrow hips, Dicey smiled to herself: Her candy bar poked up out of the back pocket of his jeans.

Cisco turned around. "What's so funny?"

"Nothing." He wasn't the kind of person to whom you could say, Look at what you did, isn't it a joke the way you did that?

"Same goes for me," he said. "I got thrown out. The lady I've been staying with? Her husband came home early. Well, she says it's early. Matter of fact, I have only her word for it that he's home. But the upshot is, there's no room at the inn for little Cisco Kidd."

Dicey didn't know what to say to that.

"Sit down here, relax for a minute, you could use a break."

"How would you know?" Dicey asked.

"You could always use a break, that's how I know. You don't need to tell me what you were doing last weekend. And what I've been doing isn't worth the telling." He sat on the gunwale of a rowboat, and Dicey sat facing him, the hot mug warm in her hands. "I should never gamble, especially not blackjack. You'd think I'd learn, wouldn't you?"

Dicey didn't know. When he asked that, he looked rueful, but mostly pleased with himself, like a little boy who knew he'd probably be caught, but went ahead anyway, just to try to get away with it, just for the adventure. Cisco was a little old to be acting like a little boy, Dicey thought. But that wasn't any of her business.

"There's a song," Cisco said. "'Never hit seventeen, when you play against the dealer, for you know the odds won't ride with you.'" He was speaking the words, but Dicey heard the melody playing in her head.

"I know it," she told him.

"How would you know that?"

"I have a—" Dicey hesitated. She didn't know what word was the true one. "A friend, who plays guitar, and knows about every song ever."

"That one, that's one of the true songs." Cisco raised his mug as if he was toasting the song.

Dicey looked at his face, all the parts of it, and remembered how the song went: "Never leave your woman alone, when your friends are out to steal her. Years are gambled, and lost like summer wages." She wondered if that was what had happened to Cisco, sometime long ago, to cut him so loose from everything and anyone.

"What are you going to do now?" she asked him.

Cisco shrugged, pursed his lips, put his elbow on his knee and his forefinger beside his nose—his eyes laughing at himself, and at her, all the time. "That, Miss Tillerman, is the sixty-four-thousand-dollar question. D'you know the story behind that expression?"

Dicey didn't.

"A tale of greed, corruption—millions of people fooled into thinking something false was true—they should have known better, everyone involved should have known better—and at the end a good man made corrupt. Or maybe just shown to have always been corrupt even though he was pretending to be good. It's very twentieth century, the story. It's the twentieth century encapsulated."

"If someone is good, then he can't be corrupt," Dicey pointed out. "The two terms are mutually exclusive." She liked that idea and felt smart for having it. She hadn't been using much of her brain recently, she realized; and she hadn't thought she minded that, but she did.

"Maybe," Cisco said. "I wouldn't have taken you for a moralist," he said.

He was misunderstanding her. But it wasn't worth your while trying to explain something like that to someone like Cisco. Like the way he kept calling her Miss Tillerman, as if making sure that she stayed the person he wanted her to be, he really paid attention only to himself. She didn't mind that. He was pretty interesting, himself.

"What *are* you going to do?" she asked again.

"I've got a job waiting in a few weeks, it's a matter of hanging on until then. So, I did think, as a matter of fact, that I might just stay on with you."

Anyone else, Dicey would have assumed he meant what she

thought he meant, but Cisco wasn't like anyone else. "What do you mean, stay?"

"Just the basics—stay, like live, you know, sleep and eat and have a roof over your head."

Dicey knew what the basics were. She started to shake her head, to say no.

"I don't mean at home, with your grandmother and your brother who goes to Yale, Miss Tillerman. And your other brother and your sister. I meant here." He pointed at the floor.

"In the shop?"

"I've got a bedroll. There's enough room for a man to lie down and sleep. You never paid me for the work I've done, and I'll do more in exchange for a place to stay. Just temporarily. So it works out fair enough, it works out about equal, as I see it."

His eyes watched her with no expression on his face, like he was holding cards in his hand and he didn't want her to know what they were. Dicey made sure her face didn't give away anything she was thinking. Her thoughts were rushing at her, like a wind that carried rain and sleet mixed in together. She didn't need to feel bad about him working if she was trading him a place to live in exchange. She didn't have any good reason for saying no to his staying at the shop. She also knew what it was like to need shelter and to have only the one chance for it. One chance on a good day, she remembered; there had been days when they had no chance. And none of those days had been in winter. For a minute, she remembered that summer almost eight years ago, so clearly that for a minute she forgot where she was. She remembered the walking and the worrying—she had the three younger kids to take care of. She remembered the maps—Connecticut, Delaware, Maryland—and the roads, and the not knowing where they could sleep or what they'd eat, or whether when they got where they were going they'd be able to stay there.

She remembered how much it mattered when someone said yes, they could stay, when someone helped them out. "Okay," she decided. "Yeah, that'll be okay, I guess."

"I thought you'd see it my way," Cisco said. "I guess you're the one who comes out ahead on the deal."

As a thank-you it left a lot to be desired. Dicey drained her mug and stood up. She didn't need people being grateful, anyway, and it was true, anyway, and she didn't have any trouble understanding how he was feeling. "I've got work to do," she said.

"Then let's get to it," Cisco answered, standing up, too.

They had been painting for only five minutes when he started in talking again. Dicey had been half-hoping he would. His first words, however, put her on guard.

"This friend, the one who plays the guitar," Cisco said, "and knows all the songs. He wouldn't by any chance be a boy."

"What's wrong with that?"

"Did I say anything was wrong with it? Don't get your dander up, Miss Tillerman. No, I'm curious. The question I'm most curious about is, whether this boy wouldn't by any chance be a boy friend, as in boyfriend, beau, suitor, swain."

By the time he got through with his list, Dicey was grinning. "What difference would that make?" She couldn't tell what Cisco was leading up to, except that he usually had something he was leading up to.

"You'd be able to answer that question better than I can. It's just, if he's a serious boyfriend . . ." Cisco waited. Dicey didn't say anything. As if he understood what her not saying anything meant, or didn't mean, precisely, Cisco went on. "If, for example, he wants to marry you?"

"Is there any reason why he shouldn't?"

"You're not wearing an engagement ring," Cisco pointed out. "Not that everyone does, but you also don't seem to do anything but work. Meaning—no dates, no evenings out, no phone calls, flowers, etcetera. A distinct lack of etcetera, if you ask me, which is pretty strange for someone who says he wants to marry you."

"Maybe I don't want to get married," Dicey suggested.

"I have trouble believing that. It's always seemed to me, there has to be an awfully good reason for a man to do it, but a woman, I mean, she's got everything to gain. Someone to support her, and be responsible, and owe her fidelity, take her out, keep her happy. She can have children."

"You don't need to be married to have children," Dicey pointed out. She could have added, My parents weren't, but she didn't.

"I know that," Cisco answered. "So what's he like, this boy? This suitor. Good-looking?"

"Yes," Dicey said. When Cisco didn't say anything, she looked up at him to catch him staring at her as if she'd just told him a secret or something.

"Then what's wrong? Why aren't you at least engaged?"

"Nothing's wrong."

"What's he doing with his life?"

"He's in school. College."

"So he's pretty eligible. If you ask me, Miss Tillerman, you ought to do it. That's my advice. I mean, I know I've seen you at your worst—in that perpetual sweatshirt—not exactly dolled up, and maybe dolled up you look better—"

"Dolled up I look exactly the same," Dicey informed him.

"And you're not my type, you're too sharp around the tongue for me. Too smart. Stubborn, too, a workaholic probably. Not that I personally mind, but then, I'm not thinking of dating you, or marrying you, or anything in between."

"Yeah, well, you're old enough to be my grandfather," Dicey reminded him.

For a minute, it looked as if Cisco was going to say something angry. Then he decided he would take it as a joke.

"You're telling me it's none of my business," Cisco said.

"Something like that."

"I still say you ought to marry this boy. You're not going to have all that many offers," he warned her.

One thing you could say about Cisco. He wasn't exactly sweet-talking her. "Have you ever been married?" she asked. He wasn't the only one who could be nosy.

"No," he said. But there was something in his voice, some difference, as if he might be lying, or as if he might wish he were married, or as if there were some sad story behind that simple no. She stared at his back, and wondered.

He turned around and his eyes were laughing. "I never met anybody rich enough," he explained.

"I don't believe you," she told him.

"You ought to believe me, Miss Tillerman."

"I don't think so," Dicey said.

His face was like a map, she thought. If time acted like wind and water to make the lines on his face, around his eyes and down from his nose to the ends of his mouth, on his forehead under the thick fall of gray-black hair, then his face was like a map of all the years he'd traveled through.

"What're you staring at?" he asked her.

"You. I was just thinking, a face is like—one of those topographic maps." She went back to her painting.

"Yeah? What do you think of the landscape?"

The idea was in her head and out of her mouth before she had time to think about it. "A nice place to visit but I wouldn't want to live there." As soon as the words were out of her mouth, she was laughing.

Cisco didn't think it was funny. She didn't turn around to

check, but she could feel him not thinking it was one bit funny. But it was true, she was willing to bet on that; everything he said about himself indicated that. And he knew it, too. She was sorry that he could know it but she wasn't allowed to say it.

After a while, he asked her, "You ever get the rent money from that dentist guy?"

"Yes," she said.

"That's too bad. I'd have enjoyed dumping his boat into the water, screwing him over a little."

Dicey guessed she could see why he'd feel that way. A man of his age, with no job, no family, no home—he hadn't done much with his life.

"So my face bothers you?" Cisco's voice asked her.

"No," Dicey said. That wasn't what she'd meant.

"You know what Abraham Lincoln said, he said that after the age of forty every man was responsible for the look of his own face," Cisco told her.

Dicey liked that. She tucked the idea away in her mind, to tell Gram, because it was an idea Gram would like hearing. This was going to be a pretty good day after all—with Cisco working, Claude's boats wouldn't take long, and she was going to go home at the end of the day with a new idea, like a flower in her hand, to give to her grandmother.

As it turned out, even though Dicey got home in time for dinner, she couldn't tell Gram anything. Gram had gone to bed, Maybeth reported. She'd gone to bed in the afternoon because she felt sick.

It was just the three of them at the table. Dicey had knocked gently on Gram's door, then looked in when there was no answer to see her grandmother sleeping. "What's wrong with her?" she asked Maybeth and Sammy, who sat facing her across the table. Nobody had much appetite.

"She's decided it must be a flu," Maybeth told her. Maybeth didn't sound worried, and she didn't look worried.

Sammy, however, did. "Gram's never sick," he explained. "We could ask Dr. Landros, she'd make a house call. I'll pay for it."

"Gram told me she didn't need any doctor," Maybeth said. "I asked her, and she told me I shouldn't call Dr. Landros."

Dicey wished she'd gotten a look at her grandmother so she could think for herself. "Does she have a temperature?"

"I didn't ask. Her cheeks were pink."

"But she's never gone to bed like this," Sammy said. "When she gets a cold, she goes to the sofa, not to bed. Besides, I don't believe she'd tell you, because she wouldn't want us to worry. And with her bathroom next to her own room, we wouldn't even know if she was being sick."

"Gram would call Dr. Landros if we were sick, if it went on too long, so I think she'd tell me. We'll see how she is tomorrow," Maybeth decided.

"Maybe you should stay home from school," Dicey suggested.

Maybeth nodded. "That's what I think."

"Wait," Sammy suggested. "Why don't you let me do that? You're the one that likes school, Maybeth, and I've got a weekly algebra test—"

"Maybeth," Dicey decided.

"But—"

"If I were sick, it's Maybeth I'd want to have staying around," Dicey said. "And so would you," she told her brother, "so don't bother arguing. When I was getting better, that's when I'd want you. But if Gram's sick—"

"She is," Maybeth said.

"That settles it then," Dicey told Sammy.

"I don't know where you get off, coming in and giving orders.

You haven't paid any attention to anything for months, and now you show up for once and start deciding things—"

"If I were you, Sammy, I'd use my energy studying for the test, not trying to get out of it."

For a second it looked as if Sammy might get angry, and then he grinned. "Yeah," he said. "Okay. I guess that means you'll do the dishes, right?"

"But—" Dicey started to say. She was tired, she'd been working all day, she had plans for her time that evening, and a long, hot bath . . . Sammy leaned back in his chair, grinning away, so pleased with himself that Dicey could have kicked him.

"You're right, Dicey," he said, adding fuel to his fire. "I ought to take school more seriously."

"I'll help with the dishes," Maybeth said.

"No, I'm okay. You did all the work making dinner, and you've got homework, too, don't you? If you two work in here I'd be glad of the company. And we could keep an ear on Gram."

The two of them worked at the table while Dicey ran hot water into the sink, whipping the detergent into the water with her fingers. For some reason, she was convinced that the more bubbles you had the more cleaning power you had. Gram had assured her that was tomfoolery, but Dicey wasn't convinced. Her eyes rested on Gram's cyclamen. Two of the white flowers had bent over at the middle of their stalks, bowing down to the dirt, the way cyclamen blooms did when they died. The leaves that ran up beside the stalks were curled together and brown at the edges. Dicey rinsed her fingers off in the tap water and pinched off the dead blooms, then the leaves. Three more blooms curled tightly over their stalks, in early bud, the hunched way cyclamen blooms started out. They budded, bloomed, and died, in a few days. So did people, Dicey thought, her hands busy with glasses and plates, utensils, then the pan Maybeth had fried the chicken in. People lived in cycles, too, longer running than flowers but shorter than trees.

At twenty-one, Dicey had run through a lot of her time. If seventy was about the usual amount of time, then she had used more than a quarter of hers up. That didn't leave all that much time to go, only forty-nine years. That was about twice twenty-one, so she was through about a third of her time, not a quarter. It felt short, and it made Dicey nervous to think about her life that way. But when she thought back, remembering, the past seemed to lie so far behind her—if she went back eight or nine years, for example, and back to Momma, it all seemed so long ago, as long ago as an old story. Thinking about it that way, nine years was a long time ahead of her.

Dicey thought about that. If the time that lay ahead moved at the same pace as the time flowing out behind her, there wasn't such a big hurry. It was when you started matching up numbers and time that you got nervous. They counted time in numbers, but that wasn't what time was. They kept cutting time up into smaller and smaller units, and numbering those units—as if, if the number got bigger you'd have more of it?

Sometimes, Dicey thought, the real trouble with people was that they were greedy.

But maybe, if that was the real trouble, that was what would keep things going? Because if being greedy was the trouble, then nobody would want to start blowing everything up, since the one thing that was clear was that there wouldn't be much of anything left to grab and be greedy about, not after a nuclear war.

So what was the real trouble was also a saving grace?

Dicey wouldn't have minded sitting down to think about that, or walking around outside in the night darkness to think about it, but she had work to do and the time to do it in. She went up to her room and brought down the books and the sheets of paper with rough plans for Mr. Hobart's boat. The trouble was, when the books showed copies of boat designs, with the measuring lines drawn lengthwise, or cross sections, and illustrations of the joints, she didn't know how to figure out how to understand them. She didn't know how to read a nautical blueprint, that was the trouble; and the books all assumed that you did.

She had a picture in her mind, and a few sketches down on paper. She had measurements penciled in on her sketches. Her hands knew the curves she wanted, the angles, planes, and joins. But when she looked at the illustrations, the grids, squares, and pictures of cuts—all those lines breaking up a boat into boxes, and she couldn't figure out why, or how to understand them—it was hard to begin when you already knew before you started that you didn't know enough.

They spent the evening in the kitchen, the three of them, each working over his own papers, all listening to the sleeping silence in Gram's room. Before they went to bed, Dicey said, "Sleep is a good sign, isn't it? It's good to sleep when you're sick." Sammy and Maybeth thought probably that was right.

CHAPTER 15

On Friday, it was Sammy who stayed home with Gram. Gram said she was getting better. She didn't look any better, and she never wanted anything to eat. She didn't even read. She just lay there in bed, sometimes sleeping, sometimes awake. "I'm getting better," Gram said, her voice—like her eyes—without snap. "There's no call to fuss. Go on about your lives. I'm just old, and it takes longer to get rid of these bugs." She was looking at Dicey when she said that, but not as if she was seeing her.

Dicey went to work. She had to, although she promised herself that if Gram wasn't out of bed soon—or at least sitting up and reading, and eating, too—she'd call Dr. Landros, whatever Gram said. Meanwhile, she had to finish this job for Claude.

Having Cisco live at the shop was no trouble at all. He was awake, his bedding rolled up and put away in the bathroom, up and dressed and ready to get to work when she arrived in the early mornings. "I told you it wouldn't inconvenience you, Miss Tillerman," he said to her, pleased with himself, like a little kid who's proved to you he could keep his own promises. They got right to work, in the mornings, and they talked.

"So what does your other brother do? The one who isn't at Yale College," Cisco asked. "And your sister?"

"They go to school."

"Everybody's in school except you?"

"And my grandmother."

"So you're the mother? Isn't that a waste of your own life?"

"No," Dicey said. Sometimes, in the course of a day, she might feel wound around with her family, trapped in some spiderweb of love and responsibility, but most of the time she would look over the years they'd spent together and feel how lucky she was. "That isn't the way it is."

"Ah," Cisco said, sarcastic. "You just support them."

At that, Dicey laughed. She couldn't support her family, not in this business anyway. "You know how little I earn," she pointed out to Cisco. "Although, Claude owes me money for the first ten boats—minus next month's rent—and when we finish these four he'll owe me another third, so—but that wouldn't support us. A family of five people is expensive."

"And one of them at Yale College," Cisco added.

"That really gripes you, doesn't it?"

"Gripes me? No, not a bit. I feel sorry for the kid. It's not as if—I could have gone to Yale if I'd wanted to," Cisco said.

Dicey didn't believe him.

"You don't believe me, but I could have," he insisted.

She didn't know why he needed to tell that lie, and to her. Maybe he was telling it to himself. It wasn't impossible, of course, but she knew somehow that it wasn't true. Partly she knew it because of the offended way he said it. But partly also because it seemed like the kind of thing Cisco would say, to let people know he was better than he seemed to be. That was kind of sad, Dicey thought, when you wanted people to think you were better than you were, as if you thought your whole life wasn't good enough.

"I could have," Cisco repeated, "but there were other things I wanted to do more. Like places to see. And doing things they don't even know about in colleges, where they spend their time thinking about things out of books, old, dusty ideas that anyone with brains figured out years ago nobody would be able to understand. So why bother, Miss Tillerman? I ask you that."

Dicey didn't know. She half-agreed with him, anyway.

"I've put my feet down on every continent of the globe—except Antarctica, but I've laid eyes on Antarctica, which is more than most people can say. I've seen all the great waters of the world." He wanted her to envy and admire him.

"I wouldn't mind that," she said, which was the truth.

He went on, telling her, "The best of them is the Pacific, mile after rolling mile of it. Every now and then you stumble on an island. I've lived on the islands there. Nothing happens except sunrise and sunset, the tides, and meals. And love—there's more love available on the islands than a man could use up in a lifetime."

Dicey figured she knew exactly what Cisco meant when he said love.

"I know what you're thinking, Miss Tillerman," his voice came over her shoulder, laughing at her. "You're wrong, you know. Like everybody else, you just don't understand the part pleasures play in life. People don't understand what life really is," he told her.

She was willing to believe that. She just wasn't willing to believe he knew better than other people. "The way I understand it, life is working," she said.

"Not if you're lucky."

"You know"—Dicey faced him to say this, because she didn't want Cisco thinking she'd just stand there and let him tell her what to think—"I think you're lucky if you have work you want to do."

"Sounds to me like you're kidding yourself. Sounds to me like you're making a virtue of necessity. Sounds to me like you can't recognize good advice when you hear it. And there's someone at your door," Cisco said, staring over her shoulder.

The man outside the door knocked, and Dicey went to answer. She didn't recognize him at first, with his thick sheepskin jacket and dark fur hat. Then she did. "Mr. Hobart. Come in."

He brought cold air in with him. "Hello, Dicey. I came down to shoot over a couple of my dogs, so I thought I'd stop by. How are you?" He took off his hat and looked around the shop. Cisco stood staring at him, but Mr. Hobart ignored the man. "You look busy."

"I am," Dicey said. She wondered what he wanted, and hoped it wasn't to talk about his boat. Guilt washed over her like waves, or like one big wave rising up from her stomach. She should have more work done for him, work she could show him; she didn't even have any plans he could look at. She didn't have anything to show him for the money he'd paid.

"So," Mr. Hobart said, making his way around the four rowboats on the floor, "how's my boat coming along?" He bent down to look closely at one of the rowboats. "Is this one you built?"

"No," Dicey said. "I told you I've never built one. We're just painting these."

Mr. Hobart looked at her, and she knew what he was going to ask her. She would have liked to lie, or to explain why she hadn't started on his boat yet, why she had to have the money and time that doing this job for Claude would give her—but she didn't want to just apologize, and that's what it would be.

"Yours is over here," she said, indicating the pile of larch.

"It looks a lot like it did the last time I saw it," he said. His eyes were on her face. He was expecting her to make excuses. When she did, his expression said he knew what he was going to answer.

"You said you wanted it at the beginning of April," she reminded him. "I said I'd have it by then."

"Yes, I did. As it turns out, however, it's just as well you haven't done any work on it," he said. Dicey could have corrected him, but she didn't. "Because I found a builder up in Massachusetts, and I've bought one of his. So I came by here to cancel the order."

Dicey didn't know what to say. She thought when you ordered something, that was a definite thing. She thought Mr. Hobart had meant what he said when he asked her to build him a boat. Mr. Hobart's blue eyes stared at her. She was trying to take it in: He didn't want her to build him a boat. She hadn't even begun to actually build, she hadn't even made the first cut in the wood, and he had fired her.

Cisco moved over to stand beside her. "Cancel it? Name's Cisco." He held out his hand to shake. After a few seconds, Mr. Hobart took off his gloves, let his gold watch shine in case Cisco wanted to notice it, then held out his own hand to be shaken.

"Tad Hobart," he said. "Call me Hobie. This concerns you?" He looked from Dicey to Cisco, and kept on looking at Cisco.

Cisco didn't answer his question. "I thought all hunting seasons were finished by this time of year," he said.

Mr. Hobart looked pleased to hear the criticism. "Not if you own the property," he said. "Happens that I own some land down here. I've got some dogs being trained. I like to keep an eye on my properties."

"So you just stopped by the shop here to renege on an obligation," Cisco said.

"There was no obligation," Mr. Hobart said. "No contract signed. It was all informal."

"Yes, of course," Cisco sounded unsurprised. "It's better if you can do business that way, isn't it? By unwritten word." Cisco wasn't even pretending to be polite.

"A handshake, and earnest money," Mr. Hobart said. Mr. Hobart at least was pretending politeness, but he didn't care if anyone believed in it.

That was something Dicey hadn't realized: She'd have to give him back the $500. That would about clean her out. Claude's check was due any day, she reminded herself, due yesterday or the day before. It was going to be okay.

"Earnest money?" Cisco asked, but he didn't wait for any answer. "But didn't you say there's no written contract?"

Unless Claude was as slow to get around to paying his bills as he was slow to get around to doing everything else. Because that $500, or actually $325, was all Dicey had. She couldn't even start to build a boat without that money. If she didn't build, she couldn't sell—then what about her business?

"There's a stack of lumber over there," Cisco said, "which represents a considerable investment. The way I understood it, that timber is for your order. Excuse me, your alleged order. There being no written contract."

The two of them were talking as if Dicey wasn't even there. They were talking as if it was all between the two of them.

"Rather like," Cisco added, sounding pleased with himself, "the alleged earnest money."

Dicey saw what Cisco was doing, and she didn't like it. "You'll get your money back, Mr. Hobart," she promised.

"But there's no need," Cisco told her. "How much was it, anyway? Fifty dollars? A hundred?"

"Five hundred," Mr. Hobart said.

"Five hundred dollars, and no contract written," Cisco said. He didn't have to add what he thought of that.

Dicey wanted to agree with Cisco. It would save her $500, for one thing, and she was angry, anyway, angry at Mr. Hobart just coming in like that to fire her.

"And what about the wood that was bought to build this alleged boat with?" Cisco inquired.

"Uh-uh," Mr. Hobart said. "She'd already bought the wood. That wasn't bought for my job."

Dicey didn't say anything. Let the two of them quarrel about it; they could have their quarrel. She'd given her word. If she wasn't going to keep her word—even if the reason she wasn't going to keep it wasn't her own choice—then she'd give back the money. She went over to the worktable. She took her checkbook out of her jacket pocket and opened it. She filled in the date, Mr. Hobart's name, and the amount, $500. Then she entered the check in the record section and did the subtraction.

That left her $115.77 in her account. After all the work, first to save up, then here in the shop to keep things going, she had $115.77 left to show for it. Bills had been sent out, she told herself—but she answered that she'd learned you couldn't count on people to pay bills. She'd given her word, she told herself—but she answered that Mr. Hobart had given his word, too.

Cisco followed her over to the table, to talk into her ear. "You don't have to do that." He didn't bother to lower his voice.

"I gave my word," Dicey said.

"If it's a hardship, Dicey," Mr. Hobart said from across the room, "I'm in no big hurry. I'm not pressing you and I hope you know that."

Dicey signed her name and ripped the check out. She reached it over to Mr. Hobart. "I gave my word on the deal," she said.

He took the check, without even looking at it. He just folded it and jammed it into the pocket of his stiff sheepskin jacket. "I am sorry, I want you to know that. You know how sorry I am about any inconvenience, don't you?"

No, Dicey didn't know that. She knew she'd been fired. He'd hired her to do something, then changed his mind. She knew he could afford to lose $500, but she also knew she couldn't afford to break her word. She couldn't afford to lose $500, but he could afford to break his word. That made no sense. It was all backward from the way it should be.

"Well," Mr. Hobart said, no longer paying any attention to Cisco. "The best of luck to you, Dicey." He smiled—white teeth appearing like the flesh of an apple between round pink cheeks. He took his gloves out of his pocket and put them on. "I'll expect to see your name, someday—maybe on a boat that's just beaten the pants off of me." His smile was smooth and easy; it stayed on his face as if he was accustomed to smiling, and keeping on smiling.

Cisco went around him to open the door. Cisco was smiling, too, smooth and easy, too, just like a newspaper photograph of a politician. "Why don't you just fuck off, friend?" Cisco asked, smiling away.

Mr. Hobart, halfway through the door, didn't much like that. Dicey tried to contain it, but laughter leaked out of her. Mr. Hobart looked at her, looked at Cisco, and decided not to say anything more. He shrugged, making sure they could see that shrugging of his shoulders under the thick, stiff jacket. That shrug was supposed to say to them, without any words, that he'd come out ahead, he hadn't lost, he was satisfied with the way things turned out. If they weren't satisfied, those shoulders said, they couldn't do anything about it. Then Mr. Hobart walked out.

All the laughter drained out of Dicey, like all that money draining out of her checking account.

She should have had a contract signed, just any piece of paper with both their signatures on it. She knew that was the way Ken did business, but she'd failed to think of it for herself. A contract would have specified what would happen if one side or the other failed to meet the terms. It was stupid not to have one.

"You can always stop payment on the check," Cisco suggested. "He's rich, he wouldn't be bothered to harass you. He wouldn't even notice any missing money, that piddling a sum is nothing to people like him."

"You didn't like him, from the first glance you didn't," Dicey said.

"I didn't," Cisco agreed cheerfully. "He's got money," he told her, as if that explained everything. "I don't much like people with money."

"Yeah, well, it shows," Dicey grumbled.

"Because they have it and I don't." Cisco grinned. "You should have kept the five hundred dollars."

Dicey wasn't surprised to hear him say that, but it still made her angry. "That would be like making somebody give you something. Like taking something for nothing."

"That's what they call good business, Miss Tillerman," Cisco told her, grinning away.

Dicey turned her back to him.

"I saw how little you've got left in the bank. I've got exceptional distance vision. You can't even pay your rent now, I'm willing to bet."

"Claude's taking that out of what he owes me. I've sent out bills, for storage, and the maintenance is on them this month," she said stubbornly.

"I guess about everybody owes you money. I guess you better hope they pay."

Dicey just got back to work. She didn't want to talk about it, and she didn't want to think about it. She didn't know who Cisco thought he was, anyway, telling her how to run her business.

But she was beginning to think she wasn't doing a very good job of running it herself. Even she had to admit that.

Well, she'd just have to work harder. Although now she wasn't awfully sure what she was working so hard for.

They worked late, finishing up the final coat of paint. Gram's light was out when Dicey finally stood in the kitchen, eating a peanut-butter-and-jelly sandwich in huge, hungry bites. Upstairs, only Maybeth's bedroom had a line of light at the bottom of the door. Dicey knocked and went in.

Maybeth, in a faded flannel nightgown with pale blue flowers printed all over it, her hair wound loosely into one thick braid to keep it out of her face, sat up in bed with a math textbook and pieces of paper spread around. The air smelled of growing things, brown earth and green herbs in pots along a window shelf.

"You were waiting up for me, weren't you?" Dicey said. "I should have been home earlier."

"You're working hard. You have a lot of work to do," Maybeth explained. "But I need to talk to you because Sammy's getting worried about Gram."

"Yeah," Dicey agreed. She would have liked to sit down but she had paint all over her. "She's been in bed now for, what? Almost a week?"

"Only two days and a half, but she's had that cough for weeks."

"She told me she's getting better."

"She doesn't eat as if she is." Maybeth looked at Dicey, her eyes round and gold-flecked in her serious face. Dicey thought, looking at her sister, how lovely Maybeth was, and gentle and patient, what good care she took of people—how Maybeth was about the exact opposite of Dicey.

"What about you? Are *you* worried?" Dicey asked. Since it was Gram, Sammy might get himself worried even if he didn't have to, but Maybeth would know.

Maybeth nodded her head, her eyes large.

"I thought," Dicey told her little sister, "if she doesn't do something this weekend, at least start reading while she's in bed, but unless she eats more, and wants to get out of bed—this weekend—then we should call Dr. Landros, no matter what Gram says."

Maybeth was satisfied. "I knew you'd know what to do."

Dicey didn't know that she was doing anything. "I'll need the truck, first thing tomorrow, but as soon as that job's done I'll come home. I should be home by lunchtime, at the latest. I'll stay here after that."

"Good," Maybeth said. "That's good. What would you like for dinner?"

Dicey didn't need to be asked twice. "Spaghetti." Maybeth's spaghetti sauce, with three kinds of ground meat in it and the tomatoes they'd put up in August, with the fresh herbs she put into it: Dicey's mouth got hungry for the taste of Maybeth's spaghetti, just thinking about it. "But Gram can't eat that."

"She doesn't eat anything, except I give her soup sometimes."

Seeing how worried Maybeth really was, Dicey started to get seriously worried herself. "I'll be home at lunchtime, or just after," she promised.

She kept her word, rousing a grumpy Cisco on the phone before she started over, hurrying through the hours it took to haul the boats back and forth. She was just going to have to leave Cisco to get the sanding done on his own that afternoon. "I can't stay," she said, when the four unpainted rowboats had been set out on the floor of the shop.

"You've finally got a date," he said.

Dicey shook her head impatiently. "My grandmother's sick."

He didn't seem troubled by that. "Well, maybe this elusive suitor will find time to see you next weekend. Although—unless you've been getting up to things you haven't told me about, and when you'd have time to, I can't imagine—if I were you I'd wonder how serious this boyfriend is. Don't you? Don't you wonder what he's up to when he's so obviously not here? What he's up to and with whom?"

Dicey didn't think Cisco had any business commenting on her private life, and she wasn't about to answer him in any way. Jeff wouldn't do that anyway.

"Men are weak," Cisco said to her. "And women play on that, women know that. If he's as good-looking as you think, and rich . . ."

"I never said he was rich."

"In that case, you're right to hold out for better."

"I thought you didn't like rich people anyway."

"I don't. That doesn't mean I wouldn't marry one. I could probably love one, too, if one loved me. That would be pretty easy, now I think of it. This guy doesn't have a sister, does he? Or a mother? What's wrong with your grandmother?"

"We don't know. Maybe just a bad flu. We don't often get sick, so we don't know what a bad flu is supposed to be like."

"You must have good genes, or you must be living right," Cisco remarked. "Well, I hope your grandmother gets better. I hope it's not something serious, like cancer."

Dicey had never thought of that, and she wished he hadn't mentioned it. He didn't look troubled at all by the idea; he looked as pleased with himself as a chipmunk. Maybe he just liked scaring people. "I gotta go," Dicey said.

CHAPTER 16

When Dicey got home, Sammy had gone to work and Maybeth was cleaning up after grilled cheese sandwiches. Dicey sent Maybeth out to do the shopping and finished the lunch cleanup herself. Every now and then she opened the door into Gram's bedroom. Gram slept on.

After a while, Dicey took a look at the books and papers she kept spread out on the dining room table—but she couldn't concentrate. Besides, she didn't have any reason to concentrate now.

She went back into the kitchen and piled all the chairs on top of the table. Then she washed the floor with a mop. Gram usually did that a couple of times a week, mopping clean the red-and-white linoleum. While the floor dried, Dicey took an empty bucket into the living room. The bed of ashes in the fireplace had gotten too high; she shoveled about half of them into the bucket and spread the rest around more evenly under the grate. If they could get Gram moved onto the sofa they'd all feel better. Taking to the sofa was what Gram did, the couple of times she'd had a cold bad enough to put her out of commission. At those times, Gram lay on the sofa, with a fire going, blankets spread over her, and a sweater on over her nightgown. She groused and gave orders, read books, and played cribbage. When she was sick, Gram made sure things still went along right.

Gram was really sick now, seriously sick. Dicey knew it in her bones. She had wanted it not to be true, so she'd let herself turn her back on the worry.

But Gram said she was getting better, and Gram didn't tell lies. So maybe Dicey was just letting her imagination get out of hand.

Dicey sat down again at the dining room table to think about boats, again, but she couldn't. She guessed she knew when to stop trying. She guessed she could tell when she'd fallen on her face for once and all. She piled the books in one of the cupboards of the sideboard and put her papers away in folders beside them. Closing the cupboard door, she twisted the knob to be sure the latch inside would catch, and hold. Doing that reminded her: They'd found a piece of lace, half-sewn onto a cambric bodice, for a night-gown, Gram had guessed, at the back of one of these deep cupboards, years ago; the materials had been folded and put away, years ago, had been left there in the dark, behind the closed door, like somebody's old forgotten dreams. Maybeth, Dicey remembered, had tried to save the lace, but it was so old that it had feathered apart even in her gentle fingers. Like old abandoned dreams somebody had put away, closed the door on.

Dicey wandered back into the kitchen. She lifted the chairs down, placing them around the table. Quietly, she opened the door into Gram's bedroom.

Gram's eyes were open. She was lying flat in bed, her head on a pillow.

Dicey went into the room, approaching the side of the bed. "How are you feeling?" she asked.

Gram's hands lay motionless on top of the white bedspread. When she spoke, her voice was as pale as her face. "Stupid question."

Dicey knew that, but she didn't know what else to say. You

couldn't say "You look terrible, what's wrong with you?" Could you? Gram had a glass of water on the table beside her bed, her light was turned on, she never wanted anything to eat—and she was just lying there, watching Dicey.

"Can I get you something?" Dicey asked.

Gram shook her head.

Dicey stood there, waiting for Gram to say something. Gram lay there, just waiting, Dicey didn't know for what.

"Maybeth says you're not eating much," Dicey said.

"Don't have much appetite, to speak of," Gram said. She sounded tired, too tired to be asked to talk.

"You told me you were getting better," Dicey reminded her grandmother.

Gram almost smiled, and she pushed herself up a little on the pillow. "I felt a lot worse two days ago. You're home early."

Dicey nodded. She didn't plan to talk to Gram about the shop. She didn't think Gram needed to worry about how badly things were going. Dicey looked around her grandmother's bedroom, a plain room, with just the double bed, the bedside table, a tall bookcase full of books, and the dark wooden bureau. The door to Gram's bathroom stood partly open, to show the sink and some towels. "Do you want me to get you something to read?" Dicey asked.

Gram shook her head. "Too tired."

"Are you warm enough? Do you want a sweater?"

"I'm fine," Gram said.

At that, Dicey almost lost her temper. "You aren't fine, anyone can see that. You're nowhere near fine. What's wrong with you, Gram?"

"If I knew, I'd be a doctor, wouldn't I?" Gram asked. "I'm waiting it out, girl. I'd be pleased if you'd do the same."

The shades were pulled down over the windows, making the

light in the room gentle, mellow, weak. There was one photograph on Gram's bureau. Dicey went over to look at it. The young man who had posed for the picture had dark hair and dark, serious eyes. His mouth was a straight line. Dicey turned around with the picture in her hand.

"Our grandfather," Dicey said.

Gram nodded.

"He was a handsome man," Dicey said, studying the broad, square jaw. You couldn't see anything from a picture except what someone looked like; and what someone looked like didn't necessarily have anything to do with what he acted like, and thought like. Stubborn, she thought, looking at the picture, and serious, and stern—he reminded her of herself, maybe, but not the self she liked best. The collar he wore looked bright white, stiff bright white, and uncomfortable, as if it were bound around his neck too tightly, like a thick collar for an unruly dog.

"Handsome is," Gram started to say—until coughing prevented her from finishing the sentence. Dicey stood, looking at the picture, so as not to stare at her grandmother—Gram, sick in bed—while she was coughing like that. Gram finally caught her breath enough to finish the sentence in a choking voice, "as handsome does."

Dicey didn't know about that. Handsome is as handsome is, that was what she thought. She knew that just because someone was handsome didn't mean he was good, or noble; but it did mean that he *was* exactly what it said, handsome. You couldn't say he wasn't just because you didn't like the way he acted, or lived.

She didn't think she ought to argue with Gram about that. She was just standing around in Gram's room, not doing anything. Standing around made her restless, uneasy. It left her free to think about the things she couldn't do anything about. Like

Gram being sick, or the boat she wasn't going to build for Mr. Hobart out of the wood she'd already paid for. She was relieved to hear the truck come up the driveway.

"That'll be Maybeth. She went shopping," Dicey told Gram. "Sammy's at work." Gram already knew that. "I better help Maybeth unload. Do you want your door open? Or closed?"

"Closed," Gram said.

Maybeth came in with two bags of groceries, which she set down on the table. "It's cold. Isn't she awake yet?" She took off her jacket and hung it on a hook by the door. "You washed the floor, Dicey. It looks nice, doesn't it?"

Dicey could have hugged her sister, who noticed things and took the trouble to say so. "Gram's awake," she reported, "but she doesn't want anything." Maybeth looked at the closed door. "She asked me to close it."

"She didn't mean it," Maybeth said.

"It's what she said, Maybeth."

"But when Gram's sick—could you unpack these, Dicey?" Maybeth didn't explain anything. She just knocked on the door of Gram's room, and went in.

Dicey put away the cans and dry foods, she washed fruit, set the week's supply of butter in the freezer and the eggs in the refrigerator. She heard Maybeth's voice, talking to Gram. Then Maybeth came back into the kitchen and filled the kettle with water. She picked up the cyclamen plant, with its windswept white flowers, and carried it into Gram's room. When she came out again, she had the water glass in her hand—she washed it out, rinsed it, filled it with fresh water, and then dropped two thick ice cubes to clink around in it, sounding as cool and fresh as a June evening. Dicey watched her sister.

Maybeth took the water into Gram's room, then came back into the kitchen to cut a slice of bread and put it into the toaster.

She poured boiling water into a mug and let the tea bag steep. Then she buttered the toast, cut the crusts off, spread it lightly with strawberry jam, and cut it into four triangles, which she arranged on a little plate. Dicey watched her sister do all these little things. Then she followed Maybeth into Gram's bedroom. Maybeth had put the cyclamen plant on the bedside table and raised the shade so sunlight fell on it. The pillow behind Gram's head had been plumped up, and the bedspread folded neatly down over the end of the bed, leaving the blanket across Gram's chest. Gram's hair had been brushed and she had changed her nightgown. While Dicey stood watching, Maybeth went to the bureau and took out a cardigan. "You should put this on, Gram," Maybeth said.

"I'm not cold," Gram objected.

"I know." Maybeth held out one sleeve, to help Gram get her arm into it.

"I said I wasn't hungry," Gram objected.

"I know." Maybeth moved the plate of toast over to where Gram could reach it easily.

"Or thirsty, either," Gram objected. "Don't say it, don't tell me—you know."

"That's right," Maybeth agreed, almost laughing.

Gram didn't look better, it wasn't that—she just didn't look as terrible as before.

"We're going to make some spaghetti sauce," Maybeth said. "You aren't going to have to eat it—but may I leave the door open? What if the smell has some nourishing value?"

"You know it doesn't," Gram told Maybeth. Gram looked at Dicey, who stood in the door, seeing everything Maybeth had done. Gram shook her head, as if to ask for sympathy for what she had to put up with. For a second, Gram really looked at Dicey.

Dicey went back into the kitchen, to start chopping up onions. If she were sick, she thought, she'd like to have Maybeth taking care of her. Dicey recognized the feeling she was feeling and knew its right name. Shame. She was ashamed of herself, for all the things she hadn't done right; she figured she should have known how to notice them. It wasn't only taking care of Gram—Maybeth was there to do that job, and do it right. It was everything that she had let go wrong, with her business mostly—from being robbed, to having to do Claude's boats, to losing Mr. Hobart's order. If she had started on his boat, he couldn't have taken his money back. She'd originally planned to start on it, then she'd changed her plans. What made her the most ashamed was the way she'd worked about as hard as she could, and that hadn't been good enough.

Dicey thought she'd better scale down her dreams. She'd better get back to being practical. She'd better see if she could sell the larch to get some of her money back from it. She'd better aim a little lower, or she wouldn't be able even to keep the shop.

Maybeth came out of Gram's room and got the spaghetti sauce ingredients out. Dicey started sautéing chopped onions in the big frying pan. Maybeth had wrapped an apron around her jeans, and was frowning as she worked the can opener around the can of tomato paste. "You're really terrific, Maybeth," Dicey said, and meant it.

Maybeth shook her head. "I can cook, and I can sing. I'm pretty. But those aren't things I do. They're things I am. I failed the first semester of history, Dicey."

That didn't have anything to do with it, Dicey thought. But Maybeth must think it did. Maybeth was like Gram, thinking that she wanted the door closed so she could hide out with her sickness in the dim light there, like some hunted animal going to ground in its burrow. "How badly did you fail it?" she asked.

"I got a fifty-one."

"Then all you need is a sixty-nine or seventy to pass for the year. You can do that, Maybeth."

Maybeth shook her head. "The best grade I've ever gotten is a sixty-four, on a homework assignment. And my map work passes."

"What if I tried to help you learn?"

"You can't. You have the shop," Maybeth explained.

"I could still, if we planned the time. Would you let me try?" Dicey asked.

"Of course. I'd like it, Dicey. But you don't have to. I don't mind."

"I know you don't," Dicey said. She wished she could learn from Maybeth how not to mind. Maybe if she tried, she'd be able to. But she did mind, and she didn't know how not to.

"It's Sammy that I mind about," Maybeth said. She stirred the chopped meat into the cooking onions. "Because he should go to tennis camp."

"We can't possibly afford that."

"I know, and so does he. But he may be good enough for a scholarship and he can't even try for it. Because they've never heard of him."

"Or seen him play," Dicey pointed out. "I didn't think tennis camp was weighing him down."

"It's not that. I just wish—"

"Me, too," Dicey agreed.

CHAPTER 17

When the spaghetti sauce had been assembled and was cooking away with slow burping bubbles, thick and red like an edible volcano, Dicey and Maybeth sat down to Maybeth's history assignment. The whole kitchen smelled of tomatoes, onion, and meat, of the oregano and basil Maybeth had brought down fresh from her window garden. Dicey went to look in on Gram while Maybeth went upstairs to find her history notebook. Gram still sat up, still sat quiet.

"It smells as good as she promised," Gram said, acknowledging Dicey's presence.

"Maybeth keeps promises."

"Oh, well, we all do. Whether we should or not," Gram said. She didn't say it as if it was important. She said it as if she was talking to herself.

"We're going to do some history," Dicey told her grandmother, in case Gram was wondering, although she didn't think Gram was even thinking about them. This time she didn't ask. She checked the glass of water, to see that it was full enough, that it had cubes of ice still floating in it.

"About time something got done about that history."

"Agreed," Dicey said. "Hungry?" she asked.

Gram's head moved back and forth on the pillow. Dicey's heart hurt her, to see Gram lying still in her bed, so weak that it looked like an effort for her to slowly shake her head and say no. Generally, Gram's noes came quick and sure, like gunshots, and her yesses, too. Dicey's heart felt swollen with sadness. There wasn't anything she could do except wait for Gram to get over this. But what if Cisco's hint was correct, what if Gram wasn't ever going to get better? Dicey turned away from the bedroom. She couldn't look that possibility in the eye, and she knew it.

Maybeth's assignment was to make a time line of the Civil War, because, she explained, they were having a unit test on Friday. Maybeth opened her textbook to a chapter titled "The War Between the States." The chapter was illustrated by a long, narrow picture, where men in blue uniforms faced men in gray uniforms, and puffs of gun smoke filled the air between them.

Dicey looked at the papers spread out on the table, class notes, homework paragraphs (graded with angry red numbers, fifty-seven, fifty-three, forty-six, with angry red notes telling Maybeth to use facts to support her ideas, to organize, to improve her spelling), and a sheet of unlined paper with a thick black line across its waist, crowded with vertical lines to mark events. Everything on that time-line paper was so massed together, Dicey could barely find the names she knew she'd recognize, like Gettysburg and Bull Run. She always remembered Bull Run because they fought two battles there, and the result had been the same both times, thousands of men dead or injured, and a victory for the South. It wasn't who won that bothered Dicey, but the thousands of dead or injured, whoever won.

If they lived then, Dicey thought, Jeff would have been one of those young men. If you lived at the wrong time, then sometimes you didn't get any chance at all to live. Like Bullet, the uncle they'd never even seen, their momma's younger brother. Bullet lived at the wrong time and died in Vietnam.

She wanted to see Jeff, to hear his guitar and his voice, just to be in the same room with him, or just to talk with him. She'd been forgetting about Jeff, but now—like the sun coming out after days and days of rain—he came back into her mind. She would call him, she decided. It was Saturday, he'd be in the dorm, she'd call him and talk for a long time with him. Everything was going wrong, going badly, but Jeff was something that was always right.

She brought her attention back to Maybeth's difficulties, and Maybeth's papers. The time line looked like a drawing of trees beside a river, with their reflections showing. Everything was all crowded together, cutting vertically through the thick time line. If it were a drawing of trees, they'd be in their thick summer abundance of branches and leaves, their trunks tangled with overgrown undergrowth.

Dicey didn't know what to say. She couldn't even tell where one decade ended and the next began. It was all a scrawl of pencil marks.

"What kind of a test will it be?" she asked.

"History," Maybeth's gentle voice explained to her.

"No, I know that," Dicey said impatiently. "I mean, essay or short answer? What kind of questions does she ask?"

"It's a he," Maybeth said, her voice sounding small.

Dicey turned her head, about to tell Maybeth to answer the question. Maybeth was staring at her, concentrating as hard as she could, trying to understand what Dicey wanted from her. She was trying so hard to understand what Dicey wanted that she couldn't possibly understand, like when you try to concentrate on remembering to breathe, each breath in and each breath out, and you find that breathing is a hard thing to do.

Dicey slowed herself down. She reached out to put a hand on Maybeth's hand that clutched a pencil, ready to write down whatever she was told to write down, and she smiled into her sister's worried face. "When he gives you a test, does he ask you fact questions? Like, to list the presidents? Give the right dates for battles and laws?"

Maybeth nodded.

"Are there map questions, where you have to put places on maps?"

Maybeth shook her head.

"How about paragraphs, does he ask you to write paragraphs?"

"No. It's all memory. And I can't remember enough."

A time line would be a good way to study for that kind of test, if it were a good time line. This wasn't a good time line.

"Okay," Dicey said. "How do you decide what to put on this time line?"

"From the topic sentences of paragraphs," Maybeth told her. "I don't think I left anything out."

Dicey, looking at the messy mass of pencil marks, thought probably she hadn't. But you couldn't memorize from that. Unless you had a photographic memory, that time line was going to be just so much gibberish, crowding across the paper from left to right.

"Maybeth, you can remember recipes, can't you?"

"That's different; it's easy. It's not just—words. I can remember music," Maybeth explained, more relaxed now. "They tell you, if there's something you're good at then that's a good way to work. But music is notes, and they're easy to remember because you can hear them. And this is—just words."

"You've been trying to do things as if they were music," Dicey said. "But that doesn't work in history?"

"No. But it's the only thing I'm good at."

So Maybeth didn't give up, but she kept doing things the same way, even when it didn't work. Dicey wondered, the idea whipping across her mind like a sail whisked across the water under a brisk wind, if she was doing the same thing with her business. She shoved that idea aside, for later consideration. Now she was thinking about Maybeth.

"Since that way doesn't work, let's toss it," she said.

"Okay." Maybeth sat, pencil ready, waiting to be told how else to do it.

"How do you remember recipes?" Dicey asked.

"Because there are things you do first, to get ready. Then there are things you do to put everything together. Then it cooks."

It didn't make much sense to Dicey, but Maybeth seemed to know what it meant. "So you separate things, into different steps," Dicey pointed out.

"No, into boxes," Maybeth corrected her patiently.

Dicey was about to start explaining it again, then a picture of a box came into her mind and she stopped herself. If Maybeth thought in boxes, and since Maybeth was the one who needed to learn those things, Dicey should try to think in boxes, too. "I don't understand," she said.

"Because time doesn't look like this," Maybeth traced the thick black line along its length. "Mr. Whoople says it does. But it doesn't because things all happen together. Like the things you do first. Music goes in a line, but time . . . Remember? There was the time we lived with Momma in Provincetown." Maybeth drew a box on the paper. "Then there was the time we came down here. Now we're here." Maybeth made boxes, all the same size, for each time she mentioned. Dicey looked at them and thought—the traveling time should be a smaller box, because there had been thirteen years in Provincetown, and eight years in Crisfield, but only a summer traveling. Maybeth had made them all the same size, so the one short summer had the same time-size to Maybeth that the long years before and after did. Maybeth was measuring time in her own way. Measuring time that way, Dicey thought that she herself was beginning another box, for the time of her own life. She wanted to fill in that box with boats. Except, the way the box was starting out, she was filling in the box with failures.

"I see what you mean," Dicey said. "But aren't there lines that connect the boxes together, or jump over some and come up later?"

Looking at her sister's blank, earnest face, Dicey knew that was what Maybeth started getting confused about, where she started getting too confused to remember. Dicey, suddenly feeling smart, feeling like she was solving problems, got to work. They taped four pieces of unlined paper together, to give them plenty of room. She and Maybeth made a box line, and then Dicey had the idea of using crayons, too. They spent the afternoon first filling in the events, the main facts, everything—speeches, laws, battles, names. Then they color-coded, choosing the right colors—like blue to underline battles the North had won, gray for Southern victories. When they were through, Maybeth looked down at her work and smiled. "It's pretty, isn't it?"

It was a long chart that showed a nation slipping into civil war, that showed the war being fought, battle after bloody battle. Dicey shook her head. She didn't think it was any too pretty.

"Look," Maybeth said. They had used brown to underline anything that had to do with the slavery question. "Look at all the brown at the beginning and then it stops until"—she bent over the chart—"the Thirteenth Amendment. As if—"

Dicey waited.

"As if it all started over slavery but then it changed to be about something else," Maybeth said.

"Do you think you can figure out what it changed to?" Dicey asked. It had been so long since she'd done school learning, it actually felt good. Maybeth bent over the long sheet of paper, separated into boxes, connected by colors. Dicey sat back, and stretched. She got up to look in on Gram, whose eyes were closed in sleep again.

"I can remember boxes," Maybeth said, still staring at the paper. "I can understand colors. Thank you, Dicey. You know everything, don't you?"

"Not by a long shot," Dicey promised her sister. She didn't know much of anything, and she had just learned how little she knew. Looking at all those facts just made her start wondering about questions she didn't know how to find answers for.

It wasn't that she was sorry not to be going to school anymore. She was just sorry she hadn't continued learning. Cisco didn't need school to learn. Gram didn't. Dicey wondered what it took to be able to not stop learning. She didn't know what the quality was, and she didn't know if she had it. She was pretty sure, in fact, that she didn't, and she didn't know what to do about that. The quality might be named curiosity. If you weren't too curious by nature, what did you do? You kept people around you who were, she thought, answering her own question.

Like Jeff. She was going to call Jeff after supper. In fact, Dicey thought, smiling to herself, she was going to call him and say yes, she'd marry him. Now. She'd tried a boat business and it hadn't worked, so she'd go ahead and marry Jeff.

Dicey held the prospect of that phone call out in front of her, like the promise of sunrise held out at the end of darkness. Knowing it was waiting out there ahead filled the time she spent between, and the things she did, with lightness. Dicey was the kind of person who saved the best until last.

At dinner she just sat and listened to Sammy and Maybeth

talk, asking occasional questions. "When does tennis start?" she asked, and "When's the spring chorus performance? What are you singing?"

When the dishes were done, and Maybeth and Sammy settled in the kitchen, Maybeth working on her history and Sammy writing an essay about a poem that started out "Success is counted sweetest by those who ne'er succeed"—"That's not true Dicey, I feel—great, absolutely—perfect when I win a match. If it's been a good match"—knowing that her brother and sister would hear if Gram needed anything. Dicey went into the living room to call Jeff.

The phone rang and rang. Lazily, Dicey wondered if Jeff was in someone else's room, talking or playing music. She pictured him there, sitting on the floor, the guitar in his arms. Finally someone picked up the phone. "Hello?"

It wasn't Jeff. "Hi, is Jeff there?" Dicey asked. She held the phone close against her ear.

"No, he's out," the voice said.

"You're not Roger," Dicey told the voice.

"That's right. I'm your proverbial passing stranger. Can I take a message?"

"Do you know when Jeff will be back?"

"God knows, tonight. It's the midwinter dance. Rog and Jeff took their dates to dinner first, and the band's been paid to play until whenever—as long as there are dancers on the floor. If I were you I'd try him some other time. Give him a couple of days to get back in shape, though—it promises to be quite a party. Any message?" the voice asked, impatient to be gone.

"No," Dicey said. She hung up.

She wasn't jealous, she was just puzzled. At least, she didn't think the jumpy, chilly feeling in her stomach was jealousy. Fear maybe, because Cisco—who seemed to know his way around—

had hinted to her that Jeff might have another girl. If Jeff did, it wouldn't be messing around, because Jeff wasn't that way. So if he did, it was serious, and Dicey had lost him. If she'd lost him, she knew who was responsible.

Mina had said her mother said something like that same warning. But Dicey had always thought Jeff wasn't like other boys, other men. And he hadn't been, either. Except, she thought now, that what she meant by not being like them might just mean that she could count on Jeff to do what she wanted, exactly what she wanted, which wasn't a terrific way to love anybody, was it?

She waited until noon the next day, filling in the morning hours by washing the windows in the living room and dining room, worrying about Gram, whose cheeks were oddly pink and who felt awfully warm to Dicey's hand, and who wouldn't even try to eat the soft-boiled egg Maybeth made for her. At noon, she dialed Jeff's number again. She didn't think he'd sleep the whole day away. He wasn't the kind of person to stay up partying all night and sleep away a day.

"Hello." Jeff's voice traveled along the phone line, and into her heart. "Hello?"

"Jeff." She was as relieved to hear him as if she had wondered if he might not have gotten back to his own room yet.

"Dicey?" He sounded surprised.

"Yeah. Hi." Now Dicey couldn't think of what to say, how to say it.

"How are you?" Jeff asked. He sounded careful, as if he was being careful. "What're you up to?"

"It's Groundhog Day. Happy Groundhog Day," Dicey said. She heard how stupid that sounded, so she went right ahead and asked: "What do you say we get married?"

There was a silence in the phone, in her ear. Dicey could imagine what was going on in Jeff's mind during that silence.

Imagining it made her smile. She hadn't known how good it would feel to give Jeff something he wanted so much.

"Why?"

What kind of a question was that? "Why what?"

"Why all of a sudden do you say you'll marry me?" Jeff asked patiently.

"I always said I would," Dicey reminded him. She knew what he meant, but she didn't want to talk about it, not now. It was too complicated. It would take too long. "Why shouldn't I?" She turned it into a joke. "You're handsome, you've got money—how could I not want to marry you?"

"No," Jeff said.

"No, what?"

"No, let's not get married," Jeff said.

That didn't make sense. Dicey couldn't understand what he said, because it just didn't make sense. She tried to hear his voice, hear it so well she could see his face in it. She hated telephones. She should have driven up to Baltimore. She should have been able to see his face. This voice—it was Jeff's voice, but it was a voice that was thinking seventeen thoughts for every word it said, as if everything Jeff said he wanted to have complete control over, so none of the words would slip away and mean anything he didn't want them to mean. His voice kept its secrets. It didn't give any clues to what his face would look like if she could see it.

"Okay," Dicey said.

There were two silences now, one on each end. She didn't understand and she needed to think.

She understood, all right. He was saying no. *That* she understood, there was no confusion to that. She could feel how understanding it had cramped up her mind entirely, and most of her body, too. The hand holding the phone, for instance, looked like the hand of a statue that wouldn't ever move. She didn't need to think. She knew what it meant, Jeff saying no like that. "Well," she said into the silence, her voice careful. "I guess there's nothing much else. I'll say good-bye, then."

"Good-bye, Dicey," his voice said. "Thanks for calling."

Why had he added that at the end? She stared at the phone, with her heart cramped up tight. She hadn't told him about Gram being sick, or about Mr. Hobart firing her, or about Cisco and the shop, or anything. He'd have wanted to hear about those things, and now he wouldn't, and it served him right.

But she knew she was kidding herself. She wasn't angry, although she was trying to think angry. When something was lost, it was lost and gone. You had to admit that to yourself. Dicey didn't even try to think she hadn't lost Jeff. Hope was painful and it interfered with moving on. She couldn't stand it if, along with everything else, she had to have hope.

CHAPTER 18

All the long afternoon—Dicey hadn't ever known how long an afternoon could be. She concentrated on just getting through it, getting through with it.

Mostly, the three of them hung around in the kitchen, worrying—without talking about it, because talking wouldn't have done any good. The aspirin Gram had taken—with Maybeth lifting her head from the pillow and holding the glass of water to her mouth and Gram not even protesting—hadn't brought down her temperature. Maybeth gave her more at two, but all Gram did was sleep them off. Awake, she'd cough, or move restlessly in her bed. She barely opened her eyes.

Sammy and Maybeth had homework to do as they sat at the kitchen table, not talking. Dicey didn't know how good their concentration was, but she figured she could make a guess. Dicey didn't have anything to do. There was no reason now to work at trying to figure out the fundamentals of boat design. She'd never thought so hard over anything as she had those boat books, and never gotten so little understanding back in return. She'd have to return them to the library, she thought, sitting at the table, shuffling the worn deck of cards, laying out yet another game of solitaire. There was nothing else to do with her hands, and she didn't want to think about anything, either. Mostly she didn't want to think about Jeff.

The no had gotten into her head. It was sinking through all the levels of her understanding, like a stone through thick water. When it hit bottom, she'd feel it. When it hit bottom, she'd know everything that no meant. Meanwhile, she laid the cards out on the table.

Gram coughed, and Sammy surged up out of his chair, slamming the palms of his hands down on the table. He marched around the end of the table and across to the door of Gram's room. "You are definitely not getting better," he said.

Dicey could barely hear Gram's voice answering, "I'm fine."

"Ha," Sammy said. "Ha, ha. Very funny. We're going to call Dr. Landros, Gram."

"It's Sunday," the weak voice protested.

"I don't care," Sammy said. He turned around. "Aren't we?" he asked them.

"I think so," Dicey answered. "What do you think, Maybeth?" Maybeth nodded her head. Dicey heard Gram rustle out of bed and close the bathroom door behind her. Then she heard the sound of Gram coughing muffled by the closed door.

Dicey got up and went into the living room. Because it was the weekend, she got only the answering service. She asked them to call Dr. Landros and ask her to telephone the Tillermans, and assured the woman that yes, it was serious. Even as she said that she hoped it wasn't, but she didn't feel any too confident. Dr. Landros would call them back as soon as she could, the woman at the answering service told her. Dicey paced back to the kitchen. She looked at the cards, and moved a red five onto a black six.

The slow afternoon moved along. By the time they realized that nobody had thought about supper, it was too late to plan what to eat. Maybeth got up and opened the refrigerator door. She stood there, looking into it, and stood there, and looked into it, until Sammy finally asked her, "What's wrong?"

"I'm trying to think." Maybeth didn't turn around.

Trying not to think would be closer to the truth, Dicey suspected. She got up to stand beside her sister. There were eggs. There was the pitcher of milk. There was a big piece of chuck, for pot roast, but it was too late to start a pot roast. The three inches of leftover spaghetti sauce in a mason jar wouldn't feed the three of them.

"I'm not hungry, anyway," Sammy announced from behind them.

"Eggs and toast?" Dicey suggested.

"An omelette," Maybeth said, as if she had just discovered the word. "With spaghetti sauce, from leftover, and I'll make biscuits—will you turn on the oven for me, Dicey? To four hundred."

Until she saw her sister find something to do, find work for her hands and a reason to do the work, Dicey didn't fully understand how tense and quiet Maybeth had been. Understanding that, she looked at her brother. His eyes were fixed on a page of a chemistry textbook, but his eyes never moved and he looked the way he looked when he was waiting to receive serve from an opponent he respected.

"Look," Dicey said, "all we can do is wait for Dr. Landros to call."

They both obeyed to the extent of turning to look at her.

"She could have called by now. Maybe we should have called her sooner," Sammy asked.

Dicey didn't argue. Maybe they should have, but they hadn't.

"It's taking her a long time," Maybeth said, and big tears rolled out of her eyes.

"Not so long, it just seems long," Dicey told them.

"I know," Maybeth said, "but it *is* long. Because I'm worried."

"So am I," Dicey admitted. "We all are. Maybe even Gram."

"I think so," Sammy said. "That's what really worries me. That"—he smiled, but it wasn't a smile for gladness—"and when you cry, Maybeth."

"I'm sorry." Maybeth wiped at her eyes with the back of her hand. "I feel better when I cry," she apologized.

"That sure cheers me up a lot," Sammy joked.

The biscuits were on the table and the omelette was cooking in its pan when they heard a car drive up. They all forgot supper. Dr. Landros came into the kitchen.

Dr. Landros was a thick, square woman. She wore workboots and worn, old gray-flannel trousers, a bright yellow plaid hunter's jacket; her hair was pulled back from her square-jawed face. She carried her doctor's bag in her hand. "I was chopping wood," she explained. "What's the trouble with Ab?"

"How did you know?" Sammy wondered.

"She's not out here waiting for me, with anxiety all over her face."

"Because she's in bed," Maybeth said.

"Then she really must be sick." Dr. Landros took off her jacket and hung it on the back of a chair. "Which is her room?"

"She's asleep," Dicey said.

"She's got a temperature," Sammy said.

"She's had a cough, for weeks," Maybeth offered.

"Let me ask her myself, all right? You three go on ahead with your dinner." Dr. Landros knocked on the door but didn't wait for an answer. She went in, shutting the door behind her. They all sat down at the table, as quiet as they could be, listening to the occasional murmur of voices in Gram's bedroom. When the bedroom door finally opened, Dicey turned around.

"It's all right," the doctor told them, before anyone could ask a question. "Can I join you for a biscuit, and maybe a cup of tea?"

Maybeth got up to start water, Sammy got up to get a plate and knife, Dicey sat in her chair savoring those words—"all right."

When she was seated, and had food in front of her, Dr. Landros explained. "I can't be sure until she's had an X ray, but my diagnosis is pneumonia."

Once it had a name, and the name wasn't something like cancer, Dicey felt better.

"Pneumonia is serious, isn't it?" Maybeth asked.

"Serious enough, especially for older people."

"But how did she get it?"

"I gather she had bronchitis, which she neglected." The doctor looked sternly around at all of them.

"But she told us she was getting better," Sammy protested. "We kept asking and she kept saying."

"You know she'd say that, regardless. You should have known better. James would have. Am I right in assuming that you didn't call James?"

They nodded. Dicey felt about ten years old, being scolded like that and knowing she deserved it.

"You take such good care of each other," Dr. Landros said, but her voice sounded matter-of-fact now, not scolding, "but you have to admit that sometimes you need to call in outside help. You can't do everything yourselves. I wouldn't be surprised if—you're so ferociously independent—I wouldn't put it past you to do open-heart surgery yourselves, on this very table."

"We would not," Sammy said. "That would be stupid."

"So is letting your grandmother bully you into not calling me," Dr. Landros said. "And could someone please pass me the biscuits again?" She split and buttered a biscuit, spread jam over each half, and then folded it back together. The jam oozed down the sides and onto her fingertips. "Take her up to Salisbury tomorrow for an X ray. I'll tell them you're coming. I've given her some penicillin and cough medicine for now; stop by my office or call when you get back, and I'll write out prescriptions for what you'll need. There's fluid in her lung, but—it should be all right. I want you to promise to call me if her temperature goes up too high, especially in the morning. It shouldn't, it probably won't, but—and call my home number, you have it. None of this shilly-shallying around. I'd rather lose an hour's sleep than a friend. I don't have so many friends."

They nodded and nodded.

"I don't think that will happen, I don't think it's near serious enough for hospitalization, that's my professional opinion, but—"

"We'll take good care of her," Maybeth promised.

"You've already taken good care of her," Dr. Landros said. "You've done everything right so far—except for not calling me sooner, but then, you could have called me even later, so I'm not going to complain. Keep up the liquids, don't let her out of bed, dress her warmly tomorrow—it's getting cold again—and call me when you're back. I'll have the X ray results by then. Thanks for the supper." Dr. Landros got up and put on her jacket.

"How *did* she get it?" Sammy asked.

Dr. Landros answered slowly. "Pneumonia isn't something you get. It's more something you get to. But I'll tell you this—I've never known anyone come down with it who wasn't overextended, somehow—overtired. When she's better I plan to tell Ab that, that she needs better self-management. I should tell her now when she's too weak to argue, but that doesn't seem fair. Does it?"

She was teasing them, letting them know she wasn't anxious. But after she'd left, the three of them looked at one another, without saying anything. Dicey didn't know about Sammy and

Maybeth, but she was feeling a mix of relief and guilt. "We'll have to do more, all of us," she said. "I guess. I guess I can."

"Me, too," they both agreed.

"I guess I don't mind, either." Dicey thought of the way she had been living exclusively for her own work. "As long as Gram gets better, and stays better. It's only pneumonia," she said. Pneumonia had a name, and a cure.

Maybeth's smile was like the sun dancing along the tops of the waves. "Is anyone else hungry? I'll make us supper."

"You already did," Sammy reminded her. He went over to the stove and picked up the omelette, limp and brown, like a rag that had been used to scrub a filthy floor. He looked at it, where it hung down from his hand. "Maybe," he said, starting to laugh, "maybe with sauce we won't notice?" It wasn't as funny as he thought it was, but Sammy continued to laugh, until his knees gave way and he leaned against the stove, waving the omelette gently, and watching it fall to pieces of its own weight.

"I was worried," he said. "And now I'm not."

Sammy picked up the mess he'd made on the floor, Dicey rinsed out the pan, Maybeth got out more eggs and whisked them with a fork; they ate supper hungrily. Gram slept, but that seemed right to them now. Maybeth announced, after they'd washed their dishes, and dried them, and put everything away, that she wanted to make a cake.

"It's late," Sammy told her.

"What about your homework?" Dicey asked her.

"It's only eight-thirty and I've done it all, and—I want to make a cake."

"Chocolate?" Sammy asked. "With chocolate frosting?"

"Yes. But I don't want you in here. You get in the way."

Dicey and Sammy withdrew to the living room. Dicey built a fire, lit it, and watched the flames rising from the paper catch at the logs, turning into thin rising trails of smoke. She felt as if her mind, and her attention, had been caught in a vise of worry, and now it had been released. She knew why Maybeth was out there putting together a cake. "I've got to make a phone call," she announced. Sammy, who had been tinkering at the piano, put his hands in his lap and turned around. Dicey dialed the shop, pulling the disk around then letting it go, hearing the rapid rat-a-tat of its turning in the receiver. Cisco answered on the third ring. "Tillerman Boats," his voice said.

"It's me."

"Miss Tillerman. I expected to see you today."

"That's why I called," Dicey said. "Did everything go okay?"

"Why shouldn't it? Do you mean, were there any armed bandits, come to remove your worldly goods? Or assault your virtue, or mine, since I was the one here, although they'd have been disappointed. You have," he explained with mocking solemnity, "a great deal more virtue to assault than I do. In either case, there weren't."

Dicey smiled. Cisco's mind never rested, or at least his tongue didn't. "How's your grandmother?" he asked.

"The doctor says it's pneumonia. I don't expect to be in tomorrow, either."

"I'll stand the watches here," Cisco said.

"Good. Thanks. I just wanted to be sure everything was going okay." Dicey hung up. When Claude did pay her, she would give Cisco part of it.

"I thought you'd call Jeff," Sammy said. "To tell him."

Dicey, staring at the phone, shook her head.

Sammy waited for her to say something, then when she didn't he suggested, "Or James."

"I thought we'd call James tomorrow, when we have the X ray results and have talked to Dr. Landros. I'll take Gram up to Salisbury tomorrow morning. You'll have to take the bus to school."

"No problem."

"Because there'll be prescriptions to fill." Her mind got busy with plans. She'd better be sure Gram brought her checkbook, to cover what Medicare didn't. "Is there gas in the truck?" She wished she knew how to call Claude and find out if that money was in the mail yet. Just so if she needed it there would be some there, for medicine or other expenses, because if you needed money to be sick with, you really needed it.

"Did you and Jeff have a fight or something?" Sammy wondered.

Dicey shook her head. "Jeff doesn't fight." He didn't; he went silent and withdrawn. She remembered how he'd done that once, the worst time she'd seen, before she'd known him long. She'd asked him, later, what had happened, and all he'd said was, "My mother has that effect on me." Jeff, when things went wrong, moved away into himself, the opposite of the way a potted plant leans toward the sun, drawing away with the same kind of silence. You'd look one day and see, like with a plant, how he leaned. And like a plant, he'd just go on with his own growing, the best he could do in whatever the circumstances were.

"Neither does Maybeth," Sammy said.

Why did Sammy say that? "Is Maybeth having a fight with someone?"

"Not with me. I never would." Sammy grinned. "No, I was just thinking—do you know why I think she didn't have a date last night?"

"Because Gram's sick."

"No. Well, yes, but—she hasn't been out on a Saturday for almost a month."

Dicey sat down on the desk beside the phone. "I'll bite. Why not?"

"Because of Phil."

"Phil Milson?"

"If he's going to be home, it'll be on Saturday. She wants him to call her, and he hasn't."

"You're that sure she wants him to?"

Sammy nodded. Dicey didn't question his accuracy. Sammy knew his sister, and understood her. "I kind of want him to, too. But he might not. Maybeth—never complains, but it doesn't seem to me that there are so many things she wants, not for herself."

"Even so, I don't think there's anything we can do," Dicey said. Maybeth endured failures like a patch of marsh grass, rooted in the mud, letting the water wash over it. She stayed planted while the water moved in its strong way, then when it was finished she'd sort of lift her head to see what was there. What the water had left. That was the same way Maybeth did school, like marsh grass, being there, being what she was, high tide or low tide, winter cold or summer warmth, being who she was.

Dicey admired Maybeth. "We don't always get what we want," she reminded Sammy.

"Tell me about it," he said. "But with me, if I can't get something one way I try another. I figure, if I do well in state matches this summer, get into the state championships, play eighteen-and-under along with sixteen-and-under, I think I'll be good enough for that, then I can apply for a scholarship next summer and have a chance. Especially," he grinned, "if I'm the champion."

"Can you do that?" Dicey asked him. She believed in Sammy, but high hopes like that—what would he do if he cooked up such high hopes and they didn't work out? "Why does it matter so much anyway, this camp?"

"Because I've been thinking that I'll want to study engineering, aeronautical engineering, and if you're at a good school, with an athletic scholarship . . . I'm not smart like James but I'm smart enough for what I want, so if I can get in with an athletic scholarship, I could do the work at a good school. Then I'd have a good chance of being admitted to the space program." His eyes lit up with hope and laughter. "You've gotta admit it would be fun, Dicey. Being in space. Exploring."

"It's not like in the movies," Dicey said. "In the movies, there's always oxygen when they go exploring, on the planets."

"Yeah, I know, or, anyway, part of me knows. The other part just gets excited. It can't possibly be like I imagine, but—imagine it, Dicey."

"And what if it doesn't work out? The camp. The scholarship. The space program."

"I'll be a tennis pro, or coach, or something. That would be okay. Or I could be a farmer here, I could work the farm, because farmers don't make much money, but they almost always make enough for food and shelter. I really like growing things," Sammy told her.

"You've got it all worked out," Dicey said. He did, and it was just like Sammy. He was right about himself, he was a tryer, he'd keep on trying different things until something worked out.

"Besides, you can never tell what'll happen. Other things turn up. Things I haven't even thought of." Sammy sounded like that possibility was exciting, too.

Dicey looked at her brother and felt a slow smile spreading over her face. She envied him, and she wondered if she could ever learn to look at things that way, as if it wasn't losing something you wanted, but making room for something new to come in. She didn't know about herself, but she admired Sammy. And liked him, too, mostly, just—liked him. "How about," she asked, "a game of checkers? How would you like to take me on in a game of checkers? I may be rusty, but you've never beaten me yet."

"Not true. I did once, when I was in eighth grade. You remember it. Don't pretend you've forgotten."

"Okay, I do, so we'll play four games out of seven. It'll be a tournament match. And the winner—" She tried to think of something. The sweet chocolate smell from the kitchen gave her an idea. "The winner will get the last piece of Maybeth's cake."

"I usually get that in any case," Sammy pointed out.

"Then what've you got to lose?"

"No, you've got it all wrong. The question is, What have I got to win?"

CHAPTER 19

The next morning, when Dicey knocked on the door of Gram's room, Gram sat up in bed, her shoulders supported by pillows. She had eaten half of a piece of toast, and finished the mug of tea. Dicey half-expected Gram to try to talk her way out of the X ray, and she wasn't planning to take any guff. "We have to go to Salisbury," she said, giving Gram no time to say anything. "You need to get dressed. I'll warm up the truck."

"I wouldn't hurry," Gram advised her. "It'll take me a while. And no, I don't want help. I can dress myself."

It was half an hour before Gram came out of her room. Dicey had washed the dishes and wiped down all the counters. She had swept the floor. She had gotten the cab of the truck warm. She had dried the dishes and put them away. She had just begun to wonder if she should worry, or knock on Gram's door again, when that door opened.

Gram looked pale, and old. She moved as if she wasn't sure her legs would hold her up for long. She wore her rubber boots and a skirt, and a thick sweater buttoned down over the skirt. Her body looked thick and round, but her face looked thin. Dicey got up to get her coat, and hat, and gloves, and finally a scarf. "Are you wearing something warm next to your skin?" she asked.

"No, and I won't. They're just going to tell me to get undressed when I get there—if I haven't boiled to death on the way up."

Dicey didn't argue. Some things weren't worth arguing about.

They drove up in silence. Gram leaned her head back against the seat and kept her eyes closed. Dicey left her off at the main entrance to the hospital. "Go sit in a chair. I'll be right there." Gram just nodded.

At the X-ray department they waited, and waited, side by side on a sofa. Their shoulders touched as they sat, waiting to be called. After Gram went off with a nurse, Dicey waited alone. She felt as if the morning stretched out endlessly, before her and behind her. She felt as if she had fallen into some time sack, hanging off time's usual line of tightly twisted minutes, and was just hanging there, outside of time. When Gram reappeared, buttoning her sweater, Dicey got up. She held out her grandmother's coat and then put an arm around her bulky shoulders, as if to help her walk. Gram didn't protest.

Back in the truck, heading home along the highway, Dicey looked over at her grandmother. "Are you all right?"

Gram nodded her head without opening her eyes. "I'll be glad to get back to bed. Which is, I trust, our destination."

"Doctor's orders," Dicey answered. "Then I'll call her office and take care of everything."

"You drape yourself over this plate," Gram said slowly. "Jaybird naked. Which is a strange phrase, now I think of it, since jays have feathers. The young woman wouldn't even stay in the same room with that machine. It's as if medicine were as dangerous as disease."

"James explained to me once that the principle is to figure out how to poison the disease without killing off the host body," Dicey said. She looked at Gram, waiting for her opinion on that—although she could guess what huffing and puffing response Gram's commonsensical mind would have. Her grandmother, head leaning back, didn't say anything. Her profile—forehead, nose, chin; cheekbones and eyebrows, eyelids closed down over her eyes—"You're as pretty as Maybeth," Dicey said. She'd never realized that before. If she hadn't thought Gram was asleep, she wouldn't ever have said it out loud.

"I was, in my day," Gram answered. She opened one eye, turning her head slightly toward Dicey. "I'd be obliged if you'd watch the road."

Gram got herself back into bed while Dicey called Dr. Landros's office. The receptionist answered her question—yes, it was pneumonia, in the left lung; the doctor had called in two prescriptions to the drugstore and they should be picked up right away; no, Gram was in no danger, no immediate danger, but she had to stay in bed for a week, and in the house for at least two weeks after that, until her lung cleared up; the doctor would stop by after office hours this afternoon; and how was James doing? Dicey, not surprised that the news was good but still relieved, looked in on Gram, who was asleep. She wrote a note saying where she'd be going. She put the note, folded to stand up, on the table by the glass of fresh ice water she'd brought in, in case Gram woke up thirsty, and went downtown to have the prescriptions filled, getting there and back fast.

By the time Maybeth and Sammy came home, Dicey had washed the kitchen windows, made two bowls of Jell-O, begun the slow simmering of a chicken for creamed chicken, and ironed four shirts. She didn't know which of the shirts belonged to which of her siblings, as she set them onto hangers and hung them off a doorknob.

"It's pneumonia for sure," she greeted them.

"Is that good?" Maybeth asked.

"They know how to treat pneumonia," Sammy explained.

"I'm starving," he announced, opening the refrigerator door. "There's mail for you," he told Dicey. "Jell-O? Is this Jell-O?"

"It's for Gram."

"Do you think she'll share?" Sammy asked.

"You might as well open this door." They heard Gram's voice. "Now you've woken me up."

Sammy looked at Maybeth and Dicey. He was grinning. "Good-o," he greeted his grandmother's complaint.

Dicey's mail was from Claude, a check for $839. The note he sent with it answered her question at the size of the check. "The rate you're going, you'll have the next ten done before you get this. I've included the fourteen dollars for the window. Temperature down here was seventy-two at noon yesterday. Eat your heart out."

Dicey wasn't about to eat her heart out; a temperature of seventy-two degrees in February was unnatural. She had a check for $839 to deposit into her account. The bank would be closed by now, but she had the check. So that was okay. And Gram had pneumonia and they'd have to keep her in bed, which wouldn't be easy, but that was okay, too. Jeff wasn't okay, or that wasn't, but that was her own stupid fault.

In the evening, while Sammy and Maybeth did homework in the kitchen, Dicey called Cisco, who assured her that everything was going along fine. Then she called James. "Gram's got pneumonia," she told her brother, "but it's fine now, she's taking medicine. Dr. Landros said."

"I'm glad she had the sense to call a doctor," James's voice announced. Then it smiled. "Or someone did."

"It was someone," Dicey said, "and only after a while, but we've learned our lesson. We're going to have to keep her in bed, and in the house, for a long time, which won't be easy, but we'll gang up on her. Anyway, that's our news. How's school?" Before

James could tell her, she remembered, "James? What did you do about that course, with the professor who liked you?"

"Didn't they tell you?"

"I haven't been around all that much."

"I wish I were home. It makes me worry, Gram getting pneumonia."

"I know. I think even she got worried. She's being pretty cooperative."

"Dr. Landros does say everything's all right?"

"I wouldn't lie."

"No, you wouldn't. What you'd do is not call me up to tell me something was wrong."

"I've called you now, James," she reminded him. "Anyway, what did happen?"

"I'm auditing the course. My adviser worked it out for me. She told me I should tell Professor Browning I couldn't handle all the work, but that I wanted to continue attending. So I dropped it."

"You don't mind?"

"Mind what? It got me out of a bind."

"Mind saying you couldn't handle it. Or did you tell your friends the truth?"

"Cripes, Dicey, I couldn't do that. What if it got back to him? No, I didn't tell anyone, except my adviser, and she'll keep it quiet. My friends all just think I'm not the hotshot I was cracked up to be, which never hurts. I mean, it never hurts to have people think you've failed. They like you to have an Achilles' heel, right? But I have to take six courses this semester, to make up the credit, and I'm working like crazy—so they'll learn better. Because it never hurts to let people know how good you are, does it?"

James's brain never rested from following twists and turns. "Boy, do you like things complicated," Dicey told him.

"Machiavellian," he answered, "that's me. You know Machiavelli?"

"No, but I know someone who does, I bet." Cisco knew just about everything; she'd ask him, the next time she got in to the shop.

"Can I say hello to Sammy and Maybeth before you hang up? We shouldn't talk, because it costs money. Dicey? I'm really glad Gram's okay, even if I didn't know ahead of time. I might even be glad you didn't tell me ahead of time—I had two tests and a paper in the last week."

Midmorning on Tuesday, Dicey went into Gram's bedroom. She was bringing in a fresh glass of water. Gram sat up in bed, not doing anything. "Can I get you a book?" Dicey asked.

"I don't seem to have the energy to read," Gram told her.

That wasn't like Gram. Dicey put down the water glass. "Are you taking your medicine?"

"Yes, and I'm feeling better for it." Gram almost snapped that at her. "So save your worrying. I just sit here and think—how much better I feel. I don't feel any too good right now, but—I've been thinking. It was like having a weight dropped on me, or like being felled, like a tree being felled."

Dicey sat down on the edge of the bed. "Why didn't you tell us?"

"Now I can get up and go to the bathroom and come back to bed—without having to lie down and take a rest during the process. Not once do I have to rest. Two days ago, I'd get into the bathroom, and sitting down wasn't good enough. Do you have any idea how cold it is lying on a bathroom floor, girl?"

"No idea at all."

"It's cold," Gram told her. "Why don't you leave me be in here? I'm thinking," she said. "I don't know what you're doing with yourself—"

"Cleaning, laundry—we've gotten behind—"

"But it's so quiet. You're being pretty quiet about it. What about the shop?"

"It's fine."

"You don't have to stay here mollycoddling me," Gram told her.

"I'm not." Dicey knew what Gram would say next so she didn't give her a chance. "This isn't mollycoddling, as you very well know. Mollycoddling is—toast in hot milk, and flowers on a tray. What I'm doing is just reasonable care."

She stood up. Gram pulled the blanket up over the sweater she was wearing in bed. Dicey looked at her grandmother and her grandmother looked back at her. Dicey could see trouble, in about one day, when Gram started wanting to get out of bed and back to work. She didn't know how she was going to keep the woman in bed. She didn't know how she was going to make her stubborn grandmother obey the doctor's orders.

"I know what you're thinking, girl," Gram said, "and I've learned my lesson. I didn't have to be as stupid as I was. So go on to whatever you're doing, and give me some quiet to think in."

So Gram wasn't trying to get up. Dicey knew that now. And Gram knew that Dicey wasn't about to leave her alone in the house, with no one to take care of her if she needed care. Dicey left the room, contented.

CHAPTER 20

That afternoon, after Sammy and Maybeth got home from school, Dicey took the truck and went downtown. She didn't know where the idea had come from, but she thought it was a good idea, so she bought a machine to play cassette tapes. It was on sale for $99—probably because it was pink and nobody wanted it, or maybe because it was shaped like one of those old railroad-car diners and nobody wanted it. For Dicey, the important thing was that it sounded good. It had a radio, too, which she didn't think Gram would ever use, and a shoulder strap in case you wanted to carry it around with you, which she was sure Gram wouldn't. Dicey opened her checkbook, stuck Claude's check into the back, and paid for the tape player, $103.95 with the tax. That got her down to $11.77, but as soon as she could get to the bank she'd have lots of money.

She went to the library next, to pick out some tapes. That was the great thing, the library had tapes you could check out. She didn't know anything about music, so she went for big names—Mozart, Beethoven, Bach. Then her eye was caught by a name she'd never heard, Vivaldi. She liked that name, and she liked the name of the music, *The Four Seasons*. She wondered about how you went about turning the seasons of a year into music, and then she wondered how, if it wasn't a song that had words, you understood the meaning just from the notes. Probably, she thought, driving home, eager to give Gram her present, there was a kind of language of music that if you studied it you could understand. Dicey felt pretty good, driving along—she had a surprise for Gram, who was really getting better, as anyone would see. The fields spread around her, spreading out from the road. Long, whitened grasses spread out over the ground, like frost. The sky above it all looked like a smudged charcoal drawing. Dicey's eyes looked around her, to see winter lying on the land, when snowflakes started to fall.

Snow was so sudden, the way it started. Even these wide, flat wet flakes, plopping onto the windshield, were just suddenly there. They hadn't been there and then they were, all at once. Dicey smiled to herself, thinking of how Sammy would be outside, hoping that school would close. She thought that if there was no school she and Maybeth would have an extra day to get ready for the history test. At least, she thought, feeling how she was feeling, she was doing all right by her family.

In the evening, while her brother and sister worked in the kitchen, because the snow had stopped as suddenly as it had started, after she had called Cisco and been assured that she needn't keep calling up to nag, she went into Gram's room, closing the door behind her so as not to disturb the two golden heads bent over schoolwork at the table. Gram had one of the tapes playing. A half-eaten bowl of Jell-O was on her table. "This toy," Gram said. "I don't know why you went and bought a thing like that."

Dicey sat down on the bed. Gram shifted over to give her room. "You do, too. You know perfectly well . . ."

"All right, I do, and I take that for granted, or, as granted. Since I can, I do. There's no need to go buying me a present."

"I know. I wanted to."

"Presents don't prove love," Gram pointed out.

"I know."

"Although the right present at the right time can show . . . I've been thinking," Gram said. "About your grandfather. John. No, more about marriage. Or the two together, since that's my experience of it. At first, I thought I'd failed—and I blamed him for that. Then, I thought he was failing—and I blamed him. It wasn't for years that I figured out that *we* failed, *we* were the ones failing, it took the two of us. I don't think he ever understood that. I think he was stuck like a pendulum in that back-and-forth blame, me to her to me . . . I don't wonder he was a bitter man."

"I'd feel better if I'd ever met him," Dicey said.

"Oh, no, you wouldn't," Gram told her. "I met him, and however much of the fault was mine, I still felt much the worse for it. Some horses just can't pull together in harness, and it's unkind to yoke them. Do you know how many years it took me to get over my fear of books, after that man?"

"Of course not. How could I?" Dicey demanded.

"You know," Gram said, "if you're not going to marry your young man, you should tell him. You should make up your mind. He might want to marry Maybeth."

"He doesn't love Maybeth."

"He could."

Dicey didn't want to think about Jeff. She hadn't thought about Jeff since—"Not and love me. We're entirely different."

Gram just shook her stubborn head.

"Besides, he doesn't want to anymore." She made herself say it right out: "Jeff said he didn't want to get married, the last time I talked to him."

For a long time, Gram didn't say anything. The music washed around the room, all the different instruments separate but also melded together. Then Gram said, "Whoever does know about these things? It's so hard to love someone—"

"Hard to live up to love," Dicey agreed.

"Then there's time, too. Who knows. Certainly not me. I wondered why we hadn't been hearing from him," Gram said.

That was more than Dicey thought she had to listen to. "You could have asked."

"If I had, you wouldn't have told me. And I'd like to know what else you haven't told me about."

Dicey didn't know how Gram knew.

"I may be sick, and weak, and old, but I'm not dead, girl."

And a good thing, too, Dicey thought. She guessed she might as well tell Gram. "Remember that man I told you had ordered a boat? He canceled the order. I gave him his money back, but Claude has paid me, so I'm fine."

She didn't know what Gram would say to that. She wanted to leave the room, but if Gram had anything to say she ought to stay and listen. She wanted to hear whatever it was Gram had to say, if Gram wanted to say anything.

"I thought I was dying," Gram said. "I did, truly. Not a heartening perception. Well, I was coughing blood. Not much, but . . . I didn't know what horrible disease it was; each one I thought of was more horrible than the one before—but I thought how much I'd miss you, all of you, miss our time together, miss finding out how the songs end, how the stories come out. But mostly, the truth is, I thought how much I'd miss me."

Gram stopped speaking and closed her eyes. "It's not very nice, but it's true, I'm who I'll miss most."

Dicey didn't say anything. She didn't know what to say.

Gram opened her eyes, and a smile swam across her face. "Not that I intend to die any too soon, now that I feel so much better. I ask you, Dicey, how can I feel so bad and have it be so much better?"

"I dunno. But I don't feel all that bad myself, and I should."

"Don't be too sure of that, girl."

Dicey laughed and got up from the bed. "I'm not sure of anything," she promised her grandmother.

She wanted to call Jeff and tell him Gram was better. He hadn't known Gram was sick, but the gladness of Gram being better was something she wanted to talk with Jeff about. Also, she would enjoy the sound of his voice in her ear, she admitted that. And why shouldn't she call him? she asked herself. Wasn't Jeff their friend? He thought a lot of Gram, as she did of him, and a friend should know about good news. Dicey went into the living room, before she could think another thought, and dialed the number. The phone was answered right away, but not by Jeff. "Roger?"

"Yes. Who's this?"

"Dicey. Is Jeff there?"

There was a hesitation she wouldn't have heard if she hadn't been listening so eagerly. Then Roger said, "He's left."

"Left?"

"For interviews, you know. Graduate schools. I'm not sure exactly where—Massachusetts, Maine, New Hampshire—he didn't leave an itinerary. He didn't tell you?"

"No."

She didn't even know where Jeff was. She couldn't place him in any known geography, and she didn't know enough to even guess what he might be doing at any given moment. She hadn't realized how accustomed she was to knowing where he probably was, at any given point of the day.

"He probably wrote it down for you, it's probably in the mail, but that's pretty funny. He's been pretty distracted with these applications, Dicey."

So Jeff hadn't told Roger how Dicey didn't matter in his life anymore. "Tell him, when he gets back—"

"Not until Tuesday or Wednesday next week. He's driving. He's looking at a lot of places."

"That's okay, just tell him my grandmother has pneumonia and is getting better. That's all I called to say."

"Will do. Do you want him to call you?"

Yes, Dicey did, but she couldn't say that. She couldn't say no, either, because that would be a lie. She found a truth to tell: "I just wanted to tell him about Gram. I figured he'd want to know that."

"Sure thing. See you," Roger said.

Probably not, Dicey thought, which was too bad, because she liked Roger. She liked almost all of Jeff's friends.

She was just sitting there, looking at the phone as if she didn't have anything else to do. But she didn't have anything else to do. There was an echoing hollowness inside her—not hunger—it was in her chest, not her stomach, an empty hollowness locked inside her rib cage. Like an empty house.

CHAPTER 21

Maybeth at breakfast Wednesday morning ate little. Dicey had the feeling that if she hadn't been there watching, Maybeth might not have eaten anything. Sammy, spooning up his oatmeal, looked over the top of his spoon at Maybeth and then at Dicey. Dicey looked at Sammy and then at Maybeth and then back at Sammy.

Maybeth looked frightened. She had drawn herself closed, like a clam retracting back into its shell when you finger it. Like a clam, Maybeth couldn't get entirely into her shell, and she knew it, and that made her more silent and less hungry.

Dicey met Sammy's eyes. "It's only a test, Maybeth," she said.

Maybeth's bent head nodded obediently.

"You've taken lots of tests," Dicey reminded her.

"I know," Maybeth said, her voice soft.

Dicey almost got angry. Why should her sister have to go to school, anyway, and be made to feel like this? "It doesn't matter," she announced. "I don't care if you pass it, and neither does anyone else here."

"Right," Sammy echoed her.

"I know," Maybeth said.

"Then don't let it get to you, okay?"

"I can't help it."

"But why?" Dicey asked.

"Because this one we've studied for—and I know more. I do."

Sammy laughed. "But that's crazy. If you know more, you should be feeling confident."

Maybeth shook her head. "It makes me nervous, because I'm not used to it. I'm sorry. Because—what if I know more and I still don't pass? Because I know how to fail because I always fail the tests. I don't know how to pass them," she explained.

Dicey wanted to promise her sister that this time would be different, but she couldn't do that. All she could tell Maybeth was the truth. "You just have to take it, and then wait and see."

Maybeth nodded. "Don't worry," she said.

"I'm not the one who's worried," Dicey pointed out, and was rewarded with a little shy smile.

After she had seen them off down the driveway, she got to work, busying herself with chores. She put together a piecrust for dessert, wrapped the dough in wax paper, and put it into the refrigerator to chill, and then looked in on Gram.

Gram was sitting up straight, with music playing—light, intricate music, like patterns of sunlight on waves. "Who is this Vivaldi?"

Dicey didn't know. "Do you want a snack?" she asked. "A nice bowl of Jell-O? We've got green or yellow. Or another piece of toast?" She looked at the dishes she was picking up. Gram wouldn't ask for anything, so she had to think of everything to ask Gram about.

"No and no," Gram said. "I feel better, but not hungry."

"Tea? Ginger ale? Water?"

"No, thanks."

"How about a book? Are you ready for a book?"

"You know, I might be." Gram sounded surprised. "Can you find me *David Copperfield*?"

Dicey thought she could.

"It's Dickens," Gram said. "I feel like Dickens. What was all that at breakfast?"

"Maybeth has a test today."

"The perversity of children seems unlimited," Gram said. Dicey stared at her. "You should be in school, and you refuse," Gram explained. "Maybeth shouldn't have to, but she wants to. You tell me if it makes sense."

"Does it have to make sense?" Dicey asked.

"No, but it would be easier on me if it did. I've left the farm to Maybeth, in my will. I've been meaning to tell you that. She's the one who might need to have it, and she'd always give a home to any of you. In fairness, I should leave it to all four of you, and I know that, but I also know that Maybeth—if she's not lucky—and there's no guarantee of luck, girl."

Dicey knew that. She knew what Gram was thinking, who Gram was remembering.

"I've been meaning to tell you what I decided about my will," Gram said. Her tone of voice said that even if Dicey wanted to argue about it, it wouldn't do any good. But Dicey didn't want to argue.

"I think it's exactly the right thing to do, Gram," she said. "And you're right."

"You're thinking about Momma."

"Maybe about all my children," Gram said. "The ones I know where they're lost, and the one I don't know."

"Is it a secret about the farm?" Dicey asked.

"Not a secret," Gram said carefully, thinking about it. "A privacy, though, between us."

"I'll get *David Copperfield*," Dicey said.

"Have you by any chance retired from business?" Gram asked.

"If you'll promise not to get out of bed," Dicey answered.

"How can I promise that?" Gram snapped. "I'm going to have to go to the bathroom, aren't I? Brush my teeth and hair, wash my face—maybe even have a bath."

She'd answered her own question and Dicey didn't need to say anything more.

While Gram read, Dicey cleaned up the mess she'd made in the kitchen, wondering how it was that Maybeth could get a piecrust made and the kitchen kept clean at the same time, then she went upstairs to see what needed doing up there. The woodwork could use a wash, she decided, seizing on a chore that would take most of the day.

"How was the test?" she asked Maybeth as soon as her sister walked in the door.

"I don't know. But it's over," Maybeth said. "It only lasts as long as it lasts. So I never mind, once it's over." Sammy grabbed a sandwich, then took the truck to work. Dicey barely had time to say hello to him. He looked in on Gram and was gone.

"There's mail for you," Maybeth told her, taking a glass of water and her day's news into Gram's room.

Dicey didn't count a phone bill as mail. She was going to have to deposit that check to pay it, and she always paid her bills right away. She put the envelope from the phone company into her checkbook, with Claude's check, and put both back into the rear pocket of her jeans. There was no need to carry Claude's check around with her, she knew, but it made her feel better. She had three months in her pocket, March, April, May. By the end of April, all her storage boats would be picked up, and who knew if a new job might turn up. Maybe she should call Ken and see if he could find somebody else to order a boat from her. She didn't think there was much chance of that; she knew there wasn't much chance; Mr. Hobart's boat had been a fluke.

But Gram was right—she hadn't been to the shop for days. Cisco was working alone.

Once she got the check into the bank, she'd write him one for—$200? No, $150, that was the most she could afford, really, and she ought to make it cash. Cisco was the kind of person who would much rather have cash, and it would be more fun to give it to him that way, anyway. Although, she reminded herself, she wasn't—properly speaking—giving him anything. He'd earned whatever she decided to pay him.

The next afternoon, when Sammy and Maybeth were home to see that Gram stayed in her bed, Dicey drove into town. She hadn't been to the shop for four days. She was ready to get working on something, even Claude's cheap boats. She could sympathize with her grandmother, being stuck in bed. Maybe over the weekend they'd let Gram move to the sofa, and light a fire in there, cover her with a blanket. Gram was being pretty docile about obeying Dr. Landros's instructions. It wasn't like Gram to be that obedient, Dicey thought, and then she thought that it was. Gram said she'd learned her lesson, and she meant it. When Gram made mistakes, she thought about them, to understand them.

Dicey walked into the shop, shedding her jacket, asking, "What coat are we on?" Then she looked around her.

Cisco sat leaning against the wall, reading, his stocking feet stretched out toward the stove. "Miss Tillerman." He stood up. "I didn't expect you. I got a library card," he said, mocking himself and her. He looked glad to see her, that, too. "I used your name as reference, which I hope wasn't imposing. How's your grandmother?"

"Getting better," Dicey said.

Looking around the shop, she saw that none of the boats had been given even the first coat of paint. The top of the worktable was piled with pizza boxes and napkins, Cisco's jacket, and empty bottles, both soda and beer. Undershirts and Jockey briefs were stretched out drying over the side of the boat nearest the stove.

"You have no idea how hard it is to wash anything in that sink," Cisco said. "The boats are all ready to start on, if you're ready."

In four days he could have finished two of them. She would have finished two of them.

"What have you been doing?" she asked. She tried to keep the anger out of her voice, but he heard it and his shoulders stiffened under the work shirt. His smile faded.

"Sanded every bleeding one of them," he said.

About one day's work, Dicey thought, chewing on her lip.

"Which still leaves you ahead, in this particular labor exchange," he pointed out. "Even if you're thinking of minimum wage. Since you can't describe the quarters as exactly luxurious," he told her.

That was true, Dicey reminded herself. It wasn't as if she'd actually hired him, she reminded herself.

"In fact, if we were figuring numbers, you'd owe me a bundle," Cisco pointed out. His easy smile returned, now that he had proved to her how right he was. "But since we never were, there's no problem. Is there?"

Dicey shook her head. If it mattered so much to him to prove he was right, he must feel awfully wrong. That was pretty weird, that feeling wrong would make him start a quarrel to prove he was right.

"I'll just put these things away." He moved into action, quick and graceful as a cat. "And we can get to work."

Cisco could work, and working with him was easy. In just the couple of hours she had before she had to get home for dinner, they got the first coat on the inside of two of the boats. Working made Dicey feel better.

She listened to Cisco talk, and watched the smooth lines of paint gradually cover the inside of the boat she was working on. Cisco, she decided, just wasn't any good at working on his own. However he felt about taking orders, and she'd just been given a taste of how he felt about it, he didn't get things done working alone. If she'd thought about it, she'd have predicted that. After all, she'd worked with enough people to know how they worked, and she knew enough about enough people to know how different people were. But when she thought of all the people in the world, so many of them and each one different, her mind went on to another idea.

"Do you ever think," she asked Cisco, "about how much you don't know?" Dicey was beginning to think it was wonderful how much she didn't know—in the sense that to think of it filled her with wonder.

"You want to hear the truth? The truth is, I don't. I'm more impressed by how much I do know. It's alarming how much my brain has stored away in it."

The answer was so like him that Dicey grinned.

"I know the grandmother is better, so tell me, how's the boyfriend?"

"I don't know," Dicey admitted.

"Uh-oh. Uh-oh and uh-oh." He kept on painting while he talked. So did Dicey. "Looks like you've painted yourself into a corner, Miss Tillerman. You played hard to get—which is about the oldest trick in the world. Granted, it's the oldest because it's the best. I have to grant you women that. Something women seem to be born knowing. You women," he said, looking across at her, the wrinkles spraying out from the corners of his eyes.

Dicey didn't know what he meant. He'd already told her she

wasn't particularly feminine, and now he was telling her she was just like every other woman. Cisco meant things only temporarily, she guessed. He probably didn't even remember that he was contradicting himself. Before, he'd said that about her to make her cross, and make her feel inadequate, as if there were things she didn't know that she ought to know; now, she thought, he was trying to make her feel as if there were things she knew, and did, to get her own way, to make her cross and make her feel guilty. She wasn't about to believe anything he told her about herself.

"My advice is: switch tactics," he said. "Try chasing him. Try it, I'm serious. Unless you want to get rid of him?"

Dicey didn't want to answer that. It was none of his business. But he outwaited her, until she shook her head no.

"Chase him a little—let him think he's the most wonderful thing in the world, desirable, wise, strong—all those things men like to hear about themselves. It's the second oldest trick. You should try that, Miss Tillerman."

Dicey didn't even want to think about Jeff. She could stand it, she could accept it, she could even understand it—but she didn't want to think about it.

"You should try working, Mr. Kidd," she snapped back at him.

"Nag, nag, nag," he said.

After a long, silent time he asked, "You going to be back in tomorrow?"

"In the afternoon."

He grimaced.

"Listen," she asked, "will you do me a favor? I got a check—for the first two-thirds of this job. Could you deposit it for me? I've got a phone bill to pay, and I can't leave my grandmother alone, so I can't get into town during banking hours. Could you?"

"If you want me to. Sure. It's no trouble. I usually pick up breakfast downtown, the drugstore does a nice breakfast for a dollar nineteen, I'd be happy to."

Dicey took her checkbook out of her pocket. She ripped out a deposit slip, dated it, entered the bank number and the amount of the check—since Claude banked where she did, she could draw on the money tomorrow afternoon if it was deposited in the morning—then signed the back of Claude's check and entered the amount into her records before passing the two slips of paper to Cisco. He looked at them, holding them in his fingers like a hand of cards.

"I'll take care of it," he said. "Are you sure you want to trust me with this much money?"

"I'm not trusting you with the money," she pointed out to him. "I'm trusting you to deposit it in the bank for me, and save me from bankruptcy."

"You can't go bankrupt," he informed her, mocking. He took out a wallet, to put the slips away. Then he grinned at her. The expression on his face had the same kind of confidence that Sammy's did when he knew that scoring the crib would win him the game.

So Dicey answered as she would have answered her brother: "Oh, yeah?"

"Not unless you're earning a living. Since this business doesn't make enough to support you, you're absolutely safe."

Listening to the twisting of his mind, Dicey remembered a question she had for him. "Do you know something called Machiavelli?"

"Some-one," Cisco corrected her. Standing beside him at the worktable, she had to look up at him. Cisco liked her, she could see it on his face. She didn't know why, but he did.

"Machiavelli was a Renaissance political theorist."

"I knew you'd know," she told him. She didn't mind Cisco, either. You couldn't expect much of him, but if you took him on his own terms, he was good company.

"Who wants to know?" he asked.

"I do. My brother used the word. I was talking to him on the phone."

"Your brother at Yale?" Cisco asked. "Well, I am impressed with myself. And so should you be."

Dicey just got into her jacket and went to the door. She could see right through him—through the vanity and pride to the fear that she wouldn't think much of him. Since it pleased him so much to be asked to deposit the check, she was glad she'd thought of it, although she'd thought of it only because it suited her own convenience. Deposits made after noon weren't credited until the next business day, the bank made that clear. She had plans for some of that money tomorrow afternoon, plans that included Cisco. Thinking of that, she smiled to herself: she guessed he'd be pretty surprised.

"I'll see you late tomorrow, then," Cisco said. "And I'll get some work done in the morning, I promise you. I don't think I could take disappointing you again. You're much too disapproving when you're disappointed," he told her.

"You can tell me all about it tomorrow," Dicey said, laughing, leaving him there in the shop.

CHAPTER 22

By Friday afternoon Gram was starting to argue that people healed at different rates, that just because most people took a week in bed with pneumonia it didn't mean she was going to need that long; she pointed out that Dicey was chained to the house, and announced that surely she could just move out to the living room, because she was going heartily crazy staring at these four walls. Leaving Maybeth and Sammy to restrain their grandmother, Dicey went downtown. She went first to the library, where she exchanged Gram's tapes for more Mozart, more Beethoven and, since they didn't have any more Vivaldi, some trumpet voluntaries, because that also was a name she liked. It made no sense to choose music because of words, but if you had no other way of choosing, words made it possible actually to make a choice, instead of just grabbing the first three tapes you came to.

The bank was open from four to six on Friday afternoons. She parked the truck in the lot and went inside, to write out the check for Cisco. She made it out to cash, and decided while she stood in line that she'd ask for it in fifties. It was more than she could afford, but it was less than he deserved, for the work he'd done. Besides, the checks for storage and maintenance would come in next week; she could pay Gram and have two months rent clear. They'd finish up Claude's boats in the next week or so, and that would be five hundred dollars more. She was okay for a while, and that was all she needed.

"How's your grandmother?" Mrs. Pommes asked her from behind the thick plastic shield that protected tellers from robbers.

"Getting better," Dicey said. She didn't wonder how Mrs. Pommes knew Gram was sick; people just seemed to know.

"And what can we do for you this afternoon?" Mrs. Pommes asked. Her earrings that day were long silver tubes that banged gently against her neck when she moved.

"I want to cash this, into fifties please." Dicey was used to writing checks, but it still made her realize that she was grown-up, a grown-up person, when she went to the bank and traded a check for cash.

"You must have had a good trip, then," Mrs. Pommes said. Before Dicey could ask her, What trip? and say, No, she hadn't had any trip, Mrs. Pommes turned away to call up the account records on the computer. They always did that and it always took time. Dicey had learned to be patient. Mrs. Pommes returned to her window and slid the check back to Dicey. "You don't have enough money to cover this," she said.

"I made a deposit this morning, from another account in this bank," Dicey explained. The trouble with computers was that they didn't always work efficiently. James said it was because they could think only in straight lines. She pictured Claude's check, going in a straight line up to Baltimore, then coming back into her account, in a straight line.

"Were you in earlier today? I guess I didn't see you."

"I wasn't, but the man who—works for me, he brought it in for me. I stay with Gram until Sammy and Maybeth get home from school, so I couldn't come in myself."

"But—" Mrs. Pommes said, and she put her forefinger against

her mouth while her face emptied itself of any expression, to disguise the worry that rose into her eyes. Her earrings hung quiet. "But you know, he cashed it."

Dicey didn't know any such thing. "I made out a deposit slip."

"But—" Mrs. Pommes looked to the teller beside her, as if asking for help, but the young man was busy with a customer. She turned back to Dicey and leaned toward the plastic window to bring her face closer. Dicey felt as if she were a prisoner in jail, on visiting day. "You had countersigned the check. He told me you were going someplace in Virginia, I can't recall the name, I'd never heard of it, but there are so many little places in Virginia one never hears of—to buy wood, where you'd heard the prices were excellent. He said you had to have it in cash. You're supposed to write 'For Deposit Only.'"

Dicey felt her head nodding. She felt her feet heavy on the floor, as if she was wearing iron shoes and not sneakers.

"I did wonder, because it was so much cash, that's an awful lot of cash." Dicey's head nodded. "But he told me about the man from Annapolis who wanted to hire you to build him a boat, who came all the way down from Annapolis to hire you, and because you wanted to bring the wood back with you, you needed cash. Because the people in Virginia wouldn't know you, wouldn't know if your check was good. Oh, Dicey," Mrs. Pommes said.

Dicey's head nodded. Her hands were like weights, holding down the check she had written.

"He was so friendly, and frank. He was so careful, too, he counted it three times, then asked me for an envelope, and then he took all the money out again and asked if I could change the hundred dollar bills into fifties, because he wondered if hundreds weren't too large. The lumberyards wouldn't have much cash on hand to make change, that's what he said. Then he counted it again . . . he must have been here for twenty minutes. I didn't know, Dicey."

Dicey made her stupid head stop nodding. "Can you stop payment on the check?"

"Not when it's drawn on this bank. It came right out of Mr. Shorter's account."

"Then how do I get my money back?" Dicey asked.

"I'm sorry," Mrs. Pommes said. "You see, when you countersigned the check you authorized the bank to pay it out. That's what countersigning means."

The money couldn't be gone. She'd earned it. She'd worked for it and been paid. It didn't make sense for the money to be gone.

Dicey didn't believe it, but she believed it. She wasn't surprised. She wasn't anything. Her head was nodding again, so she took up her own check. She jammed the paper into her pocket. She stepped away from the window. She didn't know what she was going to do about this. She didn't know anything.

Maybe Cisco was at the shop; maybe he'd just decided to cash the check to do things his own way. He liked doing things his own way; she knew that. She decided to go over to the shop, just in case, although she didn't expect to find him there. Banks should *tell* you, she thought. They told you about all those other things, service charges and penalties for overdrawn accounts; about how long you had to wait for checks to clear and how long you had before it was too late to question your monthly statement. But they never told you to write "For Deposit Only." Now that she knew it, Dicey saw how much sense it made, and she wouldn't make that mistake again. If she'd thought about it, she guessed she might have figured out you could write something like that on the back of the check—but she'd never even known she should be thinking about it. She'd always taken her paychecks in herself to deposit and no teller had ever stopped to say she ought to write "For Deposit Only."

The shop was as empty and clean as if he'd never been there. He hadn't even done any work on the boats, Dicey thought. That, somehow, seemed like the last straw. That was the knock-down blow. She stood in her shop, her hands jammed into the pockets of her jacket, looking around at the emptiness, and she knew this was the end of it for her.

Knowing it soaked into her and she soaked it up like a sponge. She thought she was going to cry—and she didn't cry, she wasn't a crier—but instead she thought she was going to throw up. She didn't do either one of those things; she just stood there. Alone, in the cold room, with the three dinghies stacked on racks, and the four rowboats spread out over the floor, and the stack of larch glowing.

She couldn't stand to stay in the shop. She couldn't stand to go home. She couldn't do anything, and she couldn't stand that, either.

Dicey drifted out of the shop and around to the creek. Standing on the short wooden dock, she looked down into the water. The muddy brown bottom was rippled by little waves, and old tires, half-buried, half-covered, lay in it. The shallow water, blown by the wind, splashed rhythmically against the flat wooden bulkheading. Thick ice painted the pilings. A few snags, which used to be trees before erosion brought them down, raised branches like the bones of hands out of the water. Where miniature coves quieted the waves, sheets of thin ice floated. It was cold out there, but no colder than Dicey felt.

She turned her back to the wind, looking at the shop, at its square cement shape. It was almost funny. It was almost perfect. She guessed that when Cisco made a promise, that was the time you could be sure he was lying. She guessed he probably enjoyed himself, stealing her money so slowly, counting it over and over. Most people would think that somebody stealing something would hurry out of the bank, and that was why he would have stayed so long, so they'd be wishing that he'd go, hurrying him out of the door. With Dicey's money in his pocket.

Dicey stared and stared at the squat cement shop, trying to see what she was going to do now. She felt as if she'd been surrounded by enemies—well, she'd known that, she'd known it wasn't easy. She'd known her enemies and she thought she was well armed against them. She felt as if there'd been a huge long battle, and the worst of it wasn't the losing, the worst of it was knowing that she was one of her own enemies.

She hadn't known enough to insure when she opened the business, and she hadn't known enough to make it hard for people to break in. She'd just known how to work and save up money. She'd actually thought she was going to be able to build Mr. Hobart's boat—in all honesty, she had to admit that while she'd been taken off guard when he ordered it, she hadn't been surprised. She'd expected something to happen for her.

Big dreams, she'd had big dreams. When big dreams exploded it was worse than when little ones got lost.

She guessed she'd be one of those people who all their lives wouldn't let go of their dreams. Not that she wasn't letting go right now—what else could she do? It wasn't as if anyone ever would buy a boat from some nobody who never built one and never went to school to learn how. She guessed she'd always be working on other people's boats, in other people's shops. She guessed she'd better get used to that.

It was as if she'd been playing her hand out, against everybody, gambling on herself, and now it turned out that she'd been gambling against herself.

Ashamed, that was how she felt. Because she knew she was

going to have to go back and explain to her family what had happened, what she had let happen.

Dicey squared her shoulders. She didn't much like having to be ashamed of herself. But she knew them—Gram and Maybeth and Sammy, and James, too, when he heard. They wouldn't be ashamed of her. It was just her being ashamed of herself. She could deal with that, she had the strength for that, and the anger.

What she didn't have the strength for was to go inside to work. She returned to the shop, but not to light a fire or open a can of paint. She hung the shutter over the glass window, then closed and locked the door behind her. She wasn't sure she ever wanted to go in there again.

CHAPTER 23

She told them after supper. Maybeth had roasted a chicken, which she served with mashed potatoes and peas. Sammy called it a second-string Thanksgiving meal, as he put together Gram's plate and carried it into her bedroom on a tray. He picked the carcass clean, and then scraped at the potato bowl, before he ate the last two pieces of the pie Dicey had made earlier in the week. Gram also ate her plate clean, finishing all the small servings.

Dicey had little appetite. She was waiting until dinner was over, and the dishes washed, and everybody gathered together in Gram's room, to tell her story. "Okay," she announced, when they were all crowded onto Gram's double bed. "Here's the news." Maybeth sat at the head, beside Gram, and Sammy sat across from Dicey at the foot.

"It's not good news," Gram predicted.

Dicey didn't even wonder how her grandmother already knew that. She didn't want to tell them what had happened, and she told them.

It was hard, saying it. She looked around at them while she explained. She wanted to stare down at Gram's white bedspread, at her fingers picking at it, but she made herself look from one to the other of her family. As he listened, Sammy's eyebrows pulled together and his lips pressed together; his eyes darkened. Gram had heard a lot of the sorry tale already, so at least she wasn't surprised. Gram was determined not to look distressed, or be distressed; she pulled calmness, like the sheets and blankets of her bed, up over her shoulders, and sat there, like a queen who was about to have her head chopped off but was still a queen. Maybeth was the only one who looked upset, with sad eyes filmed by tears she wouldn't shed. "Oh," Maybeth said, "Oh. Oh, Dicey," as the story went on.

"All in all, I've been pretty stupid," Dicey concluded.

"That's your side of it," Gram said.

"I don't think I can deny it," Dicey told them all. She felt better, for the telling of it, and for announcing that she accepted responsibility. "I'm sorry."

"Oh, Dicey," Maybeth answered. "I'm sorry, too." Dicey felt her sister's sympathy fall over her, like sunlight, as warm and tangible as a fall of sunlight.

"Thanks, Maybeth," she said.

Sammy didn't say anything. He got up off the bed and just stood there. When Dicey turned her head to look, she could see—in the blankness on his face, in the set of his shoulders, and the tension in the muscles of his legs—how angry he was. She sat up straighter. Sammy, standing there, Sammy, angry—he looked like someone you wouldn't want to cross. Strong, and ready, and dangerous.

"I'm glad you're on the same side I am," she said, trying to make a joke. "There's nothing we can do, Sammy."

"Where is this guy now?"

"Long gone, is my guess. Probably Atlantic City."

"Where's Atlantic City?"

"Farther than the truck can go," Gram said, "so get that idea right out of your head, young man."

Sammy walked across the room to the kitchen, then turned

around and walked back, then turned again. He paced the room like a young wolf. All at once, Dicey could see him, really see him—playing the kind of tennis he told her about. She'd watched him play some matches, but he'd always been her little brother. Watching, she had sat tense, wanting him to win so much that she hadn't really watched him. Now she could see how formidable he could be, and there was a little flame of anger in her that he couldn't get the scholarship to camp. He couldn't even try for it.

Sammy paced and they watched, held by his anger, until he turned around at the door. "Okay," he said. "Yeah. But I'd sure like to get my hands on him. And your money."

"He's probably gambled it away by now," Dicey told him. That was what Cisco would do, and he'd keep gambling until he lost it all. He wouldn't win, but if he did win he'd give her back hers, she suddenly knew that, too. She wouldn't get it back, she knew that. She wasn't holding that false hope out for herself. But if he had been able, he would—except he'd never stop trying to get more, not until he'd lost it all. "I shouldn't have trusted him," she said. "I should have known better."

Gram shook her head. "Don't fool yourself, girl. It's not your failure. It's his. Yours would have been not to trust him."

"That doesn't make sense," Dicey protested.

"I didn't claim it did. Things don't have to make sense—and that's lucky, because they tend not to—not when there are people involved. What are you going to do now?"

"I don't know," Dicey admitted. She couldn't think ahead. The future stretched out empty in front of her, and she couldn't look at it.

"I've got money for the phone bill," Maybeth offered.

Dicey almost said, Thanks but no thanks, I'll manage somehow. But she didn't. When someone offered you something, to help you, you owed them something, you owed them being able to help you out. "I'd appreciate that," she said. "I don't like not paying my bills."

"I know," Maybeth told her. "You always like to do things your own way."

That, Dicey thought, was the trouble. Maybeth had put her finger right on the trouble that got Dicey into this trouble.

"That's not bad, Dicey," Maybeth said. "I don't think it's bad, I just think it's true."

"I hope it's not bad," Dicey admitted, "because I think I'm stuck with it."

So she had better plan to get back to work and finish up Claude's boats. What else she'd do, she didn't know. But she wouldn't go back to work as if that was the only important thing—she'd learned that much from all these mistakes. She'd lost Jeff, she'd cost herself Jeff, and she was so sorry about that—almost as sorry for how badly she must have made him feel as for herself, losing him.

She'd have to accept that, and she guessed she could. She might well have lost Gram, who'd have neglected herself into the grave if Sammy and Maybeth hadn't been around to prod Dicey into action. Dicey was shocked at herself, although she didn't let it show. She got up from the bed, saying, "I'm going to bring the cribbage board in here, in case anyone wants to challenge me to a game. Gram?" While she was saying that, she was talking to herself, inside her head. She thought she'd learned long ago, and learned hard enough, that she didn't want to neglect her family—but she guessed she'd have to expect herself to keep on making mistakes.

In the living room, digging through the desk drawer to find the cards, picking up the cribbage board from the bookshelf, she accepted that: She would make mistakes. But she was going to be as sure as she could be not to make the ones she really didn't want to make. It could be a question of which mistakes you made, and how you used them. Since she was going to keep on making them, she wanted to take them that way.

Dicey almost ran back into Gram's bedroom, almost laughing out loud. She was twenty-one years old, and she'd just figured out that she wasn't finished learning. She was this old, and she'd just understood that growing up didn't mean you had things answered, settled. She wondered, coming back into Gram's room to play a cutthroat game of cribbage, how old you were before you began to get things settled. She looked at her grandmother, wondering.

"In my experience, older than dead," Gram told her.

Dicey just threw back her head and laughed. "You're crazy."

"That's as may be, but I'm not so far gone that I can't skunk you—if the cards lie right," Gram announced.

Dicey took up the challenge.

The next morning Dicey went to work. She took her bike because Sammy, too, had work to get to and he needed the truck, but she didn't leave the house until they'd all had breakfast together, and she planned to be back by five. She rode the miles into town along the level road, pedaling hard, partly to use up some of her energy but partly also to keep herself warm. The air was clear but biting cold. Filmy clouds filtered the weak February sunshine.

Dicey worked the day away. With no hurry, no pressure to finish up fast, she didn't slow down. It felt slower, but it wasn't. Time went by at the same ticktocking pace, but Dicey's inner time was measuring itself out differently. She covered wood with paint, in long, slow strokes. The paint flowed from the brush onto the wood smoothly, silkily. She dipped and stroked, dipped and stroked. Sometime in the middle of the day, she realized that it was good to paint, even these boats of Claude's; it was good to do a job right. She guessed, solitary and silent, that what she did when things went wrong was get to work. Since that was also what she did when things went right, she guessed that was just what she did.

Working, she knew what she was going to do. On Sunday night she wrote to Claude, telling him that she was giving up the shop, assuring him that the work she'd contracted to do for him would be finished by the end of the month, apologizing for such short notice. She didn't offer Claude any option to charge her March's rent. If she offered, he'd take it, and Dicey had better use for the money she'd earned. Things came up, like illness or tennis camp; she needed to save up her money against the things that might come up.

The dinghies she was storing she would move into the barn at home. The larch she'd try to sell—maybe put an ad in the paper. She had about enough money to pay for an ad. Until she sold it, she'd store that, too, in the barn.

Once she'd finished this job for Claude, she'd go looking for work for herself. She had a lot to learn. Maybe she'd just spend her whole life learning from the mistakes she'd keep on making. Maybe there wasn't anything you could do about that, except to make sure you learned.

By Tuesday evening she'd finished the last coat on the last of that batch of boats. She rode home feeling pretty good: That made twenty-four done, with only six to go. The only question was, should she do the final six in the same grouping of four, leaving just two at the end, or should she split them three and three, making two smaller jobs? She thought about that, pushing the pedals of the bike around and around, watching her own breath blow white out of her mouth. She could feel her pulse, the steady beat of her blood. She felt, riding her bike along the quiet road between the hibernating fields, how her inner time fit into the flow of the day around her, outer time, how her lifetime fit into geologic time, how time washed all around her, as complex as a symphony, all the different instruments time played on, all fitting together. Harmony, that was the word.

As soon as she thought that, Dicey felt the differences of her knees jerking up to push down, her feet pushing back and forth on the pedals, her shoulders forcing her hands to force the handlebars steady . . . She felt out of sync.

She *was* out of sync. Probably everybody felt out of sync, if they started to think about it. That feeling might even be part of the harmony. Dicey rode along, pedaling, pedaled along, riding—and she discovered that she had decided not to sell the larch. Not even for money, not even for cash money being held out to her. Because she was going to build her boat, build it for herself. She turned into their rutted driveway, slowing down, gripping the handlebars firmly and rising off the seat to keep better balance as she bounced toward home. There was every likelihood that the boat she built would sink, or list uncontrollably, even if she got it far enough along to put it into the water.

Never selling a boat, that wouldn't be bad. But never building one, that would be the real failure.

"I got a seventy-one and a quarter," Maybeth greeted her, turning around from the pot of soup she was stirring. "I'm making minestrone for supper."

For a minute, Dicey didn't understand. Then, "You can pass history," she said. "Because we can keep on studying, and it works. But where did the quarter point come from?"

"I didn't look, I just kept looking at the grade on the top of the paper," Maybeth admitted. "I didn't know I could get seventy-one and a quarter percent of everything right."

Dicey went into Gram's room, but Gram wasn't there. She went out to the living room and saw her grandmother enthroned on the sofa in front of the fire. Gram had a blanket spread over her and a book on her lap. Sammy sat at the desk behind her, doing some schoolwork. "You heard Maybeth's news," Gram asked at the exact same time that Dicey asked, "Did you hear Maybeth's news?"

CHAPTER 24

Dicey decided to split the last six boats four-two, getting the worst over first. She spent a day exchanging the finished rowboats for four unfinished ones and restocking her paint supply from Claude's storerooms. Then she spent a day sanding. Getting the work done. Sammy had agreed to help her get her own things out of the shop on Saturday—the three dinghies, the lumber, the tools. They would move them to the barn. She would be able to work in the barn. Everything was going to be taken care of. Once everything was taken care of, she'd build her boat.

She walked into the kitchen out of the lingering twilight of Friday evening, to the smell of spaghetti sauce and the sound of singing coming down the hall from the living room. Listening to Maybeth and Sammy sing, the same way that Gram—she knew—sat listening on the sofa, Dicey felt a sadness rising up in her. Their two voices carried the same melodic line, Sammy's rich, woody bass below Maybeth's golden soprano. It was about the loneliest song Dicey had ever heard. "Who will sing for me?"—the song kept asking that question, and never gave any answer.

She took a deep breath and hung up her jacket. The table was set, but there was a bowl of flowers in the middle of it. She recognized the bowl. It was a white china one Gram used for fancy dinners, on Thanksgiving and Christmas, for the days on which first Dicey, then James and Maybeth turned sixteen, and the day Dicey turned twenty-one. She didn't recognize the flowers.

Yellow tulips with red streaks, tiny white irises, shining daffodils—the flowers looked like a handful of spring, set out in the middle of the table. Dicey went down to the living room.

They were just as she'd imagined, Maybeth and Sammy side by side on the piano bench facing Gram, who lay along the sofa. The fire burned warm. Dicey sat down on the sofa arm by Gram's feet, not wanting to interrupt. When they moved on to a new song she joined in. In this song, the rhythm was almost ragtime. "'Oh, Lord, you know I have no friend like you.'" You could hear in the singing the way banjo and tambourine would sound, jollying the music along. "'This world is not my home, I'm only passing through,'" Dicey sang, watching the miniature mountain range Gram's toes made under the plaid blanket twitch in time to the music. "'I can't feel at home in this world anymore.'"

True enough, Dicey thought, hearing almost how the guitar would sound behind the music, sounding like a combination of banjo and tambourine. She didn't feel at home, even though this home of hers—people and place—felt entirely comfortable and good. She knew who was missing, and she couldn't do anything about it. "'Oh, Lord, you know I have no friend like you,'" they sang, starting the song again because it sounded so good.

Grief, Dicey had learned, faded. There were things you couldn't do anything about, except outwait the worst of their grief. She looked around the room, wondering what was different—because something was different. Flowers, more flowers, that was what was different. A huge armload of flowers, the kind of armload a giant might gather, of puffy white flowers, were in the big red milk pitcher on the desk. Tall, proud, white roses, with leafy ferns, stood on the table by Gram's shoulder, in a gold-rimmed glass vase.

"What's with all these flowers?" Dicey demanded.

For a minute, nobody said anything. Then Sammy decided he could tell her. "It's Valentine's Day. From Jeff. He said mine were the closest he could get to tennis balls. They're pretty hairy for tennis balls."

"Did you see the bouquet in the kitchen?" Maybeth asked.

"Yes, I did." Dicey wondered if there was a fourth gift of flowers, somewhere.

"House looks like a funeral home," Gram commented. "I know, I'm an ungrateful old bat."

"You're not old," Sammy told her.

Dicey understood, watching Gram and Maybeth and Sammy watch her, that there wasn't any fourth gift of flowers. Whatever they might think of it, it seemed to her that that was fair enough. It wasn't as if she'd sent anyone a card. She didn't think much of Valentine's Day and she'd always said so—Valentine's Day was just somebody's way of making money. "Why don't we ever grow flowers?" she asked, to change the subject and tell her family it didn't bother her.

"They aren't any too useful," Gram pointed out.

"How much does that matter?" Dicey wondered. "How about daffodils? They're bulbs and all you have to do with them is plant them. That's right, isn't it? You don't have to take care of them. Couldn't we plant some daffodil bulbs around the yard?"

"You have to do that in the fall," Maybeth said. "It's too late now."

Dicey guessed the message from Jeff was pretty clear.

"But we could next fall," Maybeth said. "I'd like to. Could we, Gram?"

"I don't see why not," Gram said.

Sammy got up from the piano and took one of the flowers out of the pitcher. He tossed it up from his left hand and swung at it with the palm of his right hand. The flower shot across the room like a comet, dribbling skinny white petals. "It makes a rotten tennis ball," he said. "If Maybeth gets to have flowers, I should be able to have chickens. Can I have chickens, Gram?"

Gram didn't even turn her head. She just ignored Sammy.

"You're ignoring me," he pointed out, picking up the disintegrating flower and batting it over the back of the sofa to land in front of the fire.

"That's right," Gram agreed.

After they'd had supper and cleaned the kitchen, after Gram and Sammy had settled down to a checkers tournament while Maybeth played the piano behind them, Dicey went into the dining room and took out the sheets of paper and the pile of books. If she was going to build a boat without really knowing what she was doing, she'd better know as much as she could. She'd gotten out of the habit of concentration, she discovered that. Even though there were no flowers in this room, she couldn't seem to sit easy with the idea of them.

She tried to get herself angry, because if you thought about it, it wasn't an awfully nice thing to do. He didn't have to send flowers at all. If he was going to send flowers, but not to her, he should know how she'd feel. Or at least he'd know how her family would feel about how she'd feel.

Dicey tried, but she couldn't get angry, because she didn't figure she'd been any too nice to Jeff. She tried, but she couldn't concentrate on the lines before her—not the lines she'd drawn on paper, nor the lines of words in the book. She felt uncomfortable, uneasy with herself. It wasn't like her to feel that way about herself.

Yeah, and it wasn't like Jeff to be unkind. So people didn't always act like themselves.

Dicey gave up trying to work and looked at the flat black windows instead.

People did act like themselves, that was what felt wrong.

Dicey got up. She went to the living room door. She told her grandmother that she was going to take the truck for a while, if that was all right. That was all right. Dicey had decided: She could gamble on what she knew was true of Jeff, what she had learned he was like, or she could gamble on what she was afraid of.

Driving along the dark road, Dicey realized that she might have things all wrong, but she thought there was a good chance that Jeff was home this weekend. He wouldn't call or write to let her know; that wasn't his way. But he would figure out a way of letting her know, if she wanted to figure it out, that he was home. From his point of view, it would all depend on whether she wanted to figure it out.

The long driveway up to Jeff's house ran beside the creek, along a low bluff. The oyster shells that covered the driveway glowed a dim white. Dicey drove slowly, partly for the well-being of the truck, partly because she wanted so much to be right that she put off arriving, in case she might find out she was wrong.

The little house was dark. It sat in its own shadow. On the other side of the low, slanted roof a full moon rode up into the sky. Jeff's station wagon was parked by the door.

Dicey knocked, and opened the door before he could answer. She really only wanted to apologize to him—in general—and let him know how things had been going, and find out how things were going with him. As she drove over, she had been thinking that maybe you had to work as hard at people as at anything else, and she owed Jeff an apology.

He sat at the table, looking out the window to where the moonlight fell over the barren landscape, dreaming so deep about something that he hadn't even heard her come in. When he heard her, he turned his head, his face like a mask in the shadows. He waited for her to say something.

Dicey didn't have anything to say. She had thought she did, but she didn't. She didn't know this face, and maybe she didn't even know Jeff. Jeff's eyes were gray, sometimes cloudy gray and sometimes clear, but never these dark, shadowed, unreadable places. She didn't know what she could say to him.

"Dicey?" he asked.

She heard it in his voice—and she already knew it, anyway. It wasn't that Jeff no longer loved her—but she was such a chicken, she hadn't even dared to know that. Maybe it was hearing it, knowing it. Or maybe it was the moon, hanging sad-faced up there in the dark sky. "I'll give it up," she heard herself say. "I promise, I will. I don't have to be a boatbuilder."

Jeff didn't stand up. He didn't say anything. He turned his back to her and looked out the window.

The creek wound like a silver ribbon through moon-frosted marshes. Dicey walked around and sat back against the edge of the table, trying to see Jeff's face. "I'm sorry," she said.

"You have no right to promise me things I never ask for," Jeff said. He didn't even look at her.

He was angry, and at her. She wasn't about to quarrel with him, not about whether he could be angry at her. "I don't understand," she told him. "Look. Jeff." He didn't move his head. "I want to marry you. That's what I want. What about you?" She was keeping it as simple and clear as she could.

"There's no need for you to have to choose, Dicey," he said, his voice as cold as moonlight.

Dicey didn't understand. "What do you mean?"

"Just what I said."

"But you haven't said anything, Jeff."

Then he did look at her. "You know, there are courses, there are some schools that teach courses. Or apprentice programs, lots of them. You never even thought about that, did you?"

"Are you angry at me for dropping out of school?"

"No. I'm angry at you because you never even thought about any other way. And then you come out here and tell me you'll give the whole thing up. As if that was even what I wanted."

He was right. Dicey didn't want him to be right, but he was. It was her turn now to look out the window, because she hadn't even tried to think about it, she had just gone ahead doing it her own way. It wouldn't do any good to apologize. He probably already knew that she regretted what she'd done—and he didn't even know half the reasons she had to be sorry. "I lost that contract, for the boat," she told him. "I'm losing the shop at the end of the month."

"I thought there was something like that," Jeff said, his voice cold and unsympathetic. That was all right with her; it wasn't sympathy she was looking for.

Dicey stood beside Jeff, looking at the twisting vines of the undergrowth and the looped creek, and at the stretching marsh, with the moon moving across the sky, as if the whole thing was a movie. Like the whole thing was a black-and-white movie, the moon moving out there among the stars, a movie someone was showing—

"Can you rent video cameras?" she asked Jeff.

She could feel his surprise. When he had reached out a hand to turn on the light and look at her face, she could see it, surprise and confusion.

"I'm sorry," she said, "it's just that— *Can* you rent them?" If you could, there were indoor courts up in Salisbury. If she rented a video camera, and they rented an hour with the pro, he could play with Sammy and she could tape it. Then Sammy could send the tape to the camp.

"Sure," Jeff said, cautious.

"Because of Sammy's tennis camp scholarship, the one he can't get—"

At the look on Jeff's face, as if his features were falling apart, she stopped herself. "I didn't mean," she said. "I just thought of it and—I thought it was hopeless and I just now thought of this and—" Jeff's face collapsed into laughter.

Dicey didn't know what was so funny. He was laughing, but he looked tired. She didn't like to see him looking so tired. She wondered how his interviews had gone and what he'd be doing next year, where he'd be living. She wondered if she was going to get to talk with him about how badly she'd done with the business, and hear his advice.

"I don't mind," Jeff said. "It's just like you. Sometimes, you've got a mind like a jumping bean. I didn't get you any flowers," he told her.

"I didn't expect any."

"I wanted to get you a tree, if I was going to get you anything, but—do you know how much trees cost, Dicey?"

Dicey shook her head. She tucked that tree away to think about.

"Why do you want to get married?" he asked her. "Now, all of a sudden." His gray eyes studied her face.

She couldn't explain. She couldn't even begin to explain. There were too many reasons, all too woven tight together into a cloth that was too . . . beautiful, or thick, or right, or complicated, she didn't know what—she knew only what its value was. She couldn't even begin to put words to it. And then Dicey knew, from looking into Jeff's eyes, that not being able to explain was the right answer.

"I didn't get you a tree, either," he said. "I got you a book."

A book? Dicey tried not to, but her face gave her away.

"Poetry," Jeff added. "You're not going to like it." He didn't seem to mind that. "Or maybe you will."

"Then why did you get it?" Dicey demanded.

"Because it's what I wanted to give you. Whether you want it or not. If you came over, I wanted to give you something I wanted to give you, not just what you want me to give you."

"What does that mean, Jeff?" Dicey asked him. She was going to try to understand, and if she really tried she bet maybe she could. "What do you mean by that?"

"I mean yes," Jeff said.

"Oh," Dicey said. She had the feeling she had missed most of the conversation. But she knew without asking, yes what.

"Oh," she said again. "Well—that's good." The conversation had ended up all right, so that was fine—that was like the wind rising to fill the sails of a boat, now she was beginning to hear all of what it meant—but how they'd gotten there she had no idea.

"In June, after graduation," Jeff said. "We could get married the first week in June."

"Okay," Dicey said. She was catching up with him. "That would be good."

"If you've got time now, I'd like to talk to you about the interviews and the options. Because if we're going to be married, it better be a coastal school, don't you think?"

"Yeah, sure. Can I call Sammy first? To tell them where I am, and about the camera, and—don't laugh at me."

"I'm not."

"Yes, you are."

"Okay, I am. But not at you. I'm laughing because—because now it's settled. It's going to be all right and I thought it wouldn't ever—we almost lost everything, Dicey."

"It was my fault," she said. "I know that. I was—I haven't been—"

"It would have been both of us, losing. It's never just one, winning or losing, it would have to be both of our faults. But now it's—how about some tea? How about if I put on a pot of water for tea?"

Dicey followed him into the kitchen. "Are you sure June will be all right?" he asked.

"June is fine for me. Or April, March—tomorrow, I'd like tomorrow."

"I can't," Jeff said. "The Professor won't be back until the end of May, and he should be there. But Monday we'll go to the bank, to get your ring."

"What ring? I don't need any ring."

"I didn't ask you," Jeff pointed out. "I have it for you, I've had it for you for years. I'm going to have to get my honors thesis written this spring, so I'm going to be pretty busy. What about you? If you don't have the shop, what are you going to do over the spring? Besides come up for weekends, and be here when I come home—besides me, what are you going to do?"

Dicey watched him set the kettle on the stove and light the gas under it with a kitchen match. She watched him reach into a cupboard for two mugs and pull out a drawer with boxes of different teas in it. She felt like she could do just about anything she wanted to, this spring, and all the rest of her life, now. She knew the feeling would pass, but that didn't make it wrong. "I'm planning to build a boat," she told Jeff. She didn't know how he'd feel about that, but it was the truth.

"That sounds right to me," he said.

"You mean that?"

"Of course. What do you think? I'm pretty confident about you and boats, Dicey. You ought to know that by now. If I were betting, I'd bet on you."

Dicey almost said, Don't do that; but if Jeff was sure of her then she was surer of herself. She figured, thinking about it, she'd probably make mistakes, but the mistakes would tell her what she needed to learn. In fact, if she was going to go to school and learn boatbuilding or design, or sign up to be somebody's apprentice, it would be smart to have made some of her mistakes ahead of time. She watched Jeff's face; and he turned to watch hers.

"I think," he said, his eyes so deep with gladness it could have frightened her if she hadn't been so glad herself, "you owe it to yourself to build your boat."

"Yes," Dicey agreed. "Among the other things I owe it to myself to do." He knew what she meant, and who; she didn't have to worry about Jeff understanding her. But when she thought of all the things she wanted to do, and do right—do right by, do as well as they could be done . . . It was all so risky, because there were no guarantees. You couldn't be sure that any of the risks would pay off. Even if you studied, and planned, and worked, even if you did the best you could, you could still lose out. There was no way to walk away from the truth of that. That's what no guarantees meant. But even knowing that didn't make Dicey feel any different about anything—which puzzled her, because it didn't make sense that it shouldn't. Then she understood—it wasn't guarantees she needed, or any of them needed, but chances, chances to take. Just the chance to take a chance.

And the eye to recognize it, she added.

The hand, to reach out and hold on to it—that, too.

And the heart, or the stomach, or wherever courage came from, she thought.

"Dicey?" Jeff asked. "What's so funny?"

She couldn't begin to explain, except with all the rest of her life. Well, she guessed now was the time to start. Now was always the only time. "I was just thinking," Dicey said. "Do you want to hear?"